STRICTLY BUSINESS

CARRIE ELKS

AVA

Why can't people just be nice to each other?

I don't understand it, because nice is good, right?

Nice means helping old people across the road and spending hours searching for a lost puppy. It's holding the door open for somebody and getting rewarded with a smile from a stressed mother juggling kids and grocery bags.

Yet people say it with a wrinkle on their nose, holding the vowel sound for a bit too long.

We should bring nice back. We need it more than ever.

I'm standing outside the brownstone building that houses my nice job, working for the funny and nice boss who's been the chief editor at Smith and Carson publishing since the 1970s. I've worked here for thirteen years myself. It was my first job after finishing college and I took it with a plan to save up enough money to move to New York and rise up the publishing ladder.

And yet here I am, at the age of thirty-six, still working in the warm, leafy city of Charleston. Not even *that* Charleston. This one is in West Virginia. And I grew up here.

It's only when I walk through the heavy wooden front door, shuffling sideways so I don't dent the box of donuts I'm carrying, that I realize something is slightly off. A grin pulls at my lips when I start to greet Sammy, the security guard come receptionist who's worked here since… well, forever.

Except Sammy isn't sitting behind the long glass reception desk that he's always buffing to a shine. In his place is a thin, bespectacled young man who keeps tapping at the keyboard in front of him and huffing.

"Hi," I say brightly because this little chink in my nice day is not going to spoil my post-vacation bliss.

He looks up and his eyes flicker over me and the donut box before he looks back down at his computer. "We open at nine," he says, his voice strangled. He's still jabbing at a key like he's trying to make a point.

"It's okay, I work here," I tell him. "Is Sammy all right? I was expecting to see him today."

He looks up, brows pulled tight. "Sammy?"

"The security guard," I say. "Security Sammy." I smile because this guy's bad mood isn't going to defeat me. "I don't think he's ever taken a day off before."

"I've no idea." The man blinks. "It's my first day. I was sent over by the agency. I don't suppose you know how to book a meeting room, do you?"

I patiently lean across the counter to show him how to use our ancient booking system. It's one of the many things I've nagged Richard – my boss – about. But he has an aversion to anything digital and an even bigger aversion to listening to me describe how much easier all our lives would be if we upgraded our systems. If he had his way, we'd still be using a calendar in the center of the office to bag the best rooms.

Not that I mind. He makes up for it in so many other

ways. He's a good boss. He lets all of us do our own things while standing up for us when we need it.

He's one of the reasons I'm still working here rather than pursuing my original career plan.

"Thank you…" he trails off as I finish his booking for him.

"Ava," I tell him helpfully. "Ava Quinn. I'm the Commissioning Editor at Smith and Carson." And also the sometimes-assistant to the chief editor, the lead for technology integration, the event planner, and chief cheerer-upper. In a small children's publisher like Smith and Carson, our roles tend to be completely different from our job descriptions.

That's why it's so difficult to recruit the right person when somebody leaves. But also why people stay here so long. No day is ever the same, and you can build your job into whatever you want it to be.

"Matthew," he mumbles. "Here for one day and then out of here, I hope."

I nod sagely. "These systems aren't for everybody. Do you know if Mr. Austin is in yet?"

Matthew blinks. "Who's he?"

"Richard Austin. The chief editor. The guy in charge."

It's interesting how the blood drains from Matthew's face. "Oh *him*. Yes, *he's* definitely in. He's the one I'm booking the boardroom for."

"Great." I smile because even if Matthew is only here for one day, he still deserves to feel welcome. "Oh, would you like a donut?"

I hold out the box. I picked the sweet breakfast treats from the Camelia Bakery, owned by my friend, Lauren. It's on my way to work. Another reason I love living here – my pretty townhouse is a fifteen-minute walk from Smith and Carson. It's in the historic district and I get to wave at Lauren and smell the sweet fragrance of the locust trees, their blooms hanging like white flowery grapes from their leafy boughs and casting dappled shadows on the sidewalk, as I make my way to the office.

"You bring donuts in for everybody?" he asks, looking suspiciously at the box I'm holding open.

"Only today," I tell him. "It's my first day back from vacation."

He quickly snatches a pink iced donut and puts it on the shelf under the counter. "You really work for *him*?" he asks, pointing at the ceiling.

"Yes." I smile patiently. "He's a nice man when you get to know him."

"If you say so," Matthew mutters. "Good luck up there."

I take the antiquated elevator up to the fourth floor. It has a sliding black iron gate and whenever I step inside I feel like I'm taking my life into my own hands. It shudders and shakes on its way up, passing the architecture company that sublets the first floor and the management consultancy firm on the second. The third floor is empty –has been ever since we moved out last year in an effort to reduce our floor space and overhead. I try not to feel wistful when I think of my old office overlooking the Allegheny Mountains.

When it reaches the fourth floor, I balance the donuts in one hand and yank at the gate with the other, sending up a quick prayer to the gods of elevators as I escape unscathed. The open-plan office is quiet as I make my way down the hall. There is still forty minutes until the office opens and will be bustling with employees and noise, but I want to catch up on my emails before things start to get manic.

Setting the donuts on the side of my desk, I sit down in my worn office chair and fire up my laptop. It takes forever to boot up and is in dire need of replacing, like the rest of our technology. Last year, I put in a proposal to have all of our laptops and computers updated, ready to introduce some new systems, but it got lost in the mess of the takeover.

Ah, the takeover. For a few months, it was all we talked

about. Whether we'd end up getting our marching orders or if we'd be transitioned into Mediatech, New York's biggest and brashest media conglomerate.

From the moment they bought us, all they wanted to talk about was our flagship series, Dandy the Lion. You've probably heard of it. There aren't many kids in America who've made it to adolescence without reading at least one Dandy book. It was my first acquisition when I was promoted ten years ago, and Dandy took the children's book world by storm.

Dandy's an old-fashioned gentlemanly lion, written by the reclusive Naomi Acre. He's funny and kind and unlike most of our other titles he makes a lot of money.

We always knew he was the only reason Mediatech bought us. They're a relative newcomer to the children's publishing world, and although they have the shiny flagship office in New York along with the high-flying editors who don't have time to buy donuts or do anything but frown at you, they don't have the one thing that we have. Cachet.

Buying us gave them that. Within weeks of the acquisition there was talk of closing this office and moving all of our work to New York.

In the end, it turned out to be a storm in a teacup. Richard went to New York for a week-long business trip, then came back and called an all-staff meeting, waving a piece of paper in his hand as though he'd just won a major battle, promising us that nothing would change even though we were now part of a larger organization.

And he was right. Nothing *has* changed. It's like we're not part of Mediatech at all. And though Richard took the glory, I know it's because I called Naomi and she called Jean-Baptiste Blanchet – the sixty-something owner of Mediatech – and told him that if we were moved to New York, she would take her Dandy franchise elsewhere.

One more reason why I love Naomi.

When my laptop notifies me that an update is urgently required, I click my mouse and sigh, because this is going to take some time. Richard's office door is closed – unusual for him – so I choose his favorite chocolate vanilla donut, slide it onto a napkin, and carry it to his door. I can hear voices inside. A deep one and a lighter, more feminine one. The deep one doesn't sound like Richard at all. It's short and stilted and sounds pissed, which Richard never gets.

Unless…

I swallow because I know his wife, Eleanor, was having tests at the hospital before I left for vacation. What if they came back bad? My heart starts to speed because I hate bad news. Richard and Eleanor are like the grandparents I never had.

Ignoring the foreboding feeling wrapping around my chest like a boa constrictor, I rap on his door and am rewarded with a terse, "Come in."

And because I'm also the chief mood enhancer at Smith and Carson, I put a smile on my face as I open the door, and cheerily say, "Hola amigo. I'm back from Spain. And along with a tan and a new sense of optimism, I also bring you donuts."

But when the door opens, Richard isn't there at all. Instead, my gaze clashes with the bluest, angriest pair of eyes I think I've ever seen.

And suddenly I don't feel very nice at all.

CHAPTER
TWO

I should probably tell you that I've seen those eyes before. Three times in person, not that I'm counting, and more times than I can remember on a computer screen when we have our monthly editorial board meetings. And let's face it, they're pretty eyes if you like that kind of thing. Which I don't.

Sure, I've seen some women go a little weak when he lands his gaze on them. And I've heard them talk about his old-fashioned movie star handsomeness. But I've checked and his nose has a bump, and his mouth is always pressed together like he disapproves of everybody and everything.

Beauty really is in the eye of the beholder, right?

He's not wearing a tie, and the white of his shirt is almost blinding. It's unbuttoned at the neck, and I can see just a hint of chest hair.

On paper, Myles Salinger is my equal. He's the commissioning editor for the children's publishing department of Mediatech in New York, and I'm commissioning editor here at Smith and Carson. But everything about his demeanor tells me he thinks he's way above me.

I first met him in New York about two months after the takeover when Richard and I flew in for a two-day meeting to discuss our future plans for Dandy. Once Jean-Baptiste accepted that Dandy the Lion was staying in Charleston with us, he wanted to know the direction we planned to take him in.

I had walked into the boardroom ahead of Richard, and in the corner were three men. Two of them were young, laughing about something. The third had his impressively broad back to me.

But it wasn't the men that caught my eye so much as what they'd drawn on the whiteboard. An uncanny likeness of Dandy the Lion bent over and being… um… taken from behind by Mediatech's biggest selling character, The Great Bear Endo.

We take great care with Dandy's image at Smith and Carson. We're not quite at Disney standards, but he's beloved by children and their parents everywhere, and that's not by accident. We don't license him for things like cereals or snacks, and we don't let his image be reproduced without our direct consent.

And we certainly don't let our art team draw a picture of him being taken from behind on a whiteboard for all to see.

"What the hell is that?" I asked. Richard was far enough behind me that he hadn't seen what I had. "If you don't get that monstrosity off the board right now, I'll be talking to your bosses."

All three faces swung around to look at me. But only one of them looked as furious as I felt. One of the younger guys swallowed hard. "He is our boss," he said tremulously, pointing at the tall man in the suit.

The one with the most striking eyes I'd ever seen.

"Then he should know better," I told them. "It's disgusting. If you don't know how to protect your assets, you shouldn't be working for a publishing company. Especially not a children's publishing company."

Pretty eyes said nothing. Just scowled at me. I scowled right back as I walked into the room and grabbed a bottle of water while they scrubbed the pornographic image off the whiteboard.

And that was that. Since then, Myles hasn't stopped scowling at me. And I've been frowning right back. We tolerate each other, but we certainly don't like each other. And no matter how much I try, I can't be nice to him.

He glances at his laptop screen. "I'll call you back," he says to whoever he's on a video call with and hits the end key before looking back at me.

"Ava," he says, sounding almost bored. "You've finally decided to grace us with your presence."

"I've been on vacation." He waves his hand like he's not interested, so I change the subject. "Where's Richard?"

"Richard no longer works for Mediatech."

Oh.

OH!

My legs lose all the strength in them. I reach behind me to find a chair to sit down in, then realize I'm still standing in the doorway of the office and the only thing behind me is air. I stop reaching and curl my fingers around the door jamb. "What happened?" I ask. "Why doesn't he work here anymore?"

"He and Jean-Baptiste agreed to part ways." Myles stands and walks around to the front of the desk, his eyes still glued to mine. He's even taller than I remember. At least six foot three. I'd feel intimidated if I wasn't…

Okay, I feel intimidated. I have to crane my neck to look up at him.

"Is Eleanor all right?" I ask.

His brows furrow. "Who's Eleanor?"

"Richard's wife."

"I'm sure she's fine, especially with the severance Jean-Baptiste gave him." Myles looks at me carefully for a moment. "Maybe you can answer a question for me," he suggests. There's no ease to his tone. No kindness. My hackles rise.

"What kind of question?"

"You're in charge of the IT system here, right?"

"Well, kind of. I liaise with the call center and sign off on the support contract."

"And security? The firewall?" He doesn't blink. Not once. That has to be painful, right?

"Yes," I tell him. "I deal with that, too."

He slowly nods. "So now we know who's responsible for losing Mediatech a hundred thousand dollars."

———

"It was mayhem," Catherine tells me. She's the head of production for Smith and Carson, and one of my closest friends in the office. "Richard clicked on a link in a phishing email and about an hour later everything went to shit."

Ryan, the sales and marketing manager, and the biggest gossip in the office, continues, "The next day, Myles arrived with a huge entourage of people. They pushed all of us off our desks and started uploading a billion patches to update the security system. Then we all got called into the boardroom and told that Richard's taking early retirement effective immediately. And while they search for a new chief editor, Myles will be working from this office."

"Hasn't he got better things to do?" I ask. He has his own books to publish, after all. And let's face it, he doesn't look at all happy to be here in Charleston.

"I can think of a few better things he could do," Catherine wiggles her eyebrows and Ryan laughs. I roll my eyes, because seriously?

"It should be you sitting in Richard's office," Ryan says, glancing over at the closed door. "Not him."

"I wouldn't want to," I tell them. "Richard knew that." Sure, I'm ambitious, but there's too much going on in my life right now. Not that I have time to think about that at the moment.

"So why didn't any of you call me?" I ask, changing the subject. I'm kind of hurt that they didn't. Or that Richard didn't. We have a good working relationship. I've been to his house. I've played with his grandkids. I thought that meant something.

"Richard said we shouldn't." Catherine shrugs. "He insisted that you deserved a break and you were going to get one. There's nothing you could have done anyway. As much as I hate to say it, Salinger has it all under control."

"We're getting MacBooks," Ryan says, smiling happily. "Isn't that cool?"

More people arrive and start to gather around my desk, helping themselves to the donuts I brought in. Eventually, somebody remembers to ask about my vacation and I'm in the middle of describing Gaudi's La Sagrada Família church in Barcelona to them when the chief editor's office door flies open and Myles Salinger is standing there, his huge frame taking up most of the doorway. His lips are pressed tightly together as he looks at my desk and all the people sitting around eating donuts on it.

"What's going on?" He blinks.

"I was just..." I try not to roll my eyes. "Giving people donuts."

I notice half of them have already slunk away. Traitors.

He glances at his watch, his shirt sleeve rising to reveal a strong forearm and an oversized silver Rolex. "Is my watch wrong?" he asks.

I have no idea, I want to tell him, but dammit, he's not ruining my day. "What time does it say?" I ask sweetly.

He ignores me completely. "Does Mediatech pay you to sit around and eat donuts?"

"No."

"Then maybe you should all get on with your work and leave the gossiping until after hours."

He whips around and walks back into the office, slamming the door closed behind him.

"Miserable asshole," I mutter.

"*Sexy* miserable asshole," Catherine corrects me.

"He is," Luella, her assistant says, dreamily. "He can shout at me any time."

———

MYLES

"They smell of what?" My brother, Liam, starts to laugh.

"I'm not saying it again," I tell him, my voice low and tired because it's been a hell of a couple of weeks. I didn't want to come here, I don't want to still be here, and I don't want to deal with the people in this office. But Jean-Baptiste insisted so here I am.

The sooner I get back to New York the better.

"Cum. You said they smell of cum."

"They do," I tell him. "Seriously."

"How can trees smell like jizz?" he asks me, sounding interested. Liam is my younger brother by a year. He lives in New York too, and we spend a lot of time together there.

"I've no idea how they can smell like that. They just do." And

I have to walk past the damn things every day because there's no parking lot for this damn office building. I just have to find a space on the road, no matter how far away it is, and park there. It's like going back in time a few centuries coming to Charleston.

Strangers actually smile at you, and it isn't a ruse to steal your wallet or phone. It's disconcerting.

"Okay… well, according to Google it must be a Callery Pear tree," Liam tells me. "It's the blossom that smells. The good news is, you should only have to deal with it for a few more weeks."

"Lucky me," I say. But I don't feel very lucky right now. Haven't felt lucky since Jean-Baptiste demanded that I come to Charleston to find out what the hell was going on at Smith and Carson. I'd asked how long it would take and he looked at me pointedly and said, "That's up to you. I want a report on how we can turn things around there."

Because the truth is, even with Dandy the Lion as their anchor series, Smith and Carson is bleeding money. It's driving Jean-Baptiste crazy, and he wants to either turn things around or close the place down. And when he gets an idea in his head, there's no dissuading him.

So I'll sort it out quietly then go back to what I was doing. And if I have to smell cum every time I get out of my car, so be it.

"So hey, isn't this the day your nemesis is due back at work?" Liam changes the subject. It's almost impossible to find a worse topic than jizz trees, yet he's somehow managed it.

He should get a medal or something.

"Her name's Ava. And yes, she's back at work." Completely unfunny story. Ava Quinn – the commissioning editor of Smith and Carson – absolutely hates me. Has since the day we first met. And yeah, I'm not her biggest fan either. She lectured two of our most talented art interns, and one of them almost quit on the spot. It took me an hour to persuade him otherwise.

I had it under control. I had been explaining to them why we don't ever make lewd drawings of our characters, and she started shouting at them. There was no need for that, I had it handled. And it's pissed me off that ever since she's done nothing but been rude. Especially when everybody insists she's the nicest person at Smith and Carson. Ha! I beg to differ.

She's the main reason I didn't want to come here. I knew she'd be a pain in my ass. It's understandable. If she got brought in over me in New York I'd be pissed as hell.

"It's okay," Jean-Baptiste said when I pointed this out. "You won't be above her. You'll both work for me."

"And how exactly is that going to work since I'll be running the office?" I asked him.

He just shrugged. "You'll make it work, Myles. You always do."

And yes, I will, because he's right. I don't like to be defeated by anything, especially not by somebody who hates my guts. But the sooner we get a replacement for Richard and I can go back to New York, the better.

"Anyway, that's not why I'm calling," Liam says. "Dad says you're not coming to his vow renewal."

"That's right, I don't have time."

"But everybody's going to be there. You have to go." Liam sounds almost pouty. "Come on, man, we'll have a blast. Play some football, go swimming in the lake. Dad's talking about reinstating the Salinger Olympics." He clears his throat. "Even mom's going."

"I'm busy," I say in a tone that invites no response. Just because my mother, along with my father's second wife, still thinks the sun shines out of his ass, doesn't mean that I do.

"I need to go," I tell him, softening my voice because Liam

is the best kind of brother. "I have a business to run and so do you."

He disconnects and I pull my laptop screen back up, trying to find the files for last month's financial returns, but the document retention system in this place is about as good as its security. Sighing, I stand up and stride to the door, whipping it open and calling out to her.

"Ava Quinn, come to my office. Now."

CHAPTER
THREE

MYLES

"This isn't going to work," I tell Jean-Baptiste. It's almost seven and I'm still in the office. Everybody else has left, including the bane of my existence.

"Of course it is. You're the only one I trust to tell me what to do with the Charleston branch," Jean-Baptiste says. I hear noises in the background. No doubt he's out at a restaurant with a client or investor. He lives to schmooze and he's very good at it. Unlike me.

My brother tells me I have a resting asshole face. That whenever anybody looks at me they assume they've pissed me off.

"Most of the branch won't talk to me. And anyway, Ava's back from vacation. She should be the one running the branch in Richard's absence. She can report to you instead."

"No." Jean-Baptiste's tone is firm. "I don't trust her. Remember how they went behind our back with Naomi Acres?"

Yes, I do. And to be fair it was pretty spectacular. Jean-Baptiste was pissed for months.

"How long exactly do you want me to stay?" Sure I can handle juggling two jobs. But this isn't a long term solution. I want to go back to New York, where I don't have to walk into an office full of people glaring at me.

Especially Ava Quinn.

"As long as it takes. I'm still thinking through our options."

Ah yes, our options. Either we close Smith and Carson down completely, and risk losing Naomi and Dandy, or we recruit a new chief editor and look into ways to save money. Either one of them is going to piss off the employees here. And I know exactly who'll have to give them the news.

"Do you at least have some candidates for the chief editor job?" I ask.

"HR is working on it."

"Good."

"And in the meantime, stick close to Ava," Jean-Baptiste tells me. "If she talks to Naomi I want to know. I'm not going to be taken by surprise this time," Jean-Baptiste warns. His voice sounds strange, as though he's eating and talking.

"Of course." My stomach rumbles, reminding me I haven't eaten since breakfast. I haven't had time. In between Ava's return kicking up a fuss and the rest of the staff going silent whenever I come out of my office, I've been trying to write this damn report for options going forward.

"Great. I'll speak to you later," Jean-Baptiste says. "Have a good evening."

He disconnects and I glance at my laptop, closing the lid but not shutting it down. I'll go out and grab something from the takeout place down the road then get back to work.

Because the sooner we figure out how to make this place run on a profit, the sooner I can get out of here.

AVA

"Seriously, he just comes out and shouts at people, like he expects them to drop everything as soon as he opens his mouth," I tell my friends as we sit in the juice bar outside of the yoga studio. Sophie surreptitiously twists the lid off of the flask she's smuggled in and pours a healthy measure of vodka into each of our glasses.

We haven't showered because the plumbing in this old building is unreliable at best. We'll all shower in our own homes where we can luxuriate in hot water and not have to compare ourselves to the model-perfect yoga aficionados who think nothing of parading around the changing rooms butt naked for what seems like hours.

So we're sitting here sweaty with our workout gear still on, breaking the rules of the studio.

This is why everybody else in the class avoids us. They're here to get fit and healthy and we're here to...

I don't know. Drink vodka-infused grass juices, I guess.

"Hmm," Lauren says, scrolling through her phone. "Myles Salinger. Alumni of Stern Business School. Seven years' experience in high finance. Ten years in publishing."

"You're looking at his LinkedIn profile?" I ask, alarmed. "Stop it. People can see when you're stalking them on there. All he has to do is click on your profile and he'll know you're connected to me."

"I'm in incognito mode," Lauren says, ignoring my panic. "I check out everybody on there. Especially potential dates."

"Why?" Sophie asks, interested.

"How many guys do you know who post statuses on Insta or Facebook?" Lauren asks.

Sophie shakes her head. "None?"

"Exactly," Lauren says. "So you have to be sneaky to find out about them. A guy's LinkedIn profile can tell you a lot. His commitment level for one."

"How does it tell you that?" I question.

"If he flits from one job to another or has big gaps in his resume, you should avoid him," Lauren says, sounding sure of herself. "But if he's had a few jobs, where he stayed at them long term, he's probably a good bet."

"Seriously?" Sophie says. "You think that?"

"It hasn't done me wrong so far," Lauren says smugly.

"You're single." I point out the obvious.

"Yeah, because the guys I swipe right on have terrible career records. There's more," she tells us, and we lean in to listen. "If he replies to comments, he'll probably reply to your texts. If he doesn't reply or like anything, avoid him."

"The Lauren Daniels Guide to Dating," Sophie says. "It's a whole new world."

"You know what's interesting about Myles?" Lauren says, still scrolling. "He left an amazing job in finance for children's publishing."

"I already knew that."

"You knew that he left something that paid him around a million a year for a job that probably pays a tenth of that?"

I blink. Even a tenth of a million is more than I earn. "He used to earn millions?"

"With bonuses and commission, almost certainly," Lauren says. "I wonder why he left?"

"They probably couldn't put up with his grouchiness," I tell her.

"Holy hell," Sophie says, leaning over Lauren's phone. "Is that him?"

"Does he look like Satan?" I ask them.

Lauren and Sophie exchange glances. They're not used to me being so annoyed. Nothing and nobody usually ruins my Zen.

"Myles Rupert Salinger," Lauren reads out, presumably on his Wiki page now. "Born November Twenty-Second Nineteen seventy-eight. That makes him, what?" She frowns and runs her finger over her chin. She can make a perfect batch of a hundred brioches without having to measure anything out but give her a simple math problem and she's stumped.

"Forty-three," Sophie says.

"Graduated from Stern Business School. Went straight to work as a venture capitalist. No wives, no kids." Lauren looks up at me. "This guy is a unicorn."

"He probably has no time for wives," I mutter. "Or he's stashed all their bodies in a dungeon somewhere. Can we talk about something other than work?" I ask, because really, I've had enough of it. Even an hour of yoga hasn't been enough to relax me. I'm considering taking Sophie's flask and downing some neat vodka.

"What shall we…" Lauren's eyes widened. "Oh my God, in all this excitement I forgot to ask. Did you make a decision?"

Sophie leans forward, her eyes wide. "Did you?" she asks me, breathless.

I nod. "I did. And I'm going for it."

"Yes!" Lauren claps her hands. "I'm so excited."

Sophie snatches my half-drunk juice out of my hand. "You can't drink this," she mutters. "It has alcohol in it."

"She's not pregnant yet, dummy," Lauren says.

This was one of the main reasons I went on vacation for two weeks. Not just because I hadn't had time off in two years, nor because I'd always dreamed of seeing Spain. But because I had a lot to think about.

I'm thirty-six years old. My gynecologist has told me that the clock isn't just ticking, it's racing, and if I want to have a baby I need to do it sooner rather than later.

So I'm going to do it alone.

"I've made an appointment at the clinic," I tell them. "To confirm what I want to do and how to go about it."

"But you don't want to freeze your eggs, right?"

"No." The fertility specialist said it would take more than one cycle to freeze them. And honestly, if I freeze them, what am I freezing them for? To wait for Mr. Right to ride in on his white steed?

We all know that's a fairytale.

I don't want to base my life choices around the possibility of a man coming into my life at the right time. I'm financially independent, I have a stable home and a lot of friends – like Sophie and Lauren – who will help. I have guy friends who are willing to provide the male role model any child would need.

And I don't want to wait anymore. I feel like it's the right time.

Or it was when I made the decision last week on vacation. Now there's this little blip of Richard retiring and Myles Salinger scowling his way around the office, but he won't stay here forever. Mediatech will recruit a new chief editor and Myles will go back to New York where he belongs and life will go on.

"I'm so proud of you," Sophie says, her eyes watery. "You'll make such a great mom."

"Have you told *your* mom yet?" Lauren asks me.

I grimace. "No. I'm not telling her anything unless it works." My mom is a very… interesting person. I love her to death and I'd do anything for her, but she's also very enthusiastic about everything. The weird thing is, she wouldn't disapprove at all. She's been a huge proponent of women's rights ever since I can remember.

But I'm still getting used to this decision. She can stay on a need-to-know basis for now.

"She'll probably be planning your birth ritual," Lauren

says, grinning. "I can picture it now. You naked in her yard, surrounded by all the women from the village."

"Your body painted with war stripes," Sophie joins in. They've both known my mom since we roomed together during college. Like me, they adore her and also fear her madcap plans.

When we finish our vodka and wheatgrass cocktails, we grab our bags and leave the studio. It's gotten dark since we came in here, but the air outside is still warm. I don't bother to put on my hoodie because it's a short walk to my town-house. Lauren and Sophie both parked their cars outside the old brownstone building so they can walk me home, even though this neighborhood is perfectly safe.

"Can you smell that?" Lauren asks. "Don't those lotus trees smell beautiful?"

They do. Fragrant and lovely and so spring-like it makes me smile.

"Better than the Callery Pear trees," Sophie agrees.

"Hey, that's the closest some of us have come to male bodily fluid in a long time," Lauren protests. "Although I guess Ava will be coming into contact with some real soon. Just without the guy."

I wrinkle my nose because I don't want to talk about disembodied semen right now. Especially as we're walking past my office. The lights in the building are mostly out, though there are still a few shining brightly on the fourth floor. I frown as I look up because everybody knows how I feel about wasting energy.

Then I slam into a brick wall and the air is forced out of my lungs.

"Fuck." Two hands circle my waist, palms directly against my skin because there's a gap between my crop top and workout shorts.

And there are those eyes again. Piercing blue, angry, and staring right at my still sweaty, red face, and pulled back hair.

I gasp for air and his big, warm hands practically lift my feet off the sidewalk and over to the wall of the Smith and Carson building so I have something to lean on.

"Ava, are you okay?" Myles asks. If he was human, I'd swear there was concern in his gaze, mixed with that constant unending fury.

"What are you made of?" I manage to mutter. "Titanium?"

He ignores me. "Can you breathe? I didn't see you coming. I was on my phone." I look down at the sidewalk, sure enough, there's his phone and a paper bag that almost certainly contains takeout. He must have put them down when he decided to go all hero on me.

"I can breathe." Or I will be able to, just as soon as he stops touching me. "Sorry, I'd been looking up. I was wondering who left the lights on."

His lips twitch. "That would be me. I'm still working."

"You okay, sweetie?" Sophie asks. Her voice sounds weird. Too sugary. I look over at her and Lauren and realize they're simpering like Victorian maids at a summer ball. Lauren is patting her hair and smiling at Myles.

He doesn't smile back. I get a grim sense of satisfaction from that. If he was nice to everybody but me I'd take it personally, but he seems to hate the world and that's okay.

Slowly he releases his hold on my waist and a rush of cold air hits my skin. He glances at my clothes, and I realize just how much I look like Julia Roberts at the beginning of *Pretty Woman*. Before she gets the glow up.

"What are you wearing?" he asks. There's a grittiness to his voice that makes my body do weird things. Like clenching my thigh muscles and feeling a deep need inside of me.

"Maybe you should look where you're going," I say, ignoring his question.

"Maybe I should." He scans me again with those all-seeing eyes. "Or maybe you should think twice about walking through the city in underwear."

I hate the way this man gets my hackles up.

"Come on, honey," Lauren urges. "Let's get you home. I'll make you some sweet tea to get over the shock."

"Good idea." Myles nods, his jaw tight. "I'll see you in the morning, Ava."

"If she's gotten over her concussion," Sophie adds, helpfully.

He doesn't say another word. Just picks up his phone and bag of takeout before walking toward the office door. Sophie and Lauren walk over to stand by my side, and I swear I hear them both sigh.

"Wow," Sophie says. "I think my ovaries just exploded."

"You have to work with him?" Lauren says. "I swear I'd combust in my office chair every time he came into the room."

"You wouldn't need to combust," I mutter. "He can incinerate you with one icy stare."

It's only when he pauses for a moment before pushing the door open that I realize he can hear us. *Shit.*

"Come on," I sigh. "Let's go home."

CHAPTER
FOUR

AVA

By Friday everybody in the office seems a little calmer. I've almost caught up with the work I missed over my vacation, which already seems like it happened in a different lifetime. I also feel like I've become Myles Salinger's personal reporting puppy. Every twenty minutes he's either messaging me – or if I don't answer quickly enough, bellowing at me from his office door – asking where different files are.

The sooner we get everything fully automated the better. Luckily, the IT team in New York seems much nicer than Myles. They actually know how to smile on the occasions that I've been on videoconferences with them.

It's almost lunchtime when my phone lights up, and Richard's name flashes across the screen. I've been calling him since Monday. Mostly to check that he's okay but also because I can't believe everything changed so quickly while I was away.

"Richard?" I say once I've swiped my thumb to accept the call.

"Ava!" He sounds jolly. Almost intoxicated. "I'm sorry I haven't returned your calls, we just got into port."

"Port?" I frown. "Where are you?"

He gives a little chuckle. "Funny story, but we're in Spain. If we'd have done it a couple of weeks ago we could have met up."

"Yes, but we weren't supposed to vacation at the same time," I point out. I frown because he sounds so… chipper.

Not like a man who's devastated because he just lost his job.

I know I should be pleased that he's happy. Richard gave me my job. He's been my mentor as well as my friend. As he keeps telling me, he's not getting any younger.

But I never expected him to be this upbeat.

"Ah, regrets, I have a few," he says. "One of them wasn't taking enough vacation time. Don't be like me, Ava. Enjoy life. I fear I've waited too long."

"But you're only sixty-two," I point out. "You've got plenty of years ahead of you."

"And there's so much of the world to see. I spent my whole life thinking the answer was between the pages of a book when it was out here all along."

"The answer to what?" I frown, because this is so un-Richardlike.

"To happiness."

I run my tongue along my bottom lip. "So, you're happy?" I ask.

"Delighted. Never been happier," he tells me.

"And you're not upset over losing your job?" I clarify.

"No, no. It's all good," he says, sounding way too jovial. "I needed the push to make a change. The only reason I stayed was to take care of you all. And now that Eleanor's tests have come back all clear, it's like a brand new start for us both."

"They came back clear?" I repeat. "I'm so happy for you."

It's wonderful news for them. I know he's been worried about her.

"Thank you. And you?" he asks. "You're happy, right? You told me you didn't want to be considered for my job whenever I left."

I take a deep breath. "I told you I had some other things going on in my life, so for the short term I needed to concentrate on those—"

"Exactly!" Richard booms. "That's what I told Jean-Baptiste. That in no way, shape, or form did you want to be running Smith and Carson. That's why they sent Salinger over. He's a good man, he knows what he's doing."

I blink. Are we talking about the same Salinger? "Well he certainly seems to be busy," I say.

"Oh wait! Eleanor wants to say hello." There's a rustle before his wife's sweet voice echoes down the line.

"Ava," she says. "How are you, darling? Did you have a good vacation?"

"Um, yeah." I blink. "Are you okay?"

"I'm wonderful. First thing we did when Richard got the pay-out was book the cruise of our dreams. We've been to Italy and Greece, now we're in Spain. It's wonderful. Everything I hoped for."

"That's lovely," I say.

"It must have been a shock for you coming back to find Richard gone," she says, sounding sympathetic.

"It was rather," I admit.

"But you're okay now?" she asks. "Richard's been worried about you."

I take a deep breath. "I'm fine," I say. "Absolutely fine."

"I told you," I hear her say to Richard. "Probably the best thing that happened to them. Change is as good as rest."

"I should let you go," I tell her. "International calls are expensive."

She laughs. "So true. Stay safe, darling. We've sent you a postcard."

"Thank you. You too." I end the call and open my top drawer, pulling a fun-size chocolate bar out of my emergency stash. Then I tear open the wrapper and shove the whole thing in my mouth at once.

It doesn't make me feel much better.

————

"You ask her," somebody whispers. I'm staring at my laptop screen, scrutinizing the copy edits that will be sent to Naomi tomorrow. They have to be perfect because a lot is riding on this year's release. Dandy the Lion needs to show Mediatech exactly how important this small publishing house is to them. And the best way to do it is by having a stellar release season.

We'll release Dandy's book in October, ready to capture the Christmas sales. The two-person marketing team is already working on a huge publicity campaign. We've upped the budget because this one needs to stick.

And I promised Naomi that nothing would change now that Richard has left. Like me, she doesn't like change. I could tell on the phone that she was anxious about everything that was happening, but I tried to reassure her it would be fine.

And it will. Even if it kills me.

"No, you do it. It was your idea," another voice replies, bringing me out of my thoughts.

"But you agreed to it. Come on, we've suffered for long enough, somebody needs to do this."

I look up from my laptop to see a small crowd gathered around my desk. It's already late afternoon and my day has passed in a blur of spreadsheets and conference calls peppered with the occasional presence of Mr. Angry himself.

I've been juggling the Dandy project along with liaising with the IT department at Mediatech. None of them can quite believe the age of the systems we've been using, and they've loudly voiced that it's a miracle we haven't had a security issue before now. They're planning on releasing a new upgrade next week, which I'm hoping will mean I can concentrate on my proper work and not spend every night working until my eyes can't stay open any more.

I haven't read a single new manuscript this week, which means I'll be taking them all home for some weekend reading. Our release plans for this year are fully formed, but next year is still wide open so we should be talking to printers and stores and distributors, not to mention schools.

I sigh because the thought of all this extra work is making my chest feel tight. I'd hoped I would have been able to talk quietly to Richard about my plans for pregnancy so we could work together on a ramp-down plan for my short maternity leave. But instead, I can't see any end in sight to this heavy, heavy workload.

"What's up?" I ask.

"It's like this," Ryan says, giving me a hopeful smile. "Everybody thinks you should ask Myles about Fizzy Fridays."

"They do? Why?" I scan the crowd of expectant faces.

"Because we haven't had them for the last two weeks and they're a Smith and Carson institution. We accept below-market pay and terrible IT equipment purely on the basis that we get free champagne on a Friday."

"And it's not even good champagne," Ella the intern points out.

"But it's free and that makes it good," Ryan interjects.

Actually, it's not champagne at all. It's a perky little cava that Richard sends me to buy in bulk from the local booze store. We keep it locked in a closet on the third floor to which only Richard and I have the key.

I guess it's only me now.

"Please, Ava?" Ryan asks, pouting. "These past few weeks

have been grueling for everybody. We need some team spirit back here. Richard may be gone, but you're still here, so do it for us."

Twenty pairs of eyes are trained hopefully on me. My stomach drops because I know I'm going to say yes. Even if it means walking into the lion's den.

"If I do this, you all owe me," I tell them.

Ryan smiles widely because he knows he has me. "Of course," he says smoothly. "Anything you want."

"I'm keeping you to that." Sighing, I push my chair away from my desk and stand up, smoothing out my skirt so it doesn't wrinkle around my upper thighs. Since my confrontation with Myles outside the office on Monday night, and his comment about my workout gear, I've been agonizing over what to wear each morning. It's so easy for guys, they just put on a suit or a shirt and pants and they're done. Women have too many choices and I fear I made the wrong one this morning.

At home, the red skirt and black shirt made me look like a professional woman who doesn't take crap from anybody. But the lining of the skirt keeps edging up my thighs and the stupid, tiny buttons on my shirt keep coming loose.

Basically, I look like I'm trying to seduce, not impress.

It's uncomfortable and for the first time in fifteen years I got wolf whistles as I walked to work. Or stumbled. Whatever.

"Maybe you should button your blouse," Ryan suggests helpfully as I gear myself up to see Mr. Angry. He was out of the office all morning – I've no idea where – then he stormed in just after lunch and slammed his door behind him without saying hello to anybody.

Ignoring Ryan's suggestion, I walk the short distance to Myles' office door and lift my hand to rap on it. But then I feel warm breath on my neck. I turn around to see that everybody's followed me.

"Um, would you all mind going back to your desks? If I'm going to do this I don't need an audience."

They look disappointed as they file back to their seats. Even Ryan's shoulders are slumped. I guess they find my interactions with Myles Salinger entertaining.

I wish I did.

A moment after I knock on his door, I hear Myles' low voice saying something that I assume means it's okay for me to enter. Taking a deep breath, I push it open and smile because this time I need something from him.

He's standing at the windowed wall behind his desk, his back to me when I walk inside, closing his office door behind me. His phone is glued to his ear and he's barking orders down it. His shirt sleeves are rolled up, revealing his strong, tanned forearms.

I grudgingly admit to myself that Lauren and Sophie are right. From a neutral point of view he really is a fine specimen of a man. His back is broad, his shirt barely containing the span of his shoulders, and his waist and hips are slim. There's a power to him that makes my own leg muscles feel weak.

Stupid leg muscles.

"It's impossible," he says to whoever's on the other end of his phone. "It was valued at three mil, I'm not paying five. Tell them to shove it, we have other options."

There's a pause as he listens, and lifts his free hand to rake his fingers through his thick, black hair. His bicep flexes, his shoulder blade rises, and I'm starting to understand Leonardo Da Vinci's obsession with the human form.

Then he turns and sees me standing in front of his door. "What are you doing here?" He does a double take, then quickly barks into his phone. "Liam, I'll call you back."

He throws his cell phone onto his desk and looks at me. His Adam's apple bobs in his throat and for a moment he says nothing.

"I did knock," I tell him. "I thought I heard you tell me to come in."

He slowly shakes his head. "I didn't hear you." His eyes rake over me, and it's like the blue turns dark for a moment. "Do we have a dress code here?" he asks.

"No." I shake my head. "We've never needed one."

"Hmm."

He doesn't sit down so neither do I. I just walk to his desk and straighten my shoulders.

When I look up he's watching me, his jaw tight.

"What is it you want, Ava?" he asks.

I meet his gaze firmly, determined to be strong. And then I stumble over my stupid words. "I, um… well, *we* were wondering actually, whether you'd be okay with…"

He sighs at my prevarication. Internally, I'm sighing, too.

I start to talk fast because it's the only way I can get it out. "It's a Smith and Carson tradition to give the team a glass of something fizzy on Fridays. To thank them for their work."

"Something fizzy?" He frowns. "Like soda?"

"A bit like that." I cough. "But it's cava."

"Cava?" he manages to draw the word out so it has a bazillion syllables. "You give them alcohol?"

"Just a glass." I don't dare tell him that after that glass everybody piles into The Hole in the Wall bar on the corner of the street and gets absolutely plastered. He's on a strictly need-to-know basis on this one.

"Does Mediatech pay you less on Fridays?" he asks.

"No." I try not to roll my eyes because I know where this is going.

"So they pay you to drink wine on company time?"

"Everybody's worked very hard this week," I tell him. "It's a nice way to thank the team. We've survived this long because we encourage team spirit. We make this a fun place to work. Fizzy Fridays are part of that."

"Fizzy Fridays. It has a name." He runs his thumb along the line of his jaw, then mutters quietly, "Unbelievable."

"You must do something similar in New York," I say, ignoring the scowl on his face. "Maybe take your staff to a bar to thank them?"

"We work until eight most Fridays. And we don't encourage drinking on company time."

"Sounds boring," I tell him, trying to make a joke. "Maybe you need to loosen up."

"I'll loosen up once I've figured out how to stop this place from going down the drain," he says quietly. "Between your finances and your systems, there's absolutely no reason why Mediatech shouldn't move your backlist to New York and close this office down."

A shudder snakes down my spine. For the first time since Monday he looks almost human. "I'm sorry, I…"

He waves his hand. "Have your Fizzy Friday. I'll be in here doing my best to save all of your jobs."

It doesn't feel like a victory. It's hollow and it feels bad and I'm already regretting coming in here. I stand and look at him, trying to decide what to say.

"Would you like me to bring you in a glass?"

"No thank you."

Okay then. I offer him a smile that he doesn't return and smooth my skirt down, feeling the burn of his stare as I walk toward his office door.

Predictably, everybody is milling around outside, trying to look busy while also waiting for me to come out.

"Are we on?" Ryan asks, his voice low.

"Yeah, we're on." I nod and everybody cheers, looking at me like I'm a soldier who just returned from winning the war.

———

MYLES

. . .

I stare at my closed door for a full minute after she leaves. The image of that tight skirt clinging to her legs is still burned into my retinas as I pick up the phone and hit the speed dial to the PA I share with three other Mediatech editors in New York. I'm not exaggerating when I say she has the patience of an angel.

"Myles," she says, sounding annoyingly perky. "Long time no talk. How are you?"

"I'm good. I just saw your message about a meeting next week. I can't make it – can you decline for me?"

"Sure. So I take it you're not coming back to New York this weekend either?" she asks.

There's no point. A four hour flight just to make calls from my apartment doesn't make sense. I can make those calls from my short-term rental here and not have to worry about packing or getting through security, even if it's the first class one.

"Not this weekend."

"And what about my other message?" Emma asks. "Your mom called. She wanted me to check your schedule to see if you're free the weekend of your dad's vow renewal."

"What did you say?" I ask, while making a mental note to never tell my brother anything. Liam is sure to have told her I'm not coming and now she's decided to get involved.

"I told her you have your schedule on private."

"Thank you."

"I don't think she believed me. I wouldn't have. What kind of assistant wouldn't be able to see her boss' schedule?" Emma clears her throat.

"It's fine. I'll deal with my mother. Next time she calls just refer her to me."

"She says you never answer. Or on the rare occasion when

you do, you never tell her anything. She says she talks to me more often than she does with you."

"I'm busy." That's an understatement. Apart from eating, sleeping, and the occasional gym visit, I've been doing nothing but work. Attempting to get Smith and Carson in order as well as doing my own work is more than challenging. On top of that, we're due to release a new Great Bear Endo book in quarter four and we're nowhere near ready for that.

"I know, Myles. But she's your mom."

A twinge of guilt pulls at my stomach. She's right. Mom can be annoyingly over interested in our lives, but she doesn't deserve to be ignored.

"I'll speak to her," I promise. Then I look at my watch. It's almost five. "You should probably be finishing up, right?"

Emma laughs. "Oh you know me. I'll be here until eight. I have to talk to the recruiters, plus there are a hundred emails waiting to be sifted through in your inbox."

"I'll deal with the recruiters and the inbox." My brows pinch together. "Can I ask you something?"

"Sure." She doesn't sound sure. She sounds slightly perturbed.

"Do you like working for Mediatech?"

"Of course," she replies smoothly, and I wonder if she even heard the question.

"And the rest of the staff in the children's publishing department, are they happy?"

"Define happy," Emma says, her voice wary..

My brows knit together. How do you define *happy*? "Should we do more to make the office a good place to work? Like… I don't know. Maybe on Fridays we could give them all a glass of champagne or something?"

Emma bursts out laughing. "What? Imagine the carnage. You want them alert and working, not rolling on the floor drunk."

"It was just a suggestion."

"I know. It's kind of sweet. And weird. But if you want I can look into staff satisfaction and how we can improve it."

"Yes, but don't do it until next week. I don't want you working all weekend."

There's a pause. I can imagine the lines denting Emma's brow right now. "Myles, are you okay?"

"I'm fine. Just thinking aloud." I glance at my watch even though she can't see me. "I need to go, I have some calls to make."

"Of course. Have a good weekend."

"You too. Don't do any work," I remind her.

"And don't you work too hard either."

I end the call, feeling like I'm on a boat in a choppy ocean, off kilter and out of control.

And I don't like it.

CHAPTER
FIVE

AVA

"Why do you have a pair of handcuffs?" I ask my mom.

I twist them in my hands, feeling the weight of them, and I have a horrible suspicion these aren't from a sex store or a children's toy department but from some black market deal, because they look exactly the same as the cops use.

Don't ask me how I know.

"For the highway demonstration," she says, as though it's a stupid question. "We're all handcuffing ourselves to whatever we can find. And if we can't find anything good enough, we'll form a circle and cuff ourselves to each other." She looks excited at the prospect. My mom lives for stuff like this. Protests and agitation and being at one with the earth. And if it involves annoying the authorities, even better.

I remember the first time she got arrested. I was twelve and had to go and stay with my friend, Alice, whose mom asked me in a very low voice if I wanted her to call child protective services, because there was clearly something wrong with my mom.

"Won't they just search you and get the key to unlock them?" I ask, sliding my finger over the lock mechanism. Once these babies are on Mom's wrist they're never getting off without the key. They're sturdy as hell.

She beams. "The key won't be on me, it'll be *in* me."

I blink. "What?"

"We swallow the keys. That way we have them somewhere safe that the authorities can't get to."

"Okaaaay…" I try to find the right words. "And how do you get them back?"

She cocks an eyebrow at me. "How do you think?"

I try to banish the image of *that* out of my brain. "Where is this protest anyway?" I ask weakly.

"At the State Capitol," she tells me, completely unaware of my horror. "There's a lot of media interest. We might even get on TV."

I pinch the bridge of my nose with my fingers. "Try not to defecate while the cameras are rolling."

"It's a natural thing, Ava," she chides. "We eat, we digest, we go potty." Another thing about my mom, despite her protests against everything, she doesn't swear. Not even the *s* word. "We're ruining this earth and not because of poop. It's the buildings and the roads and the one-use plastic. If I don't try to save it for you and future generations, who will?"

"Thank you, I think," I say.

"You can always come along. I can order another pair of handcuffs, these only took two days to get delivered." She sounds hopeful.

"I have to work," I remind her.

"Of course." Though she's fundamentally against capitalism in any shape or form, she has a grudging respect for what I do. She tells her friends, it's for the kiddies. They need books.

If I have to work for 'the man', then at least I'm doing good in the world.

I don't tell her that yesterday's Fizzy Friday descended into absolute chaos. Thankfully, everybody had made it to the bar before the singing started. I'd been stone cold sober and had cleared up the office after everybody left. If Myles had seen the mayhem it would have confirmed every prejudice he has about us. When I finally arrived at the bar an hour later, somebody had set up the karaoke machine and three of our editors were throwing up in the bathroom.

Myles was still working when I left. I went to knock on his door but I could hear the echo of his voice in yet another video call. Instead, I wrote him a note telling him there was some champagne left if he wanted a glass and that he'd find it in the fridge.

And then I'd wished him a happy weekend. Surely I deserve a halo for that.

"So, tell me more about your vacation," Mom says, bringing me out of my thoughts. "Does everybody really sunbathe topless in Spain?"

"It's spring. Nobody was sunbathing."

"But you got a tan," she points out. "It must have been warm."

"It was." It was perfect. Here in Charleston we know about warm sunshine. The average temperature in the summer here is eighty-five degrees. But it can be an unpleasant kind of heat. The kind that covers you in sweat the moment you walk out of your door in the morning, and by the evening you return all sticky and covered in dust and small insects.

"And how about the men?" she asks, lowering her voice. "I bet they were handsome."

"I thought you were against relationships between men and women," I say, confused by how excited she looks at the prospect of me having some kind of vacation fling.

"I never said that. I just said that marriage was oppression, and it is. An outdated institution that gives all the advantages to men and none to women." She lowers her voice. "But we all have needs, darling. Sexual ones. You can't ignore mother nature." Her eyebrow lifts up about two inches. "And if anybody needs to have their needs met, it's you."

"Mom!"

"How long has it been now?" she asks me. "There was Michael, but that was years ago. Then Daniel, but the less said about that man the better. And I have to admit, I've forgotten the names of the rest of them."

She hasn't forgotten, I just never told her. I learned pretty quickly not to bring men home to meet my mother. They usually left shaking and talking gibberish.

"My needs are perfectly fulfilled, thank you."

"Are you sure? Because you look pretty twitchy to me."

"I don't." I look down at my hands and realize I'm twisting my fingers. Hastily I pull them apart. "I'm just jet lagged from the flight."

"You came home a week ago."

"It was a long flight."

She sighs. "With a lot of carbon emissions. At least you don't fly very often. I saw a documentary the other day about all these business people in New York who have private jets. It's disgusting."

My thoughts turn to Myles Salinger. I try to imagine bringing somebody like him home to meet Mom. She'd probably kill him.

Then my mind drifts back to the way he looked as he took that call, his body strong and powerful. Everything about him so perfectly honed it should be illegal. I'm a sturdy woman but I suspect he could pick me up with one arm and not even bat a lash. I'm still holding the handcuffs and I imagine him clipping them around my wrists, his eyes flashing as he tells me I have to do exactly as he says.

"Are you okay, darling?" Mom asks. "Your cheeks have gone all red."

"I'm fine." I hand her back the cuffs. "I just need to get going. I have a lot of work around the house to get done."

———

"So, we'll see you tomorrow at three," the receptionist says. I say goodbye and turn the business card over in my hands. *New Dawn Fertility Clinic. Making it happen your way.* So this is it. I'm going to do this. A little frisson of excitement rushes through me.

Within a year or two, I could be a mom. I'll be completely responsible for another human being's life. The weird thing is, I'm not afraid, I'm excited.

I'm ready for this.

Pulling up my online calendar, I type 'private appointment' in the box that covers from two-thirty p.m. to five. It shouldn't take that long, but I don't want to come back to the office and have everybody ask me where I've been and if I'm okay and whether I had a job interview somewhere else.

This way I can come back when everybody's gone home for the day and catch up on my work.

Sliding the business card into my purse, I stand and walk to Myles' office and rap lightly on the door.

"Come in."

I definitely heard it this time. Even so, I gingerly push the door open, steeling myself for some kind of rebuke.

He's sitting behind his desk, his jacket off, his shirt sleeves rolled up. It's a pale blue this time. The shirt, I mean, not just the sleeves. I've never seen a man fill out a shirt the way Myles Salinger does. Everything about him is suave and sophisticated, but the way the fabric strains against his muscles is – to use his words – mildly indecent.

It makes me think about things I shouldn't. Like how

warm his skin must feel through the cotton fabric. And how hard his muscles are. Like steel, I imagine.

"Take a seat," he says, and I do as I'm told. I'm wearing pants today. Fifties style ones, tight but with full coverage, at least to my calves. On top, I'm wearing a white shell blouse, loose and airy, because the warmer days are really kicking in.

"Thanks. I just wanted to let you know I'll be out of the office for a couple of hours tomorrow. I have a doctor's appointment."

He blinks. "Is everything okay?"

"I hope so." There's no way I'm telling him what the appointment is for. By the time I have to have *that* kind of conversation, hopefully he'll be long gone and I'll have a new boss. "I'll make up for the time afterward."

"You don't need to do that. And you don't really need to ask me either. I'm not your boss."

"But you're in charge of the office," I point out. "And you seem to get annoyed when we're not earning our money." Like when he got fed up about donuts and Fizzy Fridays.

He blinks. "I wasn't annoyed. I'm just getting used to how differently things are done here." His eyes capture mine. "Are you sure you're okay? Is there anything I can do to help?"

"No." I say it so fast it surprises us both. "I'm fine. It's routine. I just thought you should know."

He nods. "I appreciate that," he says softly. "Thank you."

"Okay then." When I stand, his gaze flickers quickly from my face to my legs and back again. If you'd blinked you'd have missed it, but I didn't blink. And a rush of warmth goes right to my cheeks. "That was it. See you later."

"Goodbye, Ava." The way he says my name sends a shiver through me.

Ugh. Maybe Mom was right. I should have found a Spanish lover.

AVA

"Let's go through your options," Doctor Simons says. "As we discussed before, egg freezing while possible isn't something I'd recommend at your age."

She's been very kind, but the way she carefully forms her words tells me I've probably waited too long to do this. "I understand," I say. "And I don't want to wait anyway. I'm ready for this."

She nods. "First of all, I want to tell you that the options for single women aren't all that different than for couples who come to us. Especially if the male partner is infertile for any reason. We treat you exactly the same and try to make your experience with us as tailored to your needs as we can."

I smile, because I'd read exactly that on their website. That's why I'd chosen the New Dawn Clinic. That, and the fact that it's just outside of Charleston, so hopefully nobody will see me coming in and out of the building.

It's not that I'm embarrassed, it's that I take a while to process things. I want to keep this to myself – and my friends

– until I'm ready to share. It's private and personal and I'd like to keep it that way.

"Let's start with the whats, and then we'll go onto the hows," Doctor Simons continues. "The first option is Intrauterine Insemination. Or IUI for short. This involves placing semen directly into your uterus via a soft catheter. It's quick and relatively painless. I've had clients compare it to having a pap smear."

She smiles at me, and I nod to show her I understand.

"IUI is the first method I'd propose for you. If that doesn't work, then our next step would be IVF, In Vitro Fertilization. This involves extracting your eggs and fertilizing them in the lab, once viable, they would be implanted into your uterus. This is more invasive, obviously, but we do everything we can to make it as pleasant an experience as possible. We have good success rates with this." She tips her head to the side. "But let's go back to IUI. You have options within the procedure that I'd like to discuss with you. You don't need to make any decisions today, but I want you to have all the information to think over."

I breathe a sigh of relief, because this stuff is difficult. I've never really been sick. The only time I see my doctor is for my annual checkup. Making decisions has never been my strong suit. It was hard enough to make the decision to come here, that I didn't even think about all the ones I'd have to make afterward.

And for the next eighteen years.

"The first thing to consider is whether you want a known or an unknown donor."

"What's the difference?" I ask.

"A known donor is somebody you know who has agreed to donate sperm. An unknown donor would come from a sperm bank. There are pros and cons to both, as well as legal implications to consider if you choose a known donor."

"I don't know anybody I'd want to ask," I tell her, relieved that at least one decision could be easily made.

"That's fine. We have an extensive collection of sperm in our bank."

I squeeze my eyes shut for a moment, because all I can imagine is Lauren and Sophie's laughter when I tell them about the extensive collection. "Of course," I manage to say.

"Our donors' education and other achievements are available, so you can choose the kind of sperm you'd like."

Okay, they'd be rolling around on the floor now. Damn my imaginary friends.

"That sounds good," I squeak.

"The final thing to think about is where you'd like the procedure to take place."

"Wouldn't it happen here?" I ask, confused.

"That's one of your options. But we're finding that a lot of our people prefer in home inseminations. One of our team would come to your house and carry out the procedure, then leave you in your bedroom." She gives a little laugh. "It's the closest we can give you to the real thing."

I want to ask if they'll hold me afterward, but I don't think Doctor Simons would find it very funny.

"Are there any other options?" I ask.

This is so weird. I mean, I know it's a medical procedure, and I'd thought through what I wanted, but hearing the exact details – and options – is making me feel strange. Not just that it's all becoming real, but that it's all so clinical.

And if I'm honest, it's not how I thought having a baby would be. I blame romance novels, along with TV shows and movies. They make getting pregnant seem so easy. A girl only has to look at a guy and she's knocked up. It's so rare that you see them struggle, or have to search for medical help.

As though she senses my unease, Doctor Simons puts her pad down and looks at me. "Of course there are. Many women prefer to try as naturally as possible. Have the frozen sperm delivered to their houses and then inseminate themselves using what we call ICI – intracervical insemination. It's much cheaper, of course, and feels less intrusive. And if you do it the right way, the chances of becoming pregnant are similar to having one of our nurses perform the procedure."

"How would I do it myself?" I ask, a huge imaginary turkey baster coming into my mind.

"There are kits available. We can prescribe them but really the best place to go is somewhere like Amazon. It helps you keep cost down because all you're paying us for is the sperm."

Okay then. "There's a lot to think about," I say.

"Yes, there is," she agrees. "But try not to feel overwhelmed. I'll email you links to our informational brochures which you can read over at your convenience. And when you're ready, we can send you information about our donors and you can start to make some choices."

"Thank you." I take a deep breath. Yes, it's overwhelming but it's also exciting. And really, the way I get pregnant isn't as important as actually having a baby. I make a mental note to look at Amazon because who knew they sold insemination kits?

When the appointment is over, I walk out into the late afternoon warmth and get in my car, immediately calling Lauren. I choose her over Sophie because I know that the bakery shuts at four, whereas Sophie's work usually ramps up at this time.

"How did it go?" Lauren asks as soon as she picks up.

"It was good. I think." I take a deep breath as a wave of emotion washes over me. "But there are so many options. I need to think about how I want to do this."

"What kind of options?"

She listens carefully as I take her through everything Doctor Simons told me. "Amazon? Seriously." A moment later she laughs. "Oh yeah, there they are. They have thousands of reviews.'

"Wow."

"You should come to the bakery," she suggests. "I'll make you some coffee and you can stuff some cake down your throat and we can talk about what attributes you want the donor to have."

"I can't." I grimace. "I have to go back to the office. I need to catch up on the work I missed."

"Can't you give yourself a break, this is tough stuff?"

"No, it's fine." I imagine Myles' face if I don't go back and finish the reports he asked to have completed for first thing tomorrow. I can't do them at home because half the information I need is in the filing cabinets, thanks to Richard's allergy to technology. "I just wanted to get it all out."

"Let's go out tomorrow instead," Lauren suggests. "We'll get hammered while you still can. Dance with some inappropriate men, drink all the cocktails, regret it in the morning…"

I laugh. "Sounds good."

"Meet you at The Hole in the Wall at six?" she asks. "I'll message Sophie to join us."

"Perfect." She's such a good friend. And as I drive back to the office, the sun peeps out from behind a cloud and everything feels like it's falling into place.

CHAPTER
SEVEN

AVA

There's an eeriness to the office at night that you don't feel during the daytime. It's not just that I'm the only person in here, though that's not really helping. It's the creaks and sighs of the old construction, the occasional whirr of a printer as it decides it's time to come back to life, along with the occasional clank of the elevator as the last people in the offices below leave for the night.

I've been working on the report for two hours, and my eyes are swimming, so I take a break to decorate Ryan's desk and chair. His thirtieth birthday is tomorrow and he's been bitching all week about having to work on his birthday, so at least he can be cheered up by a bunch of banners and balloons.

The elevator clanks again, and it makes me jump. Then I jump even more when the door to our open plan office opens and Myles walks in. Instead of his usual suit, he's wearing a pair of gray sweatpants and a navy hoodie. His hair is freshly washed and brushed back from his face, which is covered by a shadow of beard growth.

He glances at the silver banner I've festooned across Ryan's desk. "What are you doing?"

"Milking cows."

His lips twitch. He looks so much younger in casual gear. Like a different person, really.

"Do you decorate for everybody's birthday?" he asks me.

"Usually. Unless they don't like celebrating. Gordon in accounting hates talking about birthdays because his wife died on his forty-second. So I just give him a hug and tell him it'll be okay."

Myles blinks. "Of course you do."

"Don't you celebrate birthdays in your New York office?" I ask him. Has he had a personality transplant to go with his new outfit? For once he's not intimidating at all.

"If we did, we'd be celebrating about a hundred a day. By the time we'd sung 'Happy Birthday' to everyone the working day would be over," he says, shrugging.

Is he making a joke? I'm not sure. I half smile just in case. "When's your birthday?"

"Are you going to blow me some balloons and cover my seat with tinsel if I tell you?"

I tip my head to the side. "If you want me to."

His lips part, but he says nothing. He's looking at me like he can't quite figure out what I am. Then he shakes his head. "A birthday and Fizzy Friday tomorrow," he says. "Is anybody going to get any work done?"

"We'll do our very best," I reply solemnly. "We wouldn't want to disappoint you."

He lifts a brow and turns, walking into his office, and I realize I didn't mention his outfit. I'll save that one for later, when he annoys me again. Because right now I need to finish decorating Ryan's desk and get back to the report.

It turns out that working alone in the office with Myles

only a few yards – and a wall – away is distracting. He's been different these past few days. Almost nice. I'm not sure whether to worry about that or enjoy it.

I keep wondering when he'll come out, so I try to look busy, which is actually harder than you'd think. Looking busy and being busy are two very different things, and trying to keep up appearances is actually hampering my productivity.

He walks out half an hour later. His hair has dried, and he's taken off his hoodie, revealing a black t-shirt that clings to his chest. "You still here?" he asks.

"No."

Both corners of his lips twitch this time. It's not quite a smile but it's not far off. He frowns as though it's painful to show any humor. "Have you seen the Reynolds file? I can't find it on the system."

"It's not on the system. I have the hard copy here."

"We need to get every single damn file onto the system," he tells me, grimacing as though the hard file is all my fault.

"Sure," I say lightly, because I just want to finish this report and get out of here. He walks over to my desk and holds out his hand, and I have to rifle through the different files on my desk to find the Reynolds one. When I finally extract it, something flutters to the floor and Myles leans down to pick it up.

"New Dawn Fertility Clinic," he murmurs, turning over the appointment card. "Is this where you were today?"

I snatch it back from him. "None of your business."

"It is if you and your boyfriend are trying for a baby. I'm trying to work out how this office can be run in the future and you're a big part of that."

"Do you think being pregnant affects a woman's brain cells or something?" I ask him.

"No, but I know that taking maternity leave affects the business. And I'm a big believer in maternity leave. I pushed

Jean-Baptiste to change policy, if you looked in the employee handbook you'd know that."

I have, and it's true. Mediatech offer a very generous paid maternity leave. Not by European standards, but way better than most companies.

"It doesn't matter anyway, I'm not pregnant yet." I look up at him, feeling like a cornered animal. "And I don't have a boyfriend."

His eyes flicker for a second. "But you're going through fertility treatment alone? Why would you do that?"

"Because I'm thirty-six years old and time is running out."

He blanches. "Can't you wait a while? Surely there must be guys knocking down your door."

I try not to laugh. "No, they aren't. Most good guys are taken at my age, and the ones that aren't have suddenly discovered that they can age down and nobody batters an eyelid. You think they want to date a someone in their mid thirties when twenty-somethings are swiping right?"

"Not every guy is like that," he protests.

"How old was *your* last girlfriend?" I ask him.

He winces. "Thirty-one. But that was a while ago."

"And you're… forty something?"

"If I tell you she was mature for her age you're going to laugh at me, aren't you?" He looks almost embarrassed. It's a good look on him.

"No. But you just proved my point." I shrug. "Anyway, even if I found the right guy, the odds are that I'll still end up a single mom in the end. Statistics prove that most relationships don't last. But I'd have to share weekends and argue over holidays and child support and the poor kid will end up paying the price."

"You've thought all this through haven't you?" he says.

"Yes I have," I tell him. "I don't have a choice. It's okay for guys, you have longevity. I need to make a decision and quickly."

He looks at me for a moment, and it feels like he's burrowing himself into my brain. I expect him to say something pithy, but he doesn't.

He does something much worse.

"I'm sorry," he says softly. "That sucks."

The way he says it touches me. It sounds genuine. And it makes tears sting at my eyes. I blink them away, because there's no way I'm crying in front of Myles Salinger.

Oh yeah? My eyes say. *May want to rethink that.*

A single tear escapes and burns a trail down my cheek. Myles' eyes widen at my sudden change in emotion.

And I am mortified.

There's only one thing worse than crying at work, not that I'd know because in all of the years of working for Richard, I haven't cried once. That one thing is crying in front of somebody who dislikes you. When you're alone together in the office and there's no escape route.

I wait for him to walk away, but he doesn't. Just stares and frowns, then does something completely unexpected.

He wipes my tears with his thumbs.

The touch of his skin against mine sends a bolt of surprise right to my toes. He's warm and gentle as he pulls me against him, so I'm sniffling against his t-shirt as he holds me tight.

Myles Salinger is hugging me.

He can hug?

Yes, he can. His chest is firm against my cheek, his arms circled around my back, and all I can do is breathe him in.

There's a whiff of shower gel in there – something deep and woodsy and very masculine. But there's something else. Something all him.

Something that makes my body ache for all the things I can't have.

He shifts slightly away from me, and that's all it takes to wake me up from my torpor and pull away from him, my face burning.

What the hell just happened? I've no idea, but I can't be here anymore. The embarrassment is overwhelming, making my head pound. I don't bother to turn off my laptop or lock away any files. Instead, I grab my purse and hightail it out of here, only turning once to look at him, before I enter the elevator.

"This never happened," I tell him, my voice gritty.

He's regained control of his expression. It's smooth and neutral and everything mine isn't. He nods as I make a grab for the handle. "Agreed."

————

MYLES

I made her cry. And I got a hard-on from hugging her. Those are the only two things that register as I watch the door swing behind her then hear the whirr of the elevator as it slowly makes its descent.

What the hell was I thinking even touching her? It's been way too long since I've touched a woman. And she'd been soft and fragrant and my body responded in exactly the way I hadn't wanted it to.

I should never have come out of my office.

Damn it, I never should have come to Charleston.

I'm just lucky she didn't notice. At least I hope she didn't.

When I'm sure she's not coming back, I sit down in her office chair and make sure everything's saved before I power down her laptop. Then I collect all the files on her desk – and the fertility clinic card – and slide them into her top drawer, locking it, but leaving the key there.

I'm getting to know Ava Quinn, and I'm almost certain she'll be here at some ungodly hour first thing in the morning to finish her report and have it to me on time. It's a matter of pride for her. She's punchy and gritty, but masks it with a veneer of respectability I'm not sure she even understands herself. She's nice and she's kind but she'll fight for those she cares about.

The way she fought me over Fizzy goddamned Friday.

And my body wants her.

Yeah, well my body can take a hike.

I turn back to my work, waking up my laptop and opening the Reynolds file to find the contract we signed three years ago. From the corner of my eye, I see a notification flash up on the screen.

Meeting Request from Mrs. Linda Salinger.

My mother is sending me meeting requests. This is where I am in life. On the plus side, any lingering remnants of desire vanish completely when I see my mom's name.

I click on it and groan when I see it's a lunch request for tomorrow. Here in Charleston. She's tracked me down and is trying to corner me.

I consider telling her I'm busy – which I am – but this is my mother. I love her, and despite my age, I still have this natural desire to make her happy. Lunch with me will almost certainly make her ecstatic, though I've no idea why.

Unconditional love, that's why.

For a moment, a fraction of a millisecond, I have a little insight into Ava's wish to have a child. But then I remember that along with that unconditional love comes sleepless nights, financial pain, emotional anguish, and the hijacking of your entire life.

I accept the meeting request and send a message to Emma to book a restaurant for us.

And then I open up the document I've been working on because I don't want to think about any of this anymore.

CHAPTER
EIGHT

AVA

"Ava, it's Matthew." Yes, the stand-in receptionist never did leave. Somehow we managed to persuade him over to the dark side with donuts and free booze. "Do you know where Mr. Salinger is? Nobody's answering his phone."

I look at his office, though I know he's out. "He isn't here," I tell Matthew. "Send him an email, he'll get it when he's back."

"There's somebody here to see him. A Mrs. Salinger." There's a little murmur on his side of the line before he continues, "Sorry, her name is Linda. Mr. Salinger's mother. She says she has an appointment with him."

"I'll come down and get her," I tell him.

"You're a star." Matthew hangs up before I can change my mind.

I'm already exhausted and it's barely lunchtime. I've been in since six this morning. It didn't escape my notice that somebody – *okay, Myles* – cleared my desk last night, and saved the report I'd left hanging on my laptop.

Thankfully he's been out of the office all morning, so I haven't had to face him after last night. If I'm lucky, I'll make it through the weekend and by Monday it will have been forgotten.

A minute later, I walk into the lobby and Matthew points at a woman standing by the window, looking out at the street. And the first thing I notice about her is that she isn't a fragile old lady at all. She's beautiful, with long blonde hair that's perfectly styled and make up that somehow makes her skin look dewy and youthful.

"Mrs. Salinger?" I say.

She turns and smiles, and it's dazzling. I wonder if Myles' smile is similarly breathtaking.

I suspect I'll never find out.

"It's Linda, please," she says breathlessly. "I'm so sorry to put you to all this trouble. I arrived a little early and thought I'd surprise Myles."

"It's no trouble," I tell her. "Why don't you come up to his office and I'll call him to let him know you're here?"

"Oh, no need to call him. At the worst I'll meet him at the restaurant he's booked. I'm just interested to see where he works." She looks around the lobby. "This is very different to his office in New York."

"This building has been here for almost two hundred years," I tell her, inclining my head at the elevator. "Shall we?"

"Oh my." She presses her hand against her chest. "A gated elevator. I remember these from when I was a tiny girl."

Unlike her son, Linda Salinger is extremely easy to talk to. By the time we reach the third floor, I've learned that she divorced from Myles' dad years ago, that she divides her time between New York, the Hamptons, and Florida, and that she loves her sons very much.

"You really brought up four boys?" I ask her.

"Six, if you include my stepsons." She frowns. "Well,

strictly speaking they're not my stepsons but it's easier if I call them that. Rupert's boys from his second marriage. They used to come stay when Deandra – Rupert's wife after me – needed a break."

"Wow. That must have been mayhem." I try not to look surprised. There's a lot going on with the Salinger family.

She laughs. "It was, but I miss those days. I couldn't turn my back on them for a minute. Otherwise they'd be balancing buckets of water on the tops of doors and gluing down the toilet lids. Myles was the worst of them, being the eldest." Her face lights up as she mentions his name. "No wonder I went gray so young."

I try to imagine Myles Salinger playing tricks on people, but my brain won't compute it. He's too serious. Too sullen.

"This is Myles' office," I say, pointing to the corner room that was once Richard's and now belongs to Myles. At least for the interim. "Would you like to sit in there? I can get you a coffee?"

"Oh no, I'd prefer to sit out here where the action is," she says, looking around the bustling open plan area. Ryan's birthday banner is hanging half-off, but he's still wearing the crown Catherine made him. Ella, our intern, is carrying files back from Myles' office, balancing them precariously like she's at etiquette school, trying to demonstrate her poise. And in the corner, the three-strong finance team is arguing heatedly over yesterday's ball game.

I pull a chair out next to my desk, and Linda sits down, still wide eyed and looking around. "So this is where my son works," she says. "It's lovely. It reminds me of those screwball comedies in the nineteen-fifties." Her eyes twinkle. "Which makes you Doris Day. Or possibly Barbara Stanwyck."

I smile, but have no idea what she's talking about.

"Do you work closely with Myles?" she asks when I sit down next to her.

"It's a small office," I tell her, dodging the question. "We all work closely with each other."

"It's okay, you don't have to be nice about him," she says, taking a sip of the water I got for her. "I know he can be a grump. I was just hoping that the change of scenery would help his mood." She wrinkles her nose. "Is he hell to work with?"

"Um… no."

Her laughter tinkles through the room. "It's okay, I won't tell him."

"Tell me what?"

The man himself is towering over us, wearing a navy suit and white shirt, no tie. He's freshly shaven and his hair is brushed back, though a few locks have fallen over his brow. He looks like he could be at home in a boardroom or the French Riviera. There's something timeless about him that makes my heart do a little leap.

"Myles!" Linda's face splits into a smile. Love for her son seeps out of every pore. "Darling, it's so good to see you."

He leans down to kiss her cheek. "You look beautiful, Mom," he tells her. "And you're early."

She pats her hair. "I wanted to surprise you, but you outmaneuvered me."

The corners of his eyes crinkle. He looks like he adores his mother.

It makes my chest feel tight.

"Since you're here, let's head for the restaurant." He holds his hand out to help her out of the chair.

"Won't we be early?"

"I'll buy you a cocktail if we have to wait." He glances at me. "Everything okay here?" he asks, his face neutral. He makes no mention of last night's shenanigans and I'm grateful for that.

"Everything's good."

"It's Friday. I assume you'll be pouring everybody a glass at four."

I nod. "If that's okay with you."

"What's that?" Linda asks Myles. "What kind of glass?"

"It's Fizzy Friday," he says dryly. "Everybody gets a glass of cava to celebrate." His eyes catch mine. "It's a tradition."

"How lovely." She tips her head to the side. "Such a nice way to end the work week." She holds her hand out to me. "It's been wonderful to meet you, Ava. Thank you for taking good care of my son."

Our gazes clash again. His expression is still unreadable, his mouth slightly parted, his jaw square and strong. And for a moment I shiver, remembering the way he held me last night.

"It's a pleasure," I murmur, and there's the slightest movement in the corner of his lips.

"I'll be back later," he says. "Call me if there are any problems."

"I will." I watch as the two of them walk out together, her face raised to him as she smiles and says something I can't make out.

Then I hear something weird. A chuckle. And damn if I can't see his face. He's laughing and I missed it. For some reason that irks me.

Next time I'm determined to be in front of him when he does it.

———

MYLES

"You look different," Mom says, her eyes appraising me over the top of the leather-bound menu she's holding. "I don't think you ever take your tie off in New York."

"I'm trying to adapt to my surroundings," I say dryly. "If you hadn't noticed, nobody wears a suit at Smith and Carson."

"It's not just that," she says. "You look refreshed. Less tired. Being away from the big city suits you."

"Charleston's a city," I point out.

"Technically, yes. But it feels like a town, doesn't it? Full of quaint shops and friendly people. It's nothing like New York at all." She puts the menu down and leans forward conspiratorially. "My only complaint is the smell. There are these trees that smell disgusting. What are they?"

There's no way I'm talking about jizz trees with my mom. "I've no idea. Maybe you were near some trash."

"Anyway, I like it. You seem more relaxed away from New York. Happier, even." She tips her head to the side. She's had some work done in the past. Nothing too obvious but it works for her. The waiter brings over our drinks – a martini for Mom and a coffee for me. She lifts her glass and smiles. "Shall we make a toast? To family and happiness."

I lift my coffee cup. "Ditto."

After she takes a sip, she puts her cocktail down and steeples her fingers, resting her chin on the tips. For a moment she says nothing.

"Spit it out," I tell her, smiling because she never could hide her ulterior motives. "Tell me why you're really here."

"To see my son. Isn't that enough?"

"Sure. You came all the way to West Virginia so I'd buy you a cocktail," I tease.

"You were on my way. I'm spending the weekend with your father and Julia."

"Why?" This is the one thing I never understood about my parents. If they like spending time together so much, why did they split up?

"Julia needs some help planning their vow renewal. There's a lot to organize."

Julia is my father's third wife. Well, fourth strictly speaking, but we call her the third, because nobody mentions dad's first wife. It's like my mom and Deandra – his wife after mom – have adopted Julia. They're thick as thieves.

"I don't understand why they don't have the ceremony and let everybody go home. Why mix it in with a family reunion?" I ask.

"Because your father wants his family there. And if you're going to the effort of traveling to see him then he'd like to spend some quality time with his boys." She gives me a sad smile. "You used to love spending time at Misty Lakes."

Misty Lakes is the name of my father's estate in Virginia. Complete with a sprawling mansion, a huge lake surrounded by cabins, and enough land to get lost in. It's where he spends most of his time nowadays, since retiring from a career in finance.

"I did when I was a child," I tell her. "It gave me the opportunity to throw Liam and Eli into the lake."

"If I ask them, maybe you can do it again," she says hopefully.

"Even if I wanted to, I can't afford to take a week away from work right now." And I don't want to go. Not at all.

"You must be owed some time off," she points out. "Your father will be so disappointed if you're not there."

"He never took a week off when we were growing up," I point out. That's why my mother and Deandra had to bring us up. And why I had to watch my brothers so much.

She reaches out to touch my hand. "Just come for a few days. The weekend, at least."

I pinch the bridge of my nose with my fingers. "Mom…"

It's like she can sense blood. In the office I'm known for my stubborn refusal to be swayed. Yet a touch of a hand from my Mom and I'm toast.

"Do it for me," she whispers. "Please, darling."

I sigh loudly, because I never should have agreed to this

lunch. I knew why she'd come here and I'm still falling into her trap. The only woman in the world who knows exactly how to play me.

"I'm not making any promises," I say. "But I'll take another look at my schedule."

She sits back and folds her arm across her chest, a triumphant expression on her face.

And I know for certain that one way or another I'll be going to Misty Lakes.

CHAPTER
NINE

AVA

Lauren was right, a night out with the girls is exactly what I need. The three of us – Sophie, Lauren, and I – are standing at a high table at The Hole in the Wall bar, watching as Ryan attempts to sink the black ball with his eyes shut, in order to win a beer.

Somebody put the jukebox on and a few of the younger staff are dancing in the corner to a Jay-Z track that seems completely out of place in this dive bar.

The Hole in the Wall has been Smith and Carson's unofficial clubhouse for as long as I can remember. It's run by Derek, an ex-soldier who started working here as a barman before buying out the previous owner when it went up for sale. He's a good guy who keeps an eye on the younger crowd as well as making sure our drinks are constantly topped up.

"So I said to her that crème pat isn't actually French cream, but she insists that Paul Hollywood says it is." Lauren sighs, describing her meeting today with a bridezilla. "I did a blind taste with her and she preferred the fresh cream profiteroles, but she still wants them the way Paul makes them."

"It's his eyes. They're hypnotizing," Sophie sympathizes. "He could persuade me to do anything."

"Just give her crème pat," I say to Lauren. "If that's what she wants."

"But it isn't the best," Lauren complains. "And I don't want to serve something that isn't the best."

This is why Lauren is so good at her job. She doesn't accept anything less than perfection. As well as running the Camelia Bakery, she also creates cakes and desserts for weddings and other events. Her food is delicious and the main reason why we all go to yoga every Monday. Sophie and I are always her willing guinea pigs when she has a new recipe to try.

"And then I made the mistake of telling her I'm friends with a weather forecaster," Lauren says, turning to Sophie, who's holding her hand up to Derek and mouthing something to him. "She wants me to ask you if it's going to be sunny on the third of September."

Sophie rolls her eyes. "You told her it's not possible to accurately forecast that far ahead, right?"

"Yep, but she says she needs to know whether to have the tent open or closed."

"Tell her to have it closed," Sophie says. "That way she might not get bitten to death by mosquitos."

Sophie is always getting asked about the weather, and it drives her crazy. Not because she's not interested in her job. She loves forecasting. She's one of the only television weather personalities who's actually qualified in meteorology. But she hates getting the blame when it rains. People hold it personally against her.

"How's the weather looking for tomorrow?" I ask. "I have to weed my yard."

"It'll be cloudy from seven to nine but no rain unless

you're in the mountains," Sophie says, and I immediately know she'll turn out to be right. "The sun should start to break through after that, and tomorrow afternoon will be glorious. Maybe too warm for yard work, so you might want to take a break after one."

"Thank you," I say solemnly. "I'll take that into account."

"You're doing yard work?" Lauren says. "You got stuff on your mind?"

She knows that I think best while my hands are busy doing something. And since I have none of her culinary skills, weeding the yard is the best way to do it.

Sophie gives me an empathetic smile. We talked about my appointment at the clinic last night, after I'd fled the office. I haven't told either of them about my run-in with Myles, or how I'd cried all over his chest.

It's still too embarrassing to acknowledge.

"Yeah. I still need to make a decision about the insemination."

"You should do it at home. At least that way you don't have to drive afterward," Lauren says, her voice too low for any of my workmates to overhear. Derek arrives with our drinks and we're all silent for a moment as we take our first mouthfuls.

"Yeah," I agree. "But I think I'll do it with a kit. It would be weird having somebody in my bedroom making a baby with me, but not feeling attracted to them."

Lauren swallows a laugh. "I guess that does feel a bit strange. But so would getting inseminated in the clinic, right?"

"At least in the clinic it would feel like more of a medical procedure." I take another sip of my drink. "I just need to adapt to the idea of it," I tell them. "I mean, it's not what we grew up dreaming of, is it? Laying on a bed and putting a turkey baster inside of you."

"I don't think they actually use a turkey baster," Sophie says.

"I know, but it's kind of the same thing," I tell her. "Just smaller."

"They should use a specially made dildo," Lauren interjects, and we both whip our heads to look at her. "Hear me out," she says, trying not to laugh at our expressions. "It'd feel more real. Plus, if they did it right, maybe it would be enjoyable."

"I don't want it to be enjoyable." I wrinkle my nose. "If I'm going to enjoy myself I might as well find a random guy and ask him to make a baby with me."

"Haven't you thought of doing that?" Sophie murmurs. Thank God the rest of the pub is too loud for anybody else to overhear.

"No." I shake my head. Although I have to admit that when I did some Googling yesterday about donors it took me down a rabbit hole. There are guys who do that for a living. Actually go to your house and… yeah. "It would get too messy."

"But you'd get some good sex out of it," Lauren points out.

"And so would he. Win-win." Sophie smirks.

"So that's your choice in a nutshell," Lauren says. "Spread your legs for a nurse, a turkey baster, or for a guy."

"A hot guy," Sophie adds, grinning. "I mean, at least you get some choice about that. You get none about the nurse."

They both laugh at the expression on my face.

"Great," I say. "Ride a hot guy senseless, or get inseminated by a dildo. Great choices." I tap my chin. "I wonder which one I'll choose."

Neither Lauren or Sophie laugh. They're both staring over my shoulder, their eyes wide, their mouths falling open.

And of course, when I turn around, Myles Salinger is standing right behind me, listening to every word I said.

______

MYLES

"Ladies," I murmur, trying to ignore the fact I just overhead Ava talking about riding a hot guy. I really don't need that image in my head right now.

Even if the guy in my imagination is me. *Christ.*

"Myles." I recognize the blonder of Ava's friends from that time outside of the office. She gives me a genuine smile. "How lovely of you to join us."

"Yes," Ava says. "It's a really nice surprise." Her voice is edged with sarcasm. I ignore it.

"Ryan asked me to come. To join in his birthday celebrations."

"He's right over there," Ava says pointedly, inclining her head at a group of our drunken employees in the corner. Ryan is doing some kind of lewd dance with a pool cue. I turn my head back to Ava and her friends.

"Yes, I see that." I take my tie off and roll it carefully around my fingers, making sure it doesn't crease. When I slide it into my pocket, I catch Ava staring at my hands. I frown and look back down at them. Is there something wrong with my hands? Have my nails suddenly fallen off?

No. They're just my hands. Long fingers, flat palms, veins that stand out too much.

"Can we buy you a drink, Myles?" Ava's other friend says.

I pull my gaze from my hand and pull out my wallet. "Let me buy you all one. What are you drinking?"

She smiles widely and I smile back. "I'm so sorry, but I don't know your names," I tell them.

"I'm Sophie. And that's Lauren." Sophie holds her hand out and I shake it.

"Myles Salinger."

"Oh, we know who you are." Sophie winks.

"Do you work in publishing, too?" I ask them, just to make conversation. From the corner of my eye, I see that Ava is frowning.

Is she still angry at me about last night? Jesus, did she know I got a hard-on?

"No, I'm a meteorologist," Sophie says. "And Lauren's a baker. She owns the Camelia Bakery on Sunset."

I look at Lauren. "You make those donuts that Ava brings in?"

She nods. "Have you tried one?"

"No, but the staff raves about them." Ava remains silent, her eyes darting back and forth when each of us speaks like she's watching a tennis match.

"Next time she brings some in I'll make a special one for you," Lauren says. "Tell me, do you prefer chocolate or citrus?"

"Citrus."

"You've got it." She narrows her eyes and touches her chin. "I'll make you a lemon custard cream donut."

"I look forward to it."

"So Myles," Sophie says. "Maybe you can help us solve an argument. Which do you prefer, fresh cream or crème pat?"

Ava gives a little laugh, like there's a joke I'm not aware of. My eyes linger on her for a moment too long. Her hair catches the light and for a moment I imagine it splayed across my pillow. Pushing that thought away, I turn back to her friend.

"Fresh cream," I say. "Crème pâtissiere is useful, but it's so easily over sweetened."

"You know what crème pat is?" Ava asks, her brows furrowing.

"I watch *The Great British Baking Show*," I shrug.

Lauren's grin widens. "Who did you want to win last season?"

"I had a soft spot for Jurgen," I tell her. "But I was happy that Giuseppe won." She elbows Ava in the stomach and Ava rolls her eyes. "Of course, it hasn't been the same since Mary Berry left."

"Right? Prue is great, but Mary was the queen," Sophie says. "Didn't you say the same thing, Ava?"

Ava lets out a long breath. "Something like that."

"Do you bake, Myles?" Lauren asks.

"I burn water," I tell her. "But I appreciate pastries and cakes very much."

Lauren sighs. "You're a man after my own heart."

"What about weather systems?" Sophie asks. "Do you like those too?"

"I appreciate a good cloud formation," I tell her, my voice deadpan. "Though I much prefer a cumulonimbus to a cirro-stratus."

"Oh so do I." Sophie nods. "Until they start raining, of course."

Ava lets out what sounds like a low level growl. I turn to look at her. "Is there something wrong with your eyes?" I ask her.

"No. Why?" She frowns.

"You rolled them. I thought you might be in pain."

Lauren sniggers and I see Ava gritting her teeth.

"I'll get those drinks now," I say. "What can I get for you all?"

"A gin and tonic for me, and Sauvignon for Sophie and Ava," Lauren tells me.

"I'm okay," Ava says quietly. "I still have some to finish."

I open my mouth to argue, but the fact is, I'm tired of arguing with Ava Quinn. I'm tired of her looking at me like I'm some kind of monster.

Overall, I'm just exhausted.

I'll buy her a glass of wine, and if she doesn't drink it, it's not my problem.

"I'll ask Ryan if he'd like something, too," I say, relieved that he's stopped his pole dancing impression and is back to potting balls on the pool table.

"Great." Lauren grins.

I nod at the three of them then walk over to the crowded pool area. As soon as I am out of reach, the three of them start talking in voices too low for me to hear, but I'm almost certain to be the subject of their whispered debate.

"Ryan," I say, holding out my hand. "Happy birthday."

Ryan blinks when he realizes who's talking to him. It takes him another second to shake my hand. "You came?" I'm not sure he's happy that I did.

"Just for one drink." I don't want them all to start acting on their best behavior because I'm here. I know they don't like me. And I'm okay with that. "What can I get you?"

"I'll have another Bud, please." He looks inordinately pleased.

In the end, I take orders from most of the people in here, because I can't buy a few of the staff drinks without buying them for the rest. I can't abide favoritism and my bank balance won't suffer. The bartender blinks when I start to give him the orders, but he and his staff are efficient, and it only takes ten minutes to hand out all of the different drinks to the right people.

When I take the gin and tonic and two glasses of wine over to the corner where Ava and her friends are standing, I see only two of them there. I hand Lauren and Sophie their drinks, then look around for her.

"Where's Ava?" I finally ask, her glass of wine still in my hand.

"Yeah, about that." Lauren shifts, looking almost guilty. "She has a headache. She just left."

———

AVA

I'm halfway home when I hear footsteps behind me. If I had any sense they'd probably scare the hell out of me, but we have a lot of runners in Charleston and I'm used to them calling out right before they overtake me, to let me know there's no harm coming.

But whoever it is doesn't call out as the steps get closer. Confused, I turn and there's no one in track pants behind me. Just one man running in a suit, his jacket flaring out behind him, his dark hair mussed by the breeze.

I turn my head back and scrunch up my face, because I really don't need to talk to this particular man right now. He knows all my secrets and I hate that. I just want to go home and sleep for a hundred years.

"Ava!" he calls out. He isn't even breathless. He probably runs marathons for fun.

I stop walking, because he knows I know he's there. A moment later, he catches up with me and I can smell his cologne in the gentle breeze that surrounds us.

"What do you want?" I ask him, genuinely baffled as to why he's running after me.

"I…" He runs his hands through his hair and blinks.

I don't think I've ever seen Myles speechless before. It's kind of thrilling but also unnerving. I look at him patiently, goosebumps lifting the skin on my bare arms because the evening has gotten kind of chilly since the sun went down.

Chilly for West Virginia, anyway. We don't get the worst of the blazing weather until mid-summer, but even now the days are warm and balmy. The evenings can be variable. Sophie has tried to explain the effect of the mountains on the weather systems here to me, but it went over my head.

"You didn't need to leave the bar because of me," he finally says.

"I didn't leave because of you," I lie. "I have a headache."

"Yeah, that's what your friends said." His eyes catch mine. Why do they have to be so piercing? Even in the gloom of the evening it feels like they can read my innermost thoughts.

And none of them are good.

"But you didn't have a headache when I arrived, so I assume I caused that headache somehow," he says, brushing his hair from his face with his fingers.

"It's not you." I swallow hard, trying to find the right words. Part of that's completely correct. How could I be annoyed at him for coming into a bar that's open to the public? That would just be rude. And he was charming to my friends.

Yet I'm embarrassed to admit that I *am* a teeny tiny bit annoyed at it. I don't want to be, but I am. I wanted my friends to see how aggravating he can be. Instead, they were both swooning over him and Googling him to see if he's seeing anybody right now.

He isn't, apparently.

The fact is, it's been a long week. I'm overloaded with work and have to make a life-changing decision soon, and I don't know what to do. I know what I want, but it's the *how to get there* that's confusing me.

"Then what is it?" he asks. "Did something upset you?"

"No." I really am starting to get a headache now. I rub my temple with my hands and wince. It's divine retribution for telling a lie.

Myles gently touches my hands and pulls my fingers from my face. His touch is warm and gentle and sends a shiver through me.

"Do you have any Tylenol?" he asks me.

"Yeah." I nod. "I'll go home and take some." I turn to walk away but he catches my wrist.

"I'll walk you there."

"Honestly, I don't need an escort," I point out. "It's a headache, not a broken leg."

He gives me a look that I recognize right away. I call it his 'stop fucking with me' look. And my now-pounding head decides to let him have his way for once. So we start walking.

Luckily, I only live five minutes away, and I can blame my silence on my head. But the pain slicing through my brain does nothing to dim my awareness of him.

He doesn't touch me again, but that doesn't matter, because it feels like he's connected to me. My body tingles at his closeness, and there's nothing I can do about it.

When we get to my front door I fumble with my purse to locate my keys, then manage to miss the lock twice because I'm so tense. He gently takes the keys from my hands and slides it easily into the lock, turning it to open.

"Take two Tylenol and get right to bed. Okay?"

"Why are you being so nice to me?" I ask softly.

He tips his head to the side. "I thought you liked niceness?"

"I do. It's just…" I shake my head, then grimace at the resulting pulse of pain. "I don't like it from you."

His brows lift but he gives nothing else away. "Take a glass of water with you to bed, too. Keep hydrated," he instructs me.

"Okay. Thank you. Good night."

He steps back, watching as I walk into my hallway. "I hope you feel better in the morning," he tells me.

I nod and close the door, about to head to my little kitchen where I keep my medicine in a decorative lidded storage box on the top shelf of one of my cupboards. But then there's a knock at the door. It's so strong and sure that I know exactly who it belongs to.

"Myles," I say, opening the door to see him standing there, his expression serious, his eyes blazing.

"If you want a baby, I can give you one."

CHAPTER
TEN

AVA

If you want a baby, I can give you one.

Those are the first words I think when I wake the next morning, a ghost of the headache that started last night still scratching at my brain.

I had stared at him open mouthed, waiting for him to start laughing hysterically. Instead his eyes had clouded as he took in my shocked expression, and he'd become uncharacteristically nervous, shifting his feet on the stoop of my townhouse.

"I mean, I can donate the sperm," he'd added. "So you don't have to go through any procedures or choose the right donor."

Still I'd said nothing. Because, seriously, what do you say to something like that?

Oh yes, please, I'd love your sperm. Give it to me now…

"Just think about it, okay?" he'd finally said when I remained silent, backing down the steps. His eyes darted to my face, as though he wasn't sure what else to say. And it was strange, but he somehow looked more appealing than when he was big bad Myles who never felt an ounce of contrition about anything.

Like instructed, I'm still thinking about his words as I pull weeds out of the hydrangea beds I planted when I first bought this place. The front yard is small, but I love having a riot of color in the summer, and in this climate they take some maintenance.

I stop digging and take a long cleansing breath. Is it really such an awful idea to use sperm donated by somebody I know?

Even if the two of us butt heads at every turn?

I'd have to carry Myles' baby for nine months. He'd see my bump swell and grow and know that the child inside of me belonged half to him, even if only genetically. Because you can be damn sure I'll make him sign away any rights.

Shaking my head, I lay my trowel down. I can't believe I'm even thinking about this. He was joking, right? Or drunk.

Except he hadn't been drinking. And from my experience I can say for certain that Myles Salinger doesn't joke. Which only leaves one conclusion…

"Ava!" My mother's voice carries across the front yard. To be fair, it carries across everywhere. She can probably be heard in Virginia. "You need to put a hat on, sweetie. Haven't you heard of global warming? The hole in the ozone layer? Skin cancer?"

I stand and stretch my arms. My mom is in her car – a convertible VW Bug painted pink with flowers daubed all across the chassis. She's had this car ever since I can remember. It's like her third limb or something.

"I put sunscreen on," I tell her dryly. "Would you like a drink? I have a jug of lemonade in the refrigerator."

"I can't stay," she tells me. "I'm off to Washington. We're doing a march against fossil fuels in the morning so Raeanne is putting us all up overnight."

"Are you driving there?" I ask, because it's a five hour

drive to Washington and I honestly don't think her car will make it. I also don't bother to point out that her car probably burns through more fossil fuels than anything else in this city. But she has an answer for everything.

"Don't be silly. We're taking the train. I just needed to pick up some supplies for my banners. We're painting them tonight around the camp fire."

"You're camping?" I ask.

She looks at me as though I'm stupid. "Yes, in Raeanne's backyard."

My mother is seventy-two and has had two hip replacements. Yet she thinks nothing of bunkering down in a tent without any bathrooms nearby. I once asked her what she did when she had to go, and I've been trying to forget her answer ever since.

Never ask my mom a question unless you want a brutal, descriptive answer.

"… So if that happens, you'll need to be ready with your credit card, okay?"

"What?" I ask. "I missed that."

"Raeanne and I are going to march naked. We think it'll get more publicity. But it's against the law, so we could end up being arrested." She looks ridiculously giddy at the thought. "She doesn't think the bail will be high, so your credit limit should cover it."

"Isn't it…" I try to find the words. "A little cold to be doing that?"

"We'll march fast. Send all the blood to the right places." She frowns as her eyes scan my face. "Are you all right? You look pale?"

"I'm fine."

"No," she says, shaking her head. "There's something wrong. I can tell. Is it work?" she asks. "Has that man who took your job upset you?"

"He didn't take my job," I point out. "I still have my job. He's just standing in until they replace Richard."

"They should replace him with you. You always did all the work there. Richard just took the credit. Can you believe we live in the twenty-first century and the patriarchy still rules?"

Somehow she's moved to a more comfortable ground, railing against the unjustness of the world.

I truly love my mom. Growing up, she was so much fun to be around. I can't really remember my dad ever being there. I only hear from him once in a blue moon.

But Mom always made sure I was happy and secure. And most of all we had fun. I used to love painting banners with her, and marching through the streets yelling slogans out of my lungs. We bonded over acid rain and the hole in the ozone layer and social injustices wherever they happened to be.

And then I reached puberty and I'm ashamed to say I got embarrassed of her. Sure, all teenagers find their parents embarrassing, but I can still remember the first time I told her I didn't want to march for her stupid cause and she looked so upset.

I hate that I did that.

I hate that I allowed my embarrassment to come between us. Even now there's a shadow of my behavior still there.

"If the police call I'll bail you out," I tell her, my throat thick. She really does believe in these causes, and somebody needs to.

Somebody needs to fight for the little guys. And I'm proud of her. Or at least I'm getting there.

"Thank you, sweetie." She leans out of the car and pats my cheek. "Are you sure you're okay?"

"I am." I offer her a smile. "Honestly."

"Hmmm." She narrows her eyes. "Come to my place next Saturday. We can go out for lunch."

"Okay." I nod. "Sounds good. Now go before they leave without you. And try to not get arrested."

She blows me a kiss. "I'll do my best. You'll know if I fail." She starts the engine back up and toots the horn so loud the whole neighborhood can hear it, before pulling away with a squeal of her tires.

CHAPTER
ELEVEN

AVA

Myles is out of the office all day Monday. I get a message from Jean-Baptiste's assistant asking me to attend the 10 a.m. management call on his behalf, along with the dial in details for our videoconference system. But there's no message from him and no sign of him being active on our systems.

I'm starting to think he's avoiding me.

When it comes to my turn to update the team, I talk through the weekly sales numbers and our upcoming events, explaining which titles we've decided to save our marketing budget for.

"We have the back to school market, of course. And there are five books we've decided to push with retailers. Our marketing team is working on store placements and special deals right now. And we're also looking forward to our quarter four releases, including the new one for Dandy the Lion. We have a special hardback edition with embossed letters which we think will really appeal to the parent and grandparent market." I look down at the notes I've made.

"We also want to buy advertising space in key areas, and we're currently in talks with Macy's about having a Dandy the Lion float in the Thanksgiving Day Parade."

"Macy's." The head of marketing nods, and I wait for him to say more. Instead, he turns to Jean-Baptiste, our boss, and says, "Actually, that's a really good idea. We should push for a Great Bear Endo float, too. The new TV show starts in September, so it would time in perfectly with our plans. I'll talk to Myles about it when he's back."

"Um, would they allow two floats from the same company?" I ask them.

Myles hadn't said a thing about a TV show. I'm annoyed that I've been blindsided, but then would I have done the same? Probably. I'm not a big bragger and neither is he. We just keep our heads down and work hard.

"I have an idea," Jean-Baptiste says. "Maybe we can have them both on the same float. They could be friends or something."

"Dandy lives in the jungle," I say quietly. "And Endo's an astronaut."

But they've already moved on to a report from the head of foreign sales and our brilliant marketing idea has been coopted by New York as their idea for their books, and Dandy the Lion has been all but forgotten.

I pause my video but still listen to the call as I click on my email window. I've already checked Myles' calendar but it's annoyingly blacked out with a private meeting all day. So I quickly type out an email, figuring I may as well get in before the New York marketing department does.

To: MylesSalinger@Mediatech.com
    From: AvaQuinn@SmithandCarson.Pub
    Subject: Marketing Plans

· · ·

Hi Myles, I hope you're okay.

When you're back in the office, can we meet to discuss marketing plans for Dandy the Lion's release? The team has some great ideas and I want to put them into action before somebody steals them.

Thanks, Ava

I hit send, then bring my attention to the meeting. It's coming to a close, and Jean-Baptiste is just updating on the shareholder meeting he had last week.

Right as he makes a joke about needing a vat full of coffee before meeting them again, a message pops up on my screen. Myles is sending me an instant message.

Myles Salinger: Hi. I just got your email. If you have some ideas go for them. I may not be back in the office tomorrow.

I frown and hit reply.

Ava Quinn: Is everything okay? And I should probably discuss this with you first, because New York is trying to steal the plans we have for Dandy the Lion.

Myles Salinger: What are they stealing?

• • •

Ava Quinn: They love the idea of getting a float in the Macy's Thanksgiving Day parade, but want to put The Great Bear Endo on it, even though we're already working on a Dandy the Lion float.

There's no response for five minutes. Occasionally three little dots appear as though he's typing, but then they go away again. The meeting ends, so all that's left on my laptop screen is our chat and the background image of the Allegheny Mountains.

And now I remember why I hated online dating so much. The Spanish Inquisition could have used those three little dots as torture weapons. It's the waiting that kills you.

Finally, a response comes.

Myles Salinger: Go ahead and contact Macy's. If New York kicks up a fuss tell them I said to do it. If they want Endo on there he can hitch a ride.

I stare suspiciously at his response. Is he trying to set me up? Get me in trouble with Jean-Baptiste? It doesn't feel right going behind their backs.

But I'm still annoyed at them for stealing our idea. That's not fair either. Maybe we'll just make some inquiries and see what happens. That couldn't do any harm, could it? Then something else occurs to me. He sounds… different. Off. And now I'm worried it really is about our conversation on Friday night.

Ava Quinn: Are you okay?

•　•　•

Myles Salinger: Why do you ask? Do you think I should be fighting for Endo's honor?

Ava Quinn: No, I meant the fact you disappeared unexpectedly. I just want to make sure you aren't hurt or anything.

Or annoyed at me.

Myles Salinger: I'm just dealing with some family matters. If I'm not back tomorrow I should be in the office by Wednesday. But if anything comes up, I'll be available by email.

Ava Quinn: I'm sorry to hear that. I hope it's nothing too bad. Always here if you need to talk.

Myles Salinger: Thank you, Ava. I appreciate that.

The typing dots disappear and I stare at the screen until his name turns dark and *offline* appears next to it.

And I find myself worrying about him. Not because he's very possibly setting me up with the New York office, nor that he didn't mention his offer at all. But because Big Bad Myles Salinger actually sounded a little bit… I don't know… tender?

It touches me, and I have no idea what to do about that.

CHAPTER
TWELVE

AVA

I don't know what I expected Myles to be like when he came back to the office, but this isn't it.

He seems moodier than ever, walking into the open plan office and giving terse nods to people before he stalks with those long legs over to his closed office and wrenches open the door, slamming it behind him loud enough that a few of us exchange glances.

I'm starting to wonder if the kinder, gentler Myles Salinger that I got a glimpse of on Friday night, and again on Monday during our messaging was only a figment of my overactive imagination.

Because he sure isn't behaving like that now. Especially, when he opens his door and cusses out the accounting team for not providing a report he needs.

"Who peed in his cornflakes?" Ryan asks. "He seemed like an okay guy on Friday. I guess it was the beer."

"It was nice of you to invite him," I say to Ryan, because it really was. And Ryan isn't always known to show unprompted signs of kindness.

"Yeah, well." Ryan shrugs. "I'm regretting it now."

At three o'clock, Myles opens his office door and calls out my name. I look up from the artwork I've been proofing and catch his gaze.

"Can you come into my office, please?" he asks me.

Ryan sends me a sympathetic smile as I close down the document I was working on and push my chair out from under the desk. Today I'm wearing a navy shirt dress that belts at the waist and ends at my lower thigh. It's elegant but modest.

And no, it has nothing to do with the fact that I knew Myles would be back in the office today. Nothing at all.

Myles is sitting back at his desk when I make it into his office, carrying my laptop in case he asks me for any details I don't have on hand. When I enter, after knocking of course, he tells me to sit and I take the chair opposite his. From here I can see the dark shadows beneath his eyes.

He looks tired.

"Thank you for standing in for me at short notice," he says. "Especially at the Monday meeting."

"No problem. It was eye opening."

He's taken his tie off and has unfastened his top three shirt buttons, revealing a vee of tan skin and a hint of chest hair. It's funny because I'd forgotten just how big this man is. His chest is so broad that it makes my body tingle.

"Did you contact Macy's?" he asks. His eyes flicker to mine. He holds my gaze for a moment too long.

And I like it.

"Yes," I tell him. "We have a videoconference on Friday. Would you like to be there?"

He shakes his head. "It's your baby. You take the lead on this one."

I still don't know whether to trust him or not. I mean, I

think I should give him the benefit of the doubt, but he's giving himself an awful lot of plausible deniability if something goes wrong.

That's why I've saved our messages. Just in case.

"There's something else I need to talk to you about," he says, his voice lowering. I feel my face flame because I know exactly what the topic is.

The offer he made on Friday night. It's been four days and I haven't stopped thinking about it. Of course, I should tell him no. As much as I'm confused about which way to go when it comes to having a child, making one with Myles is asking for problems.

And yet the words don't come to my lips.

"Okay. Shoot."

"I have to take some leave next month. Will you be able to stand in for me?"

"Oh, right." I frown. "Yeah, sure. Just send me the dates."

He tips his head to the side. "Are you sure it's okay?" he asks. "You seem… I don't know, disappointed."

I manage to collect myself. "Not at all. It's just been a busy few days. Is that it, or do you have something else you want to talk to me about?"

He shakes his head. "That's it."

But what about your sperm? The words flash into my mind, and I try to push them away.

"Is everything okay?" I ask. "With your family problems?"

"Everything is fine, Ava." He glances at his laptop screen. "And you? Are you okay?"

"Yes, I'm good." Is he goading me? I feel like I'm dancing on tiptoes around the elephant in the room. Am I going to have to bring this up first? Maybe I should walk away and pretend the offer on Friday night never happened. Standing, I decide to do just that, and grab my laptop and notebook, then turn to head to the door.

But then I look back over my shoulder and he's staring right at me. And damn it, I don't want to walk away.

"Friday night, did you really say what I think you said?"

"What do you think I said?" he asks, his voice mild.

"You know." I give him a pointed look.

The corner of his lip twitches. "Yes, I did."

"And we're not going to talk about it?" I ask him, clutching my laptop to my chest.

He stands and damn if my neck doesn't have to crane just to keep eye contact. "I told you to think about it. I assumed you're still thinking."

"What if I have questions?"

He regards me coolly. "Then you can ask them, Ava. But not here."

"Then where?"

"Somewhere that isn't work. That isn't an appropriate conversation for the office, is it?"

No it isn't. And we all know the walls here don't just have ears they have loud hailers, too. "Then where should we talk?"

"I could come to your place. Or you could come to mine?" he says.

The thought of being at his place talking about making a baby feels so… *intimate*. And I know that's stupid because this *is* intimate. The only way it could be more intimate is if we actually did the deed.

And now I'm blushing.

"How about we walk and talk?" I suggest. "The evenings are beautiful right now, and if we meet before the sun goes down it'll still be warm."

"I still don't know the city well." He looks almost embarrassed. "Where should we meet?"

"How about we grab some food from a vendor and walk by the river," I say. "It's a pretty walk and there's lots of history there, too."

The hint of a smile crosses his lips. I feel my gaze lingering on them for too long.

"Yeah, that sounds good," he says. "Where should I meet you?"

I show him the best parking lot on my phone and we agree to meet at seven. He'll probably come straight from the office, but I'll go home first. Mostly because it would be weird if I waited for him and we left the office together.

We don't need everybody talking about us. This is hard enough.

"What food do you like?" he asks. "I'll buy if I'm there first."

I blink. "Tacos. But you don't have to buy my food. It's not a date."

He looks at me for a moment, and my cheeks start to flame. Sometimes I hate my complexion. It's like having a flashing banner saying 'embarrassed person here.'

"I know it's not a date," he says calmly. "But if I'm possibly going to impregnate a woman, I'd at least like to buy her dinner first."

———

He's waiting for me when I arrive, and I try really hard not to ogle him as he stares out at the Kanawha River. He's still in his work clothes, but he's taken off his jacket and tie, and his sleeves are rolled up to make the most of the evening warmth. The glass of his watch flashes orange as it catches the setting sun.

He glances up and his gaze softens when it lands on me. He's holding a paper bag and I know that there are two tacos in there. If my mom was here I'd be getting a lecture about going Dutch, but seriously, I like that he's bought my dinner.

Even if this isn't a date.

"Hi," I say when I reach him.

"Hey." He holds up the bag. "I bought dinner. Don't kill me."

"Wasn't planning on it. Plus, tacos always put me in a good mood."

"I wish I'd known that before." He smiles and damn if my knees don't shake a little. I swallow hard and try to not roll my eyes. Even my body is deserting me right now.

He glances at my hands. "Why are you shaking?"

"Because I'm nervous." Nervous and thinking about how this is all so wrong. I should go home.

"Have a drink." He pulls a bottle of soda from one of the bags, twisting the cap off and handing it to me. "Do you want to sit down?"

I shake my head. "No, I'm fine." I swallow down a mouthful of liquid. Full of sugar, thank goodness. "I'm sorry, this is all so weird."

"If it makes you feel any better, I've never done this before either," he says.

I look up at him, taking in his expression. It's still soft and kind and damn if that doesn't make my legs shake all over again. "I'm glad to hear that," I say. "Shall we walk? We can eat when we find a good spot." I'm hoping this conversation will be easier if I don't actually have to look at him. I'm not sure where this weird attraction has come from, but I can't shake it off. Even worse, I'm not sure I want to.

"Sounds good to me." He holds his elbow out, and I take it. My fingers graze his bicep and it's as hard as steel. We start to walk along the riverbank path. It's made of concrete and there's a grass bank that slopes down to the river. It's quiet here tonight, but sometimes you can barely move from all the people, especially on nights when they have concerts here.

"You okay now?" he asks.

"Getting there."

He tips his head to the side. His profile is almost perfect, apart from a slight bump on his nose. I feel a weird compulsion to trace the line of it with my fingertip.

"What can I do to make you feel better?" he asks me.

"Be less intimidating?" I suggest.

He finally laughs, and it's everything I thought it would be. The corners of his eyes crinkle, his cheeks lift, and I can see the whiteness of his teeth. Something twists inside of me, and I tell myself it's just the thought that I might be able to have this man's genes.

We reach the first sign with historical information on it. He glances at the words, taking them in. I don't bother to read it; I've done this walk hundreds of times before. I know that this is where the first gas well was sited, and that the driller ended up creating an inferno.

"Interesting," Myles murmurs.

"There are more of those little stories along the path if you'd like to read them."

He tips his head to the side. "So how do you want to do this? You ask and I answer?"

So we're back to it. A reminder that we're not just here to enjoy the evening. I mean, I'm glad he's not dancing around the issue, but I was just getting used to his company.

"Okay." I nod, ignoring my disappointment. "That would work."

"Go for it. Ask me anything you want."

We start walking again. There's a slight breeze in the air and it lifts the ends of his hair.

I take a deep breath. My chest feels tight. "Your offer," I whisper. "Were you serious?"

"Yes."

I wait for him to say more but he doesn't. So this is how he's playing it. I glance at him from the corners of my eyes.

"You're willing to donate sperm to me?" Damn, it's so weird saying it out loud.

"That's what I offered," he says mildly as we pass a copse of trees. "So yes."

"And do you know if your sperm is…" I widen my eyes, trying to find the right words. "Good?"

He bites down a smile. "I haven't had any complaints."

I roll my eyes. "I thought you were trying to make this easy on me."

The smile fades. "I'm sorry. And I am almost certain my sperm is good. I could schedule a checkup if that would make you feel better."

"I'll think about that. But I have more questions. Can I…"

He waves his hand for me to go ahead.

"Why would you do this for me?"

"Does there have to be an ulterior motive?" he asks, glancing at me. "Maybe I just want to do a good thing. You need something that I have. It feels like the right thing to do."

"But are you willing to sign away your rights as a father?"

"If that would make you more comfortable, then yes."

I blink. "If you don't sign away your rights you're leaving yourself wide open. I could chase you for child support. That would be crazy."

"If you needed money I'd give it to you whether I had rights or not," he tells me. "If you have a child that's physically mine, it's my obligation to make sure you're both taken care of."

My chest tightens. "But you know you'd have no right or expectation to do that. I could turn down your money."

His lips curl. "I'm confused. Are you going to be chasing me for money or throwing me out for offering it?"

"I don't know. But this is important. We need to agree on these things up front. Otherwise there's every chance that things can go wrong."

"Understood." He nods. "I'll ask my lawyer to draft something up. You get a lawyer and have them review it." He glances at my mouth. "That's if you want to go ahead."

It's another pivotal moment. Just like the one when I decided that I was actually going to do this alone. We stop walking and I look up at him.

"Won't it feel strange?" I ask. "Knowing you have a child in the world that you have nothing to do with."

He presses his lips together, and I realize how gloriously handsome he is. Especially when he's not looking angry.

"I've thought about that," he says. "Maybe you can keep me updated occasionally. Photographs, that kind of thing. And if you need anything you have to agree to ask. I know you don't like being helped, but..." he trails off and takes a long breath. "If I can help I want to."

"I never knew you could be altruistic," I tell him.

The corner of his lip quirks. "Maybe I'm not being generous. Maybe I want to know my existence isn't futile. Isn't that what having children does? Continues your bloodline? Gives you a little entry in the history of the world? Maybe I'm the opposite of generous, seeing as I'm agreeing to have a baby then walking away."

He's half smiling but there's something in his words I don't quite believe. "I can't imagine walking away from a child that's mine," I whisper.

"I wouldn't walk away if I didn't know that child had an excellent mother. And I know that's exactly what you'll be."

And there it is. The killer shot. I have no idea where this kind, caring version of Myles Salinger has come from or how long it's here to stay, but I'm here for it.

The sun has almost met the horizon. Tiny lights sparkle from the boats floating on the river and in the buildings on the other side of the water.

I take a deep breath. "Are you sure you want to do this?" I ask him again. "Because from where I'm standing it's a completely one sided agreement. I get everything I want and you get..." What does he get?

"It's not one sided," he tells me. "You were right the first time. I'm really not that altruistic."

He's lying. Because he's getting nothing out of this at all. The nice girl inside me should feel bad but it's outweighed by hormones and the desire to have my own child.

I'm going to have Myles Salinger's baby. Seven words I'd never thought I'd utter. And yet here we are, talking about sperm and lawyers and ceding rights, and somehow it doesn't seem so stupid at all.

"Okay then. Let's do this."

He nods. "Thank God. Can we eat now?"

CHAPTER
THIRTEEN

AVA

"You cannot tell a soul," I tell Lauren and Sophie. We're sitting in the corner of the yoga café, sipping at our juices. Lauren didn't spike them this time, and that's a good thing, because if I'm going to do this then I need to take care of my body to give myself the best chance.

"I don't understand. You don't even like the guy. You walked out of the bar because he offered us a drink." Sophie frowns. "And now you're going to have a baby with him?"

"I don't dislike him. I just…" I widen my eyes, trying to think of the right words. "I just don't quite understand him. I think somewhere deep inside there's a good guy waiting to come out."

"Into a sperm cup," Lauren says, sniggering.

I roll my eyes. "Stop it."

"If you're doing this you can't be squeamish. He's going to come into a cup and you're going to put it inside you and…" Lauren wrinkles her nose. "Well, leave it for a while."

"I know that. But I'd be doing that even if I ordered frozen sperm. I'd just be defrosting it instead."

"Like a microwave meal," Sophie says, looking amused. "Can you defrost it in the microwave as well? Or do you have to leave it at room temperature?"

"Probably tastes better than a TV dinner," Lauren says, grinning. "I mean, the guy's perfect. I bet he has perfect sperm, too."

"We shouldn't be talking about his sperm," I say. "It's intrusive."

Lauren and Sophie exchange a glance. "So tell us," Lauren says, leaning forward. "How is this going to work?"

"He provides the sample, I do the rest," I say simply.

"Yeah, but I want logistics. Is it going to happen at your place or his? Will he jack off in the same room as you or in the bathroom? Will he stay while you inseminate yourself?"

"We'll do it at mine," I tell them. "Because I want to be as comfortable as possible. And I assume he'll do what he needs to do in the bathroom then bring it out." As for staying while I do the deed, I have no idea. I hadn't thought about that.

Just talking about it makes me blush. He's going to be touching himself in my house. He'll make himself come. The thought of it makes me shift on my chair.

"I still can't believe you bought the kit from Amazon," Sophie says. "How amazing is that?"

"It's not that complicated," I say to her. "Pretty much a specimen cup and a syringe." All wrapped up and sterile, ready to be used. It's not the reason I made the decision, but doing it this way is so much cheaper than using the clinic, too. If it works, that means I'll have more money for the future, which can only be a good thing.

"How big is the specimen cup?" Lauren asks. "Just so I can picture it."

Sophie giggles.

"It's the usual size," I tell them.

"But is *he* the usual size?" Lauren asks, wiggling her brows. "Or do you have to get extra large specimen cups, like you can get extra large condoms?"

I give her what I think is a withering stare, but she just grins. "Sorry, it's just so..." Lauren shrugs. "Exciting and different and unlike you."

"Yeah, I never thought you'd go for something like this," Sophie admits. "Not that I think you're wrong for doing it, but it feels so... personal. Did he really say he'd sign away his rights?"

"His lawyer has already sent me the draft agreement," I tell her. I got it yesterday via email. Five pages of legal verbiage which essentially states Myles will sign away all rights except in case of my severe illness or death. That seems fair to me. If I die, he wants to know his child is still being taken care of, so he should have the right to either have a say over a guardian, or become the parent himself.

"So," Lauren says, leaning forward, "when will you do the deed?"

"It depends on when I'm fertile." The kit came with some handy ovulation strips to test for that. "But based on my cycle, it should be in two weeks."

"Wow." Lauren's eyes widen. "So soon?"

"As long as we've both signed the agreement and all our tests come back clear, then yes." A buzz of excitement washes through me. "There doesn't seem any reason to wait." And every reason not to. My eggs are getting old, if this doesn't work I'll have to find another way.

Sophie breaks out into a smile. "I love how you're so certain about this. You're gonna be the strongest momma bear around."

"And we'll be the evil aunties," Lauren says. "Leading your baby astray."

"Can we at least wait until there is actually a baby?" I ask.

"Sure," Lauren says, pushing her juice away with disgust. "Come on, let's go home. You need to get as much sleep as you can, because you sure as hell won't get any once you have a kid."

———

My bravado disappears two weeks later when there's a knock at the door and I know Myles is on the other side of it. All of our documents have been signed and registered, and according to his reports he's not only free from STDs but his sperm is gloriously frisky and abundant.

Okay, the medical term was high and motile, but we all know what that means. Basically, Myles Salinger only has to look at a woman to impregnate her. I'm surprised all the women in the office aren't already knocked up. I have high hopes that this could be a one and done situation.

"Hi," I say, opening the door. He's wearing a black v-neck sweater over a white t-shirt and jeans cover his long, muscled legs.

"Hello." He gives me the softest of smiles. Is he nervous or am I just projecting? Because talking about doing something and actually doing it are two very different things.

And today Myles is going to try to impregnate me without even touching me. This is so weird.

"Would you like a drink?" I ask him as he follows me inside the townhouse. It's small but perfectly formed. More than enough for one person – or even two once the baby arrives. There are a lot of steps but I'll put baby gates in. It'll be fine.

"Water?" he asks, following me into the kitchen. Like the rest of my house, it's small and it makes him look like a giant. Another inch or two and his head would be skimming the ceiling.

Grabbing a bottle from the refrigerator, I pour out two

glasses and pass him one. He takes a sip but says nothing, his blue eyes regarding me with interest.

"So…" I say.

"So," he replies. Bastard. Ugh, he's going to make me do this.

"I don't know how you want to play this, but I've put the … ah… *equipment* you need in the bathroom. But if you'd prefer to lay down, I've made up the spare room. Oh," I say, touching my finger tips to my chin. "Do you need the WIFI password to, um, watch something?"

My cheeks flame. We both know what I'm talking about.

"I have plenty of 5G. But I don't need to watch something." Is he biting down a smile? "And the bathroom will be sufficient." His eyes rake over me. "Where should I bring it when I'm done?"

"My bedroom. I'll show you."

"And then I'll let myself out?"

"Yes, please." I frown. "Unless you want to stay." I don't want to be rude. Or make him feel used. Why aren't there etiquette books for this?

"What do *you* want?" he asks, his voice husky. "Isn't that the most important thing?"

I take a deep breath and think about his question. "I don't know," I admit. "It's my first time."

His gaze flickers. Then he swallows hard. "How about we play it by ear?" he suggests. "I'll bring you the sample and if you want me to leave, I'll leave. If you want me to stay, then I'll stay. There are no right answers. I've never done this before either."

He's being so nice, at any other time I'd be worried. "Sounds like a good plan."

He finishes his glass of water and I show him where my room is before leading him to the bathroom. It was converted from a bedroom, so it's a good size, with a double walk in shower, a toilet and sink, and a chair where I throw my clothes every evening before I wash off the day.

"I've left the container by the sink," I tell him, pointing at the small plastic cup with a white lid. "You just need to take it out of the wrapper and unscrew the lid."

He nods. "Got it."

"Do you need anything else?" I ask him.

"I think I'm good." He glances at the counter.

"Where will you do it?" I ask. "On the chair?"

For the first time he smiles. "I don't know. Why do you ask?"

"In case the baby ever asks for his or her origin story," I joke. I don't actually know the answer to that. Maybe I'm just trying to drag this out because the next part is going to be excruciatingly embarrassing.

"I think we can keep this part to ourselves, can't we? Don't want to cause psychological problems at such a young age." He's kidding too, and I like it. Somehow he makes things feel better.

"Sounds like a plan. So when you're done, I'll be in the bedroom."

"It's usually the other way around. Bedroom then bathroom," he jokes.

"Conventional is boring," I tell him. "Myles?"

"Yeah?"

"Thank you for doing this."

He doesn't say anything for a moment. Just looks at me until I feel embarrassed for saying anything.

"You're welcome," he eventually says.

I pull the bathroom door closed and head for my bedroom, where I've set up the rest of the kit. A syringe and a plastic cap that I'll put inside of me to keep the sperm where I need it.

I lay down on my bed and stare up at the ceiling for a moment. I'm wearing pajamas – mostly because they'll be the easiest thing to take off when I need to do the deed. It feels a bit ridiculous to be in them at one in the afternoon, but what else should I wear for this?

A minute passes. Then a second and a third. I start to wonder how long it's going to take. Maybe he can't get it up. Maybe he's having second thoughts. Has he left without saying anything?

I sit up, frowning, then hear a knock on the door.

"Come in," I say, my voice thin.

He pushes it open. He looks exactly like he did when he arrived at my front door. Unflustered, unflushed.

"Did you change your mind?" I ask him. "Because it's okay if you have."

He holds up the container. It's full of… *yeah*, I look away quickly, embarrassed.

"Oh. That was quick," I squeak.

"Exactly what a guy wants to hear," he says dryly. "Shall I put it on your nightstand?"

"Yes, please."

He puts it down next to the syringe and I still can't look at it. It feels too intimate, too personal.

And that's stupid because I know exactly what I'm going to do with it in a moment. And if I think this is intimate then that's out of this world.

"Are you okay?" he asks, his brow furrowing.

"Yeah." I nod. "It's just a lot to think about, you know?"

"I know." He glances at me. "If you've changed your mind, you don't have to do this either. I mean, I had fun either way." He actually winks and it makes my whole body tingle.

Why can't he be like this every day? People would love him.

"Well that's a good thing," I manage. "Imagine if providing a specimen was like having a pap smear every time."

"The human race would die out." He glances at his watch. "I don't want to hurry you, but you only have a few minutes. I'll leave you to it."

"Okay."

"Good luck," he says. "If that's not a weird thing to say."

"Everything about this is weird. Thank you though." I smile at him and he smiles back, then turns to walk out of my bedroom.

I take a deep breath. "Wait…"

"What?" He glances over his shoulder.

"Can you hang around until it's done? I'd just feel better if I wasn't completely alone. You could make yourself a coffee in the kitchen or something." I pull my lip between my teeth. "Unless you have somewhere else to be."

"I'll stay," he says softly. "Now stop prevaricating."

He leaves the room this time, closing the door behind him, and I pull my pajama pants off and scramble over to where he left the specimen. The instructions are simple. I'll be doing an ICI – intracervical insemination. Just a syringe, no tube needed.

In the end, it takes me as long as it took him to provide the sample. Mostly because I had to psych myself up to actually open the specimen cup, and then because my hands were shaking every time I tried to use the syringe. But within a few minutes, the deed had been done and I put everything into the waste bag provided, threw it in my trashcan, and had lay back on the bed.

"It's done," I call out.

"Sorry?" he yells from the kitchen.

Of course he can't hear me. I grab my phone and type him the same message.

It's done. – Ava

• • •

His reply comes a moment later.

Shall I go now? – Myles

Actually, can you come up here for a moment? I'm decent. – Ava

I hear the sound of his footsteps on the stairs followed by a soft knock on my door. "Come in," I call out.

He opens it and leans on the door jamb, his freshly made coffee in hand. "You okay?" he asks, looking concerned.

"Yeah." I nod, feeling fragile. "This is going to sound stupid, but could you hold me for a minute?" I wait for him to laugh or ask why, but he just puts his coffee on my dresser and walks over to the bed. Toeing his shoes off to reveal surprisingly bright purple socks, he offers an almost boyish smile as he climbs onto the bed beside me.

His arms wrap around me and he pulls me against his chest, my cheek resting against his muscles. He smells of fresh shower gel, and I assume he washed up before he came over.

For some reason that touches me.

He strokes my hair and it feels so nice. We both lay there silently, Myles staring up at the ceiling, me with my face against his lovely body. It's not post coital bliss, but it's sweet, nonetheless. If I had to give my baby an origin story, this would be it.

Your father held me close and made me feel safe. That's good, right?

"What do you think?" Myles asks after a while. "Did it work?"

"I don't know. I don't feel any different."

"I guess we'll have to wait and see," he says. "And if it doesn't work this time, there's always next month."

"Yeah. If you still want to do this."

"I do if you do," he says.

I nod against his chest. "Yeah, I do."

"That's good," he murmurs. He sounds sleepy. I feel a little tired myself. Maybe it's from all the emotions surrounding today. The anticipation, the anxiety, the knowledge that something may have fundamentally changed inside of me.

Or maybe it hasn't.

Whatever it is, my eyes get heavy as Myles softly strokes my hair. He dips his head and breathes me in. And if it was anybody else holding me this way I'd be getting turned on. But this is Myles Salinger, and my nipples going hard has nothing to do with him.

The thought dissolves in my mind, as the heaviness of sleep washes over me. My eyelids flutter, my breath evens, and Myles continues to hold me.

And then the worst thing in the world happens.

AVA

"Hello?" my mom's voice echoes through the hallway. "Ava, are you here?"

Why did I give her my second key? Why did I tell her to let herself in if I don't answer?

More importantly, why am I laying in my pajamas in Myles Salinger's arms with the seed of his loins inside of me?

The answer to the first two is easy. Because she's my mom and I've never done anything like this before. If I'm on the top floor it's easier for her to let herself in than for me to run down two flights of stairs to open the damn door.

And the answer to the third question? I'll get back to you, but I'm not going to lie, it feels good to be in his arms. He has this ability to make everything feel okay. I don't know how to explain it except I want to stay here forever.

But instead I lift my head up, my horrified eyes meeting his. Except, he doesn't look horrified. More amused than anything.

"That's my mom," I whisper.

"That's good," he says, his tone serious. "I hoped it wasn't a burglar. They don't usually shout out your name on arrival."

"Are you in your bedroom?" Mom calls out. I can hear her footsteps now. "You left the coffee pot on. Do you know how much energy gets wasted keeping coffee hot?" She huffs as she reaches the hallway. "And let's not talk about the carbon footprint of a coffee bean. You'll never drink coffee again."

She's wrong, but this isn't the time for that conversation. Before I can think of what to do next – or extricate myself from Myles' warm and strong arms, she pushes open the door.

"Oh." Her mouth drops open as she takes in the scene before her. Me, wearing a pair of pajamas and Myles, fully dressed, our bodies tangled up like we've just done something we shouldn't have.

Thank God I threw away the specimen container and syringe.

"Mom…" I frantically search my brain for something to say. "This is Myles. Myles, this is my mom."

It's like a switch has been flipped. He lets go of me and sits up, sliding his legs to the floor. But instead of running like I thought he would, he stands and smiles.

"It's a pleasure to meet you," he says, holding out a hand. My mom takes it. And I start to wonder which hand he used to pleasure himself with.

Dear God, is my mom shaking *that* hand?

"Myles, as in the Myles who works with Ava?" she asks.

"I'm afraid so."

"The man who brought us the Great Bear Endo," she murmurs.

"Guilty." He doesn't look at all perturbed by her. "But you'll be pleased to hear his adventures in space are all carbon neutral."

Mom quirks an eyebrow. "How can they be carbon neutral?"

"He runs his spaceship on vegetable peelings." Myles' expression is totally serious. "We're doing our bit to save the world, too."

"He's not as nice as Dandy," Mom says, and I send her a secret high five. "That lion is such a gentleman."

"You're right." Myles nods. "Endo could learn a lot from Dandy."

I don't know if it's the tone of his voice, or the fact that all three of us are in my bedroom where I've just tried to impregnate myself with Myles'… *yeah*… but my lips start to twitch. We're talking about imaginary animals and the imaginary ways they're trying to save the world and I can't deal with it.

I cough, trying to hide my laugh, but it fails miserably. Myles turns to look at me, his brows unknitting when he realizes I'm not, in fact, choking but guffawing.

"What's funny?" Mom asks.

"Myles made a joke earlier," I manage to say. "I was remembering it."

"What's the joke?" she asks Myles.

He shoots me an exasperated look. "It was crude," he says carefully. "I wouldn't want to repeat it in your company."

She laughs. "Don't be silly. I grew up in the sixties, I've heard everything."

He leans forward and whispers in her ear. I can't hear what he's saying but I can see my Mom's face, and her eyes as they practically bulge out of her head.

"Oh my," she says, covering her mouth and giggling like a school girl. "He really is dirty." She taps him on the arm. "You bad boy."

Myles' grin is boyish and I feel a weird sensation in my stomach. Like it's being tipped upside down and turned inside out.

"Why don't we go grab a coffee?" he says, offering his

arm to my mom. "Ava isn't feeling so good. We should let her rest."

She hates chivalry, so I wait with glee to see her bat him away. Instead, she takes his bicep and actually gives a little 'ooh' as she squeezes it.

My stomach flips because I know exactly how good that bicep feels. He obviously has this effect on all the women in my family.

"You didn't say you were sick," she says to me, still clinging tightly to my could-be-baby-daddy.

"I'm not," I croak. "I'm just tired."

"Sleep," he tells me, looking serious for a moment.

"I'll make sure she does," Mom says, before looking at me over her shoulder. "I'll come check on you before I leave."

They walk out into the hallway and I hear my mom's voice.

"Tell me more about the Great Bear Endo," she says, her tone half an octave higher than normal. "Is it true you devised him? No wonder everybody calls you the golden boy of children's publishing."

I lay back on my bed, letting my head hit the pillow before I give a grunt. This has turned out to be the weirdest afternoon ever.

This baby will never understand what I put myself through to become its mom.

———

The problem with getting potentially impregnated by your co-worker is that you still have to see him on Monday morning. I didn't think to ask how we should treat each other in the office. There's nothing in the legal agreement we both signed to say that we have to be nice to each other, or that we have to treat each other the way we have this past year.

To add to the confusion, I'm actually looking forward to

seeing him. I haven't heard from him since he left my apartment on Saturday. A few times on Sunday I thought about texting him, but what would I say?

Thanks for the sperm. And for beguiling my mom. She didn't even ask why I was in my pajamas.

In the end, I went to an extra yoga class with Lauren, who has her eye on an account executive who's recently moved into the Charleston area and attends yoga regularly. For a woman with a big mouth she didn't even talk to him, so I've somehow agreed to go next week again.

And now it's Monday and everything in the office is the same as last Monday. Except for one thing.

Myles Salinger jacked off in my bathroom and donated his sperm to me.

Through the window in the door I can see that he's in his office already, talking to the computer screen. He looks as calm and collected as ever, his jacket slung across the back of his chair, his sleeves rolled up as he nods to whoever's on the other end of his video call.

Then he frowns and says something, his lips pressing together into a thin line. He shakes his head and starts talking rapidly, and I figure whoever he is talking to is getting ripped into.

Dragging my eyes away, I open up my laptop and wait for it to boot up. I have a full schedule this week. We have to agree on our final production run for Dandy the Lion as well as the marketing plan. If we're going to book advertisements and commission a designer for our Macy's float, I need to get it all agreed on before Friday.

I spend most of the morning talking to our printing company and the distribution team. By the time lunchtime rolls around my neck is aching from hunching over the phone.

"Ava?"

I look up to see Myles standing in the doorway of his office. "Can I have a quick word?" he asks.

Nodding, I stand and smooth out my skirt, aware of everybody in the office watching me as I walk to Myles' office. I feel awkward and unsure, like there's a neon light above my head telling everybody my business.

"Can you close the door, please?" Myles asks when I walk in. I do as I'm told and take my usual seat opposite his. His hair looks unusually mussed, like he's been running his hands through it.

"I have some bad news," he says. "I wanted to share it with you first."

For a moment I expect him to say they got his sperm count wrong.

"New York has decided to go with Endo for the float. I'm sorry."

I swallow, my throat tight. "Even though it was my idea?"

"All of our ideas belong to the company. You know that."

Yes I do. It's in my employment contract, after all. But it doesn't matter because I also thought there was some honor in this world. That they wouldn't just take something that was mine and give it to somebody else.

"I was due to meet with the Macy's people this week," I say.

"The marketing team in New York will be taking the discussions over," Myles tells me. "I'm sorry, Ava. There's nothing I could do."

"How long have you known?" I ask him.

"They confirmed it this morning."

"That's not what I asked. How long have you known that I was bashing my head against a wall? You told me to run with it and now you're telling me to stop."

"They told me last week that it would probably be Endo," he admits. "But I asked them to reconsider."

"So you knew on Saturday?" I feel raw, like he can see beneath my skin.

He nods. "Yes."

"And you didn't tell me?" I feel hurt. And it's stupid because he doesn't owe me any loyalty.

"I couldn't. It was under embargo until they confirmed today." His eyes meet mine and I see pity there. I don't want it. Not at all. "Ava, I did fight to have Dandy there, too."

My guts twist. I look away because I don't want him to see the tears in my eyes. "It's okay. You won. Well done, Myles."

"Ava…"

I knew how to deal with nasty Myles. I knew not to let myself get vulnerable with him. I knew not to let myself believe we were anything other than rivals.

"I need to go work on our marketing plan," I mutter, because everything is hinged around the Thanksgiving Parade. It was going to be the anchor of the plan. The rest of our marketing revolved around getting the float, and now I'm going to have to start from scratch all over again.

"Ava!" he thunders, and I blink because as aggravating as he is, Myles doesn't shout. "Will you listen to me for a minute?" he asks when he has my attention. "Please?"

I look at him but say nothing. There's a little battle being waged here and I'm not going to lose.

Not again.

"The reason I hadn't told you until now is because I've spent the morning arguing with finance to increase your marketing budget. I know you'll be having to fight for space for Dandy, and I'd like to help you with that. Why don't we sit down and talk this through together? We can make a kick-ass marketing plan for Dandy between us."

My throat feels too tight to breathe. I shake my head and clench my jaw, knowing that in about ten seconds I'm going to run out of air. "It's okay," I manage to get out. "I'm happy for you, I really am. I just need to think."

"I didn't want this to happen," he tells me. "I didn't ask for it." He swallows hard. "I'm sorry for upsetting you."

"Can I go now?" I ask, because I can't let him see me like this.

His gaze softens. "Sure."

"Thank you," I whisper, and high tail it out of there before I risk looking vulnerable. This feels bad. Worse than coming back from vacation to find Richard and Sammy gone. Worse even, than finding out that Myles Salinger had replaced my boss.

Because now I'm taking it personally, and I have no idea where to put the emotions anymore.

CHAPTER
FIFTEEN

AVA

I got my period. – Ava

I send him the message because he asked for me to let him know, then throw my phone to the side because I'm feeling sorry for myself. As though nature likes to point out that she knows better than anybody else, my period has also arrived early. And heavy.

Myles and I have barely spoken since he told me about Endo getting the Macy's Parade. It's not that he hasn't tried. But I've been feeling so weirdly upset about it. I was hoping it was hormones.

Turns out it's just me.

This is why you shouldn't mix your home life with your work life. My head is so messed up it's hard to think straight. I feel like a failure at work and a failure at home.

I can't even inseminate myself properly.

I knew that the chances were slim, especially for the first

time. But it's the hope that kills you in the end. I thought that for once in my life something would go right, and then life turned around and gave an evil cackle.

It's okay, I'm feeling sorry for myself, and I know that. Tomorrow I'll paint on a smile and hype myself up and stop being such a wet blanket.

But tonight I just want to sulk.

After ten minutes I realize Myles isn't going to reply. I don't know why I thought he would. He's probably relieved that he won't have to be permanently connected to my miserable ass forever.

His sperm had a lucky escape.

It's only eight-thirty, but I decide to go to bed and sleep off the rest of this miserable day. I shower and wash my hair before I drag on my period pajamas, the soft over worn cotton cool against my heated skin. Then I brush my teeth and grimace at my reflection in the mirror. My skin is shiny and blotchy. Even my complexion hates me tonight.

As I'm pulling back the covers, I hear noise from downstairs. It takes me a moment to realize somebody's knocking on the front door. When I finally reach the door and open it, it's somehow a complete surprise and yet not a shock at all to see Myles standing there.

"Hi." I shift my feet, embarrassed by how bad I look.

His gaze flickers over me. "Nice pajamas. Can I come in?" He's holding a plastic bag.

"I'm not great company." I wait for him to say I never am, but he doesn't.

"I assumed you wouldn't be. That's why I brought bribes." He holds up the bag. "Ice cream, sweet tea, and a family pack of chocolate."

"What kind of chocolate?" I ask, feeling ever-so-slightly better.

"Cadburys. The best."

He knows about my Cadbury's addiction? "Is it the stuff made by Hershey's or the good stuff?"

He reads the back of the bar. "It's imported from England. Bourneville, actually. Now, can I come in or do you want me to feed you on the step?"

I step aside to let him in, and his warm body brushes past mine as he enters the hallway. Closing the door behind him, I take a deep breath and catch his eye. "You don't have to do this. I'm a grumpy ass bitch and you don't owe me anything."

"I figured it was this or an apology note from my sperm for not doing their job."

My lip twitches. "It wasn't your sperm. It was me. I probably did it wrong. I spent too long thinking about it and not enough time… well… doing the deed."

"It's only one month." He shrugs. "We have plenty of time ahead of us."

We. The way he says it makes my heart do a little twist. "Yeah." I nod. "We do."

"Were you in bed when I knocked?" he asks, following me to the kitchen and putting the bag on the counter.

"I was thinking about it."

He checks his watch but says nothing about the fact that it's not even nine o'clock yet. "Then go on up. I'll follow you in a minute."

"To my bedroom?" I lift an eyebrow.

He gives me the sweetest smile. And I swear if he wasn't my kind-of-nemesis and also the donor of sperm, I'd be falling a little bit in love with him right now.

"Yes. Get into bed and I'll bring everything up. You have a TV up there, right?"

I blink. "Yes."

"Find something for us to watch on Netflix. Anything you like. Serial Killer documentary, romcom, whatever."

"You're staying?" I frown, because this is so not how I expected things to go.

He shrugs. "Haven't got anywhere else to be."

Ten minutes later, we're laying under my covers watching a documentary about a woman who killed her husband and buried the different parts of his body all over her yard. Myles winces when they talk about finding his appendage beneath the hydrangea bush, and I get a grim thrill from watching him. He's taken his jeans and socks off, but kept his shorts and t-shirt on, and our thighs are pressed together. Somehow his arm has ended up around my shoulders, and I'm kind of nuzzling against his chest.

"Myles?"

"Yeah?" He swallows, his eyes still on the screen. His hand idly traces patterns on the top of my arm.

"I'm sorry I've been a bitch at work."

His lip quirks. "You were angry. I get it. I was angry, too." His voice is low and smooth but I can feel the vibration of it through his chest.

"Yeah, but I didn't need to take it out on you. I know New York has the final say."

He exhales deeply. "Yeah, but they're wrong on this. We both know that Dandy has the longevity that Endo doesn't. Sure, he's flying high now, but he won't be a treasured favorite in thirty years."

"You think Dandy will?"

He looks down, his blue eyes catching mine. Being this close I can see a tiny scar on the corner of his lip. It takes all the strength I have not to reach out and touch it.

Don't spoil this. He's come here to take care of you, nothing more.

"Yeah, I do. Dandy's iconic. He's like Curious George and Paddington and all those other characters who stand the test of time. He's got the right mixture of heart and soul."

"Naomi's a genius," I say, referring to the author.

"It's not just Naomi, it's you." He's still drawing circles on my arm. It's distracting in the best kind of way. "I know how closely you work with her. How she only ever listens to you. Why do you think New York wanted you in the offices there? They know you get the best out of her."

"Yeah, well now you know why I don't want to move to New York."

"Because of the baby?"

"I can't afford to live in New York with a baby. I'll just about manage here."

"I still don't get why you didn't move there ten years ago," he murmurs, lifting the remote control and pausing the documentary. "Didn't you want to climb the ladder?"

"I like it here. Everybody knows everybody. People smile at you."

"I noticed. At first I thought they were all grimacing."

I smile and he smiles back at me and my chest does another squeeze. Why can't we always be like this?

"And what's with the cum trees?" he asks me. "Those things stink."

"Cum trees? You mean the Callery pears?"

"Yeah." His brow dips. "I gag every time I walk past them."

"They're a Charleston fixture. You just have to remember not to park near them while they're in blossom. That's how we can tell the out of towners from the locals."

"I guess I failed."

I tip my head at him. "I can't imagine you've ever failed at anything."

He has this intense look on his face, like he wants to say something but has no idea how. And then I realize that he's probably thinking about the donation. Maybe he feels like he's failed, too.

But he shouldn't.

I open my mouth to tell him that, but my lower abdomen chooses that moment to squeeze like a vice. I wince and grit my teeth, the breath knocked out of me.

"You okay?" he asks, concerned. "Is it cramps?"

"Yeah." I nod. "Sorry, I told you I'm not great company."

He climbs out of bed and I try to not look at the thick ropes of muscles on his thighs. They're not stupidly huge, just defined and in proportion with the rest of him. And as he turns around I get a glimpse of his ass beneath his boxers and my breath catches again.

He pulls his jeans on and I feel a sense of disappointment wash over me. So he's going. I know I have no right to feel disappointed. He's been so sweet, bringing food over and cuddling me in bed.

Like a boyfriend without the emotional attachment. Something about that thought makes my chest ache.

"Thank you for coming," I say softly. "I appreciate it."

He looks back at me and frowns. "What are you talking about? I'm just going to get you some Tylenol and a hot water bottle. I assume you have one."

"Do you have a sister?" I ask.

He frowns at the abrupt turn of conversation. "No. Why?"

"How come you know about hot water bottles making things feel better?" And then I realize it's not a sister, it's probably a girlfriend. Or a wife. Has he ever been married?

"I was the oldest son of a single mom. I've been buying tampons and Midol on the way home since junior high."

"You were?"

He shrugs. "It's no big deal. It's just a period, right? I don't think I can catch cooties from it."

My throat feels tight, but I say nothing as he finds some Tylenol, then five minutes later is back from the kitchen with my fluffy hot water bottle. I only really use it in the depth of winter when the wind whips around the house and gets in through the many cracks in the walls.

He hands it to me before he shucks his jeans off again. It looks like he's staying for a while. I put the hot water bottle on my stomach and within a few minutes it works its magic, loosening the tight muscles and soothing the ache.

"I should put your next ovulation window in my phone," he says, as I nestle back against his hard chest. "When is it?"

"Between fourteen and eighteen days from now," I say. I'm a clockwork kind of girl. I guess there's something to be grateful for.

He scrolls through his phone and opens the calendar app, moving his finger over the dates and clicking on the one two weeks from now. Then he frowns, his finger hovering but not moving.

"Shit. I'm away that week."

"You are?"

"Yeah. Remember I told you about taking a vacation?"

"It's okay. We can try the following month." If he hasn't come to his senses and decided to pull out of our agreement by then.

"No." He shakes his head. "That's not happening. Just let me think for a moment." His jaw is tight, his eyes narrow, and there's this determined look on his face. "You'll have to come with me."

"What? Where?" I twist in the bed, still clutching the hot water bottle to my stomach. "What are you talking about?"

"To my family reunion." He's still deep in thought, sounding as though he's talking to himself as much as to me. "There's good WIFI, we can work from there."

"Myles," I say, my voice low. "I can't come with you to your family reunion."

"Why not?"

"Are you serious?" I question, trying not to laugh. "First of all, because the clue's in the name. A family reunion. *Your* family. And anyway, New York will never let us both be out of the office."

"I'll explain that it's a team building exercise. Or a chance to brainstorm off site." He's so unruffled it's stupid. If he didn't smell of peppermint and coffee I'd think he was drunk. "They want me to persuade you to come to New York, I'll tell them that I'm working on that."

A long breath escapes from my lips. "And your family, what will you tell them?"

"The same thing."

"And if I'm ovulating when we're there? How will you explain having to do the deed?"

"I wasn't planning on inviting them to watch, Ava. It's none of their business. I'll tell them there's some work we have to do and that's why you're there. They're used to me being a workaholic, it won't surprise them."

"We should just skip the month," I tell him, thinking his idea is insane. "You don't have to ruin your reunion by taking me."

He looks at me for a moment, then shakes his head. "You're coming. I want you there. We made an agreement and I'm going to keep it."

"Won't your family think I'm an interloper?"

This time he laughs. "My family is made up of interlopers. Half the time I've no idea who most of the people are. You don't have to worry, you'll fit right in."

"I'm not sure if that's a compliment or not."

His smile is crooked. "It is."

My cheeks heat up and I feel like he's caught me fishing for a complement. "At least we know it'll only take you three minutes to provide the sample," I say jokingly, just because I can't stand this tension between us. "They'll hardly notice you're missing."

He lifts an eyebrow. "It took me three minutes because I wanted to get the job done. When it counts I can last a lot longer."

"You can?" I squeak. This is a dangerous path. If I open up that door I'm not sure I can close it again.

His eyes are blazing. I can't decide if he's angry at my joke or annoyed by something else. "Yes," he says shortly. "I've never had any complaints, Ava."

The stupid thing is, I know he wouldn't have. He has a dedication to being the best at all things.

And he'd be good at sex, too. I have no doubt about that. He'd probably have me screaming in three minutes flat.

Let's face it, I haven't had anything approaching a screaming man-induced orgasm for a very long time.

He's staring at me and I'm staring right back, my cheeks flaming. Neither of us wanting to be the first to look away. My heart is doing a little polka in my chest, dancing in double time. And all I can think of is just how warm and heavy he'd feel between my thighs.

How good a kisser he'd be. How he'd dedicate himself to my pleasure the same way he dedicates himself to everything else.

"Shall we watch the show?" I finally ask. "I want to find out if she gets caught."

I couldn't give a damn about the show, actually, but I need to stop thinking about his sex face. A dismembered body should help with that.

He reaches for me and I scramble into his arms with embarrassing haste. His arm loops around my shoulders, pulling my face against his chest and this time he traces my spine with soft, maddening fingers.

And when I wake up early the next morning, he's gone.

———

MYLES

"I hear you're bringing a plus one to Misty Lakes," Liam says when we've finished our video conference with his clients. It's just the two of us now, and I'm in the apartment I've rented in Charleston, because the kind of meeting we just had can't take place at work.

"She's not a plus one, she's a work colleague. And I need her there because we'll be working."

"Bullshit. I know exactly who you're bringing. And I remember you telling me exactly how gorgeous she is."

Liam has this ability to push through the armor I wear to keep the world out. It's infuriating.

"She's not my plus one," I say again.

"So what is she? Because there's no way you're bringing her for work reasons. I know you and I know you'd prefer her to be in the office right now. Things are moving fast."

I sigh. "Okay. But you have to keep your mouth shut about this."

Liam's eyes light up. "What is it?" he asks. "If you're not banging her, then why the hell do you want to bring her with you?"

"Because we're trying to have a baby."

I get a sense of grim satisfaction from the way Liam's mouth drops open on the screen. Shutting my brother up takes a lot of work yet I've done it with a few words.

"Satisfied?" I ask a minute later when he still hasn't said anything. "Because I have work to do. I need to go."

"No way. You're not leaving me hanging," he finally says. "So you *are* banging her?"

"I didn't say that."

"But you're having a…" He shakes his head. "A baby. And I don't know if mom gave you the birds and bees talk, but you kind of need to knock boots for that."

"No you don't. I'm donating sperm. She's inseminating herself with it. There are no knocking boots going on."

"Whoa." Liam holds his hand up, his palm looking huge on the screen. "Let's backtrack. Why the hell are you donating sperm?"

"Because she wants to have a child."

"So why don't you fuck her?"

I wince. Mostly because he's so direct. But also because that thought crossed my mind, too. "Can you try to not be so crass? This is the potential mother of my child we're talking about."

"You've finally gone mad," Liam says, sounding almost serious. "I knew it would happen, I just didn't know when."

"Shut up and listen," I demand. "You're not to say a word to anybody about this. And you're not to make Ava feel weird either. She's already nervous about this, I don't want her feeling any worse." Then I take a deep breath and explain exactly what's happening. Liam's expression doesn't change one inch. He still looks somewhere between shocked and disbelieving.

I guess I can't blame him. I'd think the same about him if roles were reversed.

And let's be honest, this is Liam. The only reason he's not a father right now is that he's paranoid about birth control. He certainly seems to work his way through half of New York.

"And your lawyer okayed it?" he asks.

"Yes. The contract is signed." And the deed has already been done once, but I don't need to tell him that.

"Wow." He shakes his head. "You're going to be a dad."

"Technically, I'm not," I correct. "I'm just a donor. Ava will be the only parent."

His brows scrunch tight. "But why? Why would you do this?"

It's the same question Ava asked me. And there's no answer I can give that will explain my reasons. I'm not even sure if I know them myself.

"Because I can." It's the easiest answer to give. "Now can you promise me you won't say anything?"

He nods slowly. "Yeah. I don't think anybody would believe me anyway."

"Good. Then we're done. I'll talk to you soon, okay?"

Liam nods, then leans forward, his face taking up the camera. "Bro?" he asks.

"Yeah?"

"Don't go falling for her, okay? Because that would complicate an already complex situation."

I let out a sigh because I'm not an idiot. "Of course I won't. You know me better than that."

AVA

"So he's taking you to meet his family but there's nothing going on between you two?" Lauren asks, an amused grin on her lips. "And he also spent the night at your house last week?"

"Nothing happened then either," I remind her. "We're… friends, I guess." I never thought I'd say that about Myles Salinger and me, yet there's a truth to it that I can't deny. "He was worried about me and came over to cheer me up."

"You could have called me," Lauren says. "I would've brought donuts."

"I didn't ask him to come over," I remind her. "He just turned up."

"Hmmm."

"What?" I ask, because her hmmms are so annoying.

"It just doesn't feel like the sort of thing a friend would do."

"You just said *you'd* do it," I point out.

"Yeah, but a *guy* friend. Who's not into you. They don't do that without an ulterior motive."

I frown. "Don't spoil it. He was just being sweet. Why can't I have a guy friend who cares for me?"

Sophie carries over our drinks. Two mojitos for them and a soda with lime for me. "What guy friend cares for you?" she asks, passing the drinks out.

"Myles," Lauren says, offering Sophie a smile as she raises her glass to her lips. Then she turns back to me. "And we've seen *When Harry Met Sally* enough times to know that women and men can't be friends."

"Not with somebody they're attracted to anyway," Sophie adds.

"*Are* you attracted to him?" Lauren asks.

"No," I lie. "He's just a good friend who's doing the nicest thing for me that anybody could. And I'm not about to ruin that friendship by getting a crush on him."

"Sure," Sophie says dryly. "Keep telling yourself that."

"I'm serious," I admonish. "He's a good guy and I'm really hoping he'll be my baby's father. Why would I mess that up by falling for him?"

"But he's not a good guy. At least that's what you told us. He's arrogant and annoying and made you feel two feet tall the first time you met him."

I open my mouth and close it again. Because they're right, he's all those things. It's just hard to remember that when he's bringing me chocolate and Tylenol and letting me sleep on his chest.

"I don't think you should go to this reunion," Lauren says, her brows pinching.

"I already said I'd go. And I want to. Myles was right, we need to keep working on this thing." And I'm not about to tell him I've changed my mind. Not after all the kindness he's shown me. The least I can do is spend a few days with his family.

"I'm with Lauren," Sophie says. "I'm scared you're going to get hurt."

I blink. "How is *he* going to hurt me?"

"You just told us he spent the night with you. Holding you and stroking your arm, and then in the morning he'd gone," Lauren says, her voice slow like she's trying to let it sink in. "And neither of you have mentioned it since."

"There!" I say, feeling triumphant. "If it meant anything we'd have mentioned it. So that means it's unimportant. Like the three of us going out together."

"I'm going to ignore the way you just told us we are unimportant," Lauren says sharply. "And concentrate on the other stuff instead. If it had been unimportant you would've talked about it. But you didn't. Maybe because you're embarrassed or maybe because you can't work out in your brain what it all really means. But, honey, you're too nice and he's going to hurt you."

I should never have told them about this family reunion. "Do you think the same thing?" I ask Sophie.

She presses her fingertips to her temple and looks carefully at me. "I think…" She frowns, as though trying to find the right words. "What the two of you are going through is a very emotional thing. Trying to make a baby together is huge. You're bonding through it. And sometimes those bonds can feel very intense when they occur this fast. Kind of like when you go through a trauma together."

She's gentler than Lauren, but somehow that feels even worse. I can ignore Lauren because she talks first and thinks later. But Sophie is analytical. She thinks things through from every direction. She's a planner and a worrier and I hate that she might be right.

"You think we've trauma bonded?" I ask.

"I think emotions are high. And maybe hormones, too." Sophie bites her lip, her brows knitting. She hates upsetting people so she always chooses her words carefully. "Myles is in a new town, probably feeling lonely, and he's offered you this lovely gift. But then he turns up when you're feeling sad and it's confusing. Your body is telling you to bond with this potential baby daddy, because that's what our bodies have done ever since humans existed."

I take a sip of my soda with lime, and really wish that it was something stronger. "Maybe you're right. I'll think about it."

"Are you still going to the reunion?" Lauren asks.

"Actually, I think she should," Sophie says.

I frown at her. "What? You both told me I'm bonding with him in all the wrong ways."

"No, I didn't." Sophie shakes her head. "I told you you're bonding with him in all the ways humans ever have. But I also think the sooner you get pregnant, the better it will be. So go to this reunion and take every bit of sperm he has."

Lauren's lips twitch. "Go swimming in his sperm. Take showers in it. Just make sure you get pregnant this time."

"You're grossing me out." I fake gag.

Lauren smiles smugly. "Then my job is done."

"Thanks," I tell her, rolling my eyes. "You've made me feel so much better."

———

"Okay, so that's it I think," I say, sitting back in my chair and looking up at Catherine and Ryan. "But if anything goes wrong here, and I mean *anything*, you have to call me. I'll only be a couple of hours away and I can be back at short notice. I don't want a repeat of my trip to Spain."

"That wasn't my fault," Catherine says, putting her hands up as though in surrender. "Richard made us promise not to tell you."

"So now you need to promise you'll call, okay?"

"Nothing's going to go wrong. Not for us anyway," Ryan

says, a smile playing at his lips. "You're the one spending days offsite with Mr. Moody."

"He's not that bad," I say, glancing at his office from the corner of my eye. The door's closed, thank God. I'd hate for him to hear people talking about him like this.

"What?" Ryan frowns. "I thought you hated him like the rest of us."

"He bought you a beer," I remind Ryan. "If he's good enough to buy you a drink then maybe he's good enough for a bit of human decency."

"What's wrong with her?" he asks Catherine.

She shrugs. "She's too nice for her own good."

"Anyway," I say, trying to pull the subject away from Myles, because he already occupies enough of my thoughts, "I don't think anything should come up. Just try to keep some order in the office for me."

"Can we still have Fizzy Friday?" Ryan asks.

"Yes. But only if you all behave." I'm aware I'm talking to them like they're six years old, but ever since they heard about Myles and me going away they've all been acting a little giddy. We made up this stupid excuse about having to write an in depth report which requires a lot of brainstorming and blue sky thinking. Somehow, everybody believes it.

I guess the alternative – that I actually want to spend time with Myles Salinger – is just too preposterous to think about.

"If you need us to invent a crisis to get you out of there, we can," Catherine says. "You know, like when you go on a date and ask a friend to call you in case you need an excuse to leave."

"It's okay. No crisis needed." I smile at her. "But thank you for being sweet."

"The offer's always there."

I look at the list I jotted down and make sure I've ticked every line. This all feels too easy and I don't like it.

"Hey, do you think he'll wear his suit and tie every day

when you're away?" Ryan asks. "I can't imagine him going casual."

"Um, I guess we'll be keeping it professional," I say. "He'll still be having video conferences with New York."

"It's such a shame," Catherine says. "If it was anybody else I bet you'd be looking forward to it. But going away with that guy." She grimaces. "You're going to need another vacation after that."

"Will you have the production costs ready for the Monday meeting?" I ask, changing the subject because I don't want to be roped into talking negatively about Myles. If they only knew what he was doing for me. He didn't need to invite me to this reunion. Heck, he didn't have to offer me free use of his sperm. And yet he's doing all this and I'm sitting out here gossiping about him.

As though he can feel my thoughts, he opens his door and looks over at my desk moments later. His brows raise when he sees Ryan and Catherine with me, and damn if they don't look guilty as hell.

"Yes, I'll make sure you have the costings," Catherine agrees, her cheeks pinking up.

Myles' jaw is tight. "Ava, do you have a moment?"

"Yup." I nod, still feeling that twisting guilt in my stomach. "You guys have any questions?"

"Nope, we're good." Ryan doesn't look up at Myles. I hope he feels bad.

"We're great," Catherine says, smiling widely.

"Okay then." I push myself out of my chair and walk to Myles' office, all while I try to ignore that Ryan's humming the tune of Darth Vader's Imperial March behind me.

"Everything okay?" I ask Myles as I pull the door closed behind me.

"Yes." He nods. "Just finalizing details for tomorrow. You might want to bring a swimsuit."

"I might? Why?"

"Because there's a lake."

"And we'll be swimming in the lake?" I try to clarify, because he's looking all clamped up.

"Yes. And there will be… events in the lake."

Okay, this is interesting. "What kind of events?" For a moment I picture him and his brothers doing a synchronized swim dance. My lips twitch at the thought.

"Think of it as team building. But worse."

A smile pulls at my lips. "Are we having a swimming competition?" I'm more than okay with that. I swam competitively as a kid.

"You get to swim for pleasure. My brothers and I will be… partaking in some competitive activities."

Okay, I'm officially intrigued. "What kind of competitive activities?" I ask.

"My brothers want to reinstitute the Salinger Olympics." He looks almost pained to say it.

"The Salinger Olympics," I repeat, trying not to laugh. "Your competitive activities have a name?" I grin. "Oh God, are they all as desperate to win as you?"

"Worse. Much worse."

I hadn't thought much about the fact Myles' family will be at the reunion, which I know is stupid but I've been busy. But the thought of seeing him surrounded by his family is delicious.

I've always been fascinated by big families. I suppose it comes from growing up in a household of two. I can remember watching *Home Alone* and wishing I could have a family so big that some of them were forgotten on the way to the airport. If Mom forgot me she would have realized before closing the door.

"How many of you are there again?" I ask him.

"A lot."

"Can you tell me their names? After all, shouldn't I know

more about them before we arrive and I make an idiot out of myself?"

"You won't make an idiot out of yourself." His voice is soft. "How about I give you the rundown on the drive there?"

"Sure. Okay." I smile again, because I'm actually looking forward to this Brady Bunchesque family gathering. More than Myles is, from the expression on his face.

"One more question," I say, because I know we both have piles of work to do before we can leave the office.

"Hit me with it."

"If you win the Salinger Olympics, will you be in a better mood?"

CHAPTER
SEVENTEEN

AVA

Swimwear, leisurewear, business wear, summer dresses, sunscreen, bug spray, and *two* sealed artificial insemination kits. I stand back and survey my two suitcases – yes two, because there's no way I can pack light. I've got five different pairs of shoes for a start, and Myles has been completely unforthcoming about the dress code. I've had to hedge my bets and hedging takes space.

I just hope it all fits in his car.

There's a knock at the door and I run down the stairs to answer it. Myles is wearing a pale blue striped shirt, the sleeves rolled up, and his hands are stuffed into his jeans pockets. It's sunny outside, and a pair of aviators cover his eyes, reflecting my image back from the glass.

"You're early," I complain. "I'm still packing."

His gaze drops to my dress. It's white with blue flowers printed all over it, tight on the bodice and flaring out from the hip. It reaches mid-thigh, and he swallows hard as he takes in my tanned skin.

I kind of like that.

"I can help you with the packing," he says as he follows me inside. As I walk up the stairs, I swear I can feel the heat of his gaze on my back. We reach my bedroom and he rolls his eyes when he sees how much I've got.

"Don't say anything," I warn him. "You're the one who sprung the swimwear requirement on me."

"I was just wondering what you've packed for the ceremony," he says smoothly.

"Ceremony?" I frown. Is he talking about the insemination? Because while it's important, I wouldn't call it a ceremony. And anyway, I'll wear pajamas like last time.

"My dad's vow renewal."

"What vow renewal?"

He blinks. "Didn't I tell you?"

"No, Myles, you didn't." I grit my teeth, because what the hell? "When is it?"

He shifts his feet. "Um, tomorrow?"

My mouth drops open. "Is it dressy?"

He won't meet my eyes. Probably for the best because I've got a death stare right now. "I'm wearing a tux."

Of course he is. "I can't believe you didn't tell me."

"I told you about the Olympics," he points out, as though a renewal of vows ceremony is no big deal. "And to bring a swimsuit."

I give an exaggerated huff and walk over to my closet, yanking it open dramatically. He watches, amused, as I rake through the dresses hanging in there, finally pulling out a champagne evening dress I wore to a friend's engagement party last summer. I have matching heels and a bag to go with it, thank God.

"Will this do?" I ask Myles, holding it up to me. "Or should I bring something longer?"

He swallows hard. "That will be fine." Then he takes a

deep breath. "Don't kill me, but you'll also need something warm for tonight."

"What's happening tonight? Another wedding? A christening? A full blown Olympics opening ceremony?" I wouldn't put it past him at this point.

"The bachelor and bachelorette parties."

I blink. "But aren't they already married?"

"They ran away to Vegas. Dad wants to do it right this time. He thinks Julia missed out on the whole bride thing and wants to make it up to her."

"Will I have to go to the bachelorette? I don't know anybody."

"You don't have to do anything you don't want to," he promises me. "But they're combined. I'll be there, you know me."

"So why do I need something warm?" I ask.

"They're having a cookout and a band. By the lake." His smile is tight. "I'm sorry. I didn't think any of this through. It's bad enough that I have to put up with my family, you shouldn't have to as well. It's not too late to back out."

"And miss out on your super sperm?" I quip, trying to lighten the mood. "No way, buddy."

Thankfully, he laughs as I pull out some more clothes, then have to ask for his help to zip my suitcases shut. The smaller one is resisting so much that in the end he picks me up and sits me on the top, making a show of pulling the zipper around the lid to close it. I'm kind of closed lipped myself, because I'm still marveling at how easily he lifted me up. Like I wasn't a good one hundred and thirty pounds.

Ten minutes later, we're finally in his car as he pulls away from my townhouse and drives toward the Kanawha River. Soon we are on the interstate, and I sit back in the leather bucket seat and watch his bare forearms as he steers left to join the fast lane. His car is beautiful, a silver F Type Jaguar convertible, with the top down to enjoy the almost-summer sunshine. I've pulled my hair back and my ponytail ruffles in the breeze, the same one that caresses Myles' hair and makes him look young and carefree.

There aren't many cars on the road, and Myles takes advantage, putting his foot down on the gas until he exceeds the limit by a bit. His lip curls as we make progress, crossing the Kanawha River then heading east toward Virginia.

"Tell me about your father's place." I have to yell as the wind almost swallows my voice.

"Misty Lakes," he says, still facing the road. "It's a big estate in the west of Virginia. There's his house, then a whole load of cabins around the water."

"Is that where we're staying?"

"Yeah. When we were kids we all got to pick a spot. Then as we got older we helped him build our cabins."

"You built your own cabin?" I ask, shocked. "Like with your hands?"

"Yeah. We all built each other's. We had to get some help for the plumbing and electric, but we did most of the grunt work."

"Why? Couldn't he afford to have them built for you?"

His cheeks plump as he smiles. "He liked to keep us busy. Having six boys is… challenging. We didn't always behave. So when we stayed with him he always gave us projects to do."

"And the Salinger Olympics," I add, because I'm still fascinated by this competition.

"Yeah, that too."

"And you have five brothers," I say. It's more of a state-ment than a question. "Tell me their names."

"There's Liam. He's the closest to me in age. Then there's Eli and Holden. The four of us have the same mother and father. After that there's Linc and Brooks. They're my step-mother's kids with my dad."

"The one he's renewing his vows with?" I ask.

Myles shakes his head. "No, that would be his third wife. Julia."

I blink because I'm already losing track. "Okay, so he's been married three times?"

"Four, but he doesn't talk about his first wife. They were married and divorced within a year."

"Wow." I lift a brow. "Your dad's an Elizabeth Taylor."

"He loves falling in love." I can't see behind his sunglasses, but I swear Myles is rolling his eyes. There's a tone in his voice I've come to recognize. "Staying in love though, that's tricky."

"How long have he and Julia been married?"

"Ten years."

"That's quite a long time to stay in love," I point out. Heck, it's five times longer than any of my relationships. But I don't tell him that.

"He likes to average ten or fifteen. I guess we'll see if this one sticks."

"You're very cynical," I point out.

"Yep. I guess I learned that from watching my parents mess up all their relationships."

I run the tip of my tongue along my bottom lip, trying to find something to say. There's a bitterness to him that I can understand. Anybody who has a fractious relationship with a parent understands the bitter – but it doesn't help.

"How close are you and your three oldest brothers?" I ask him, deciding a change of subject is needed.

"Liam and I were really close growing up. He lives in New York, so I see him a lot when I'm there."

"What does he do?"

"He works in finance." There's a truck ahead of us, and Myles indicates left to pass. "Holden is also in New York, too. But Eli lives in Boston right now."

"What does he do in Boston?"

"Plays hockey."

"Ice Hockey?" I ask.

"Yep. For the Razors."

"Wait one minute," I say, holding my hand up. "Your brother's a professional hockey player? Why didn't you tell me?"

"I don't know. You didn't ask."

"Maybe I should cheer him on at the Olympics," I muse. "Because he always wins, right?"

"It's not the Winter Olympics," Myles replies, smiling. "And no, he doesn't always win."

"Who wins the most?"

"We haven't done this for years. But when we did, I guess I did."

"So I should support you then?"

He swallows, and I watch the prominent Adam's apple in his throat bob up and down. His profile is absolutely delicious. The sun is shining onto his face, making an almost-halo around his square jaw and slightly bumped nose. I fight the urge to take his sunglasses off – not only because that would make me a weirdo but also because we'd almost certainly end up in a ditch.

"You can support whoever you want."

The thing is, I know who I want to win. Him. Every time. A few months ago, I would have paid good money to see him fall on his ass. But a few months ago I wouldn't have been here, sitting in his beautiful car, driving to a family reunion just so he can knock me up while we're there.

That's definitely one not to tell the grandkids. How would I explain it anyway? We're crossing so many lines I'm not even sure where we stand anymore.

Four hours later he takes a right onto a gravel road, surrounded by trees that shoot up and over to form a canopy above our heads. Dappled sunshine fights its way through the leaves, and the highway suddenly feels a long way away. He's slowed down and I swear I can hear the chirping of birds, even though his engine probably drowns out the sounds of nature.

Then, just as suddenly as we drove into it, we're out of the forest, and I have to blink to adjust my eyesight. Ahead of us there are acres of green grass and rolling hills, and on top of one is a beautiful house that looks like it belongs in one of those upmarket lifestyle magazines.

"Misty Lakes," Myles says, as though I don't realize that this beautiful piece of architecture is his dad's home.

"Where are the lakes?" I ask him, because there's no sign of glinting water from here.

"On the other side of the hill with the house. Give it a minute, you'll see them."

Sure enough, as we drive up the road toward the house, I catch glimpses of blue. It expands as we drive closer, until there's nothing else but sparkling water, one small lake and one large. The large one is surrounded by trees and cabins – belonging to Myles and his brothers, I assume. He pulls into the driveway and parks, and I notice that all the other cars here are as sporty as his.

The Salinger brothers have a thing for speed, I guess.

When he kills the engine, I suddenly feel anxious. Like he's bringing me home to meet the parents. And even though I remind myself that I'm not Myles' girlfriend and I'm only here for one reason, the feeling doesn't dissipate.

"Remind me of your dad's name," I say as he walks around to open my door. His fingers curl around mine as I climb out of the seat.

"Rupert."

"And your stepmom is Julia?"

"His *wife* is Julia. We don't call her our stepmom."

I'm about to ask him why, but then a couple walks onto the front steps of the house and I realize exactly why. Julia is young. Younger than Rupert. Not very different in age to Myles.

Yeah, calling her his stepmom would be weird.

A second later, the front steps are filled with men. Tall, broad men who bear an uncanny resemblance to Myles. They're grinning and shouting at him, and I start to feel overwhelmed because I'm never going to remember all their names.

Myles squeezes my hand. "Relax," he murmurs. "You'll be great."

"Darling! You made it." I look up to see one familiar face in a crowd of strangers. Myles' mom looks as beautiful as I remember as she walks down the steps, beaming. "Ava, it's so lovely to see you again." Linda reaches out to clasp my hand. "Let me introduce you to everyone while Myles gets your things."

"Aren't we driving down to the cabins?" I ask.

She laughs. "Oh no, there's no road. You have to walk down to them."

Myles reluctantly lets go of my other hand as Linda leads me up the steps. "Rupert, have you met Ava Quinn?"

Myles' dad catches my eye and smiles. There's a presence to him that you don't see in many men. It's in the way he looks at me, as though I'm the most important person on the steps. It isn't lecherous or weird, just warming.

And now I'm starting to see why he's had so many wives.

"Ava, it's a pleasure," he says, leaning forward to kiss my cheek. The man even smells perfect. "This is my wife, Julia."

Julia Salinger leans forward to hug me. "Thank you for bringing Myles," she whispers in my ear. "I wasn't sure he'd come."

Well that's weird. I accept her thanks and store away the question created by the interaction for Myles later. "I wouldn't miss it for the world. I have high hopes for the Salinger Olympics."

She rolls her eyes. "I swear those boys would make a competition out of a funeral." It's also weird how she calls them boys when some of them look older than her. But then I turn around to see Myles and Liam laughing uproariously at something, and somehow they all do look boyish.

Myles' eyes land on mine and I feel my stomach contract. He mouths 'okay?' and I nod.

"Let's go inside. I want to introduce you to everybody," Julia says, putting her arm through mine. Myles' mom takes my other arm and we walk inside.

I'm in a Mrs. Salinger sandwich and I'm not sure if that's a good thing or not. It gets even more complicated when they introduce me to Deandra, a pretty fifty-something brunette who's cooking at the stove.

"Hi," Deandra says, smiling at me while she stirs. "It's so lovely to meet you. I've heard a lot about you."

"You have?" I blink, because what is there to hear?

"You publish the Dandy the Lion books, right?" Deandra asks. "I read them to my pre-school class every Friday. They love them."

"Oh, that's right," Linda says. "Myles told me about those. You're a publishing sensation."

"That's the one character he would have loved to publish," Julia joins in. "He always says so."

Before I can respond, Julia pulls me away and introduces me to her friends and family. I nod and smile but I know that I'll never remember anybody's name.

"Is there anything I can do to help?" I ask, when I realize everybody is either cooking, making wedding favors, or polishing silver right now.

"Oh no," Linda says. "We've got this. I'll take you back to Myles in a minute so you can freshen up. You've had a long drive."

"We need you to bring his grumpy ass to the party tonight," Deandra says, nodding. "He usually finds an excuse to avoid us all."

"I've never known somebody to have so many work meetings," Linda agrees. "Remember the Christmas after Rupert and Julia eloped?"

Julia bites her lip, as though embarrassed.

"It's nice that you're all friends," I say. "Being ex-wives and his current wife."

Deandra beams. "Honestly, Rupert has many faults, but he has an excellent taste in women."

"Why thank you." Linda beams. Even Julia's cheeks pink up.

"I'm very lucky to have them both," she says.

I'm fascinated by this set up. Every divorce I know has ended up in acrimony. Most of my friends' estranged parents won't even be in the same room with each other, let alone help with reunions and vow renewals.

It's hard to get my head around, but I like it. I like that there's kindness and love here, along with a big portion of mutual respect. It's like having sister wives without the husband sharing. And it must be great for the boys to have their parents all get along so well.

"You should have a reality show," I blurt out, then immediately regret it.

"We should." Deandra laughs. "Three wives, six boys, and a…"

"Handsome man you can't resist," Rupert says, walking into the kitchen. He puts his arm around Julia's waist and the blush she had earlier deepens. He kisses her cheek and murmurs something in her ear and it's like she blooms.

The man could make the polar ice caps melt.

A smile pulls at my lips as I look over his shoulder. A younger man with dark hair and the wickedest grin you could imagine walks in and grabs a pastry from a cooling rack. Deandra slaps his hand and he winks at her.

"Liam, those are for tonight."

"I'm just testing them," he tells her, pushing it whole into his mouth.

Two more men walk in. One of them wearing a hoodie with the Razors logo, so I assume that's Eli. He's even broader than Myles, if that's possible, and almost as tall. His hair is shorter, though, and there's a big scar from the corner of his eye to his ear.

And that leaves…Holden? Yeah, that's right. The brother who also works in New York. I can't begin to imagine the kind of attention the Salinger brothers must attract when they go out en masse. It would be like Henry Cavill co-opting the Hemsworth brothers and adding Jamie Dornan into the mix. They're testosterone in human form.

And they're going to be part of my baby's gene pool. I take a moment to marvel at that, but then I realize that the baby will never know any of this. The other side of his or her family. The love and the acceptance and the kindness.

That makes me feel sad.

Myles walks to my side and looks down at me. "You want to head to the cabin?"

"Hey, you need to introduce us first," Liam says, grinning as he grabs another pastry. "Liam," he says, offering his free hand. I take it and he circles my hand with his warm, firm fingers.

"Ava," I tell him.

"Oh, I know who you are." He winks.

"And this is Eli," Myles says, introducing me to his second younger brother.

"Hi," I say, smiling. "Love the hoodie."

"I've got a box of them in my car for the team. You're more than welcome to one."

Oh, I like him, too.

"Holden," the one who looks the youngest says. He looks shyer than the others, but the trademark Salinger smile is still there. I shake his hand and try to decide which of the brothers I like the most.

Apart from Myles, of course. And it's a tie, which is good because I don't like playing favorites.

"What about your other brothers?" I ask him, desperately trying to remember his half-brothers' names. "Are they here?"

"I sent Linc and Brooks outside to collect firewood," Deandra says, shaking her head. "They were fighting again."

"Over what?" Julia asks, looking worried.

"I have no idea. Could have been whether the sky is blue, could have been over a football team." Deandra shrugs. "You know those two."

"Fighting as in arguing?" I ask. "Or fighting as in…"

"Punching the heck out of each other." Deandra shrugs as though it's an everyday occurrence. "I told them that if either one of them has a black eye for the photographs, they'll know what a real punch feels like."

Myles' mom was right. His dad does have great taste. I love them all.

"I'll introduce you later," Myles promises. "Shall we go to the cabin now?"

"Sure." I smile at them all. "Let me know if I can do anything, okay?" I say to Julia.

She smiles warmly back. "I will."

And then we head outside to get our luggage.

CHAPTER
EIGHTEEN

AVA

"Your family is amazing," I tell Myles as he carries his own bags plus one of mine down the bark-covered footpath that weaves through the trees. I'm left carrying my laptop bag and pulling the smaller of my two suitcases, which sounds easier than it is because little pieces of bark keep getting stuck in the wheels and making me stop short.

"Leave it," Myles says. "I'll come back and pick it up in a minute."

"Nope, I've got this," I tell him, brushing the bark away. "You're already carrying enough."

He shakes his head and leads me through the wooded path, the sparkle of the lake on one side of us, a thick layer of trees on the other. "So tell me," I say, huffing because the damn suitcase has caught up again. "You built the cabin closest to the house, right? Because you got first pick of the sites."

"Nope." He smiles smugly. "Mine's the furthest away."

"Figures," I mutter, tugging at my luggage. If I hadn't

stuffed so much into it I'd probably be able to lift it, but it's just too heavy. It's also making a weird noise every time I move it, as though the wheels are groaning at the effort they're having to make.

"My family likes you, too," he says, returning to my earlier remark. "My mom wants you to stay in the house. She says you shouldn't have to slum it."

"It's a cabin, it's not exactly slumming it," I point out, smiling. "You have hot and cold running water, right?"

"When it works. But if you want to stay at the house I can arrange it."

I swallow hard. "It's okay. I can work with that."

I'm not going to lie, the lure of a warm bed and an even warmer shower at the main house is alluring. But if I don't stay in this cabin, it's going to make things even more awkward when I ovulate. How would I explain the booty call to his mom and his stepmom and… Julia? Which reminds me.

"Julia called you boys," I tell him. "You and your brothers. It sounded a little strange."

"She's known us for a long time."

"She and your dad have been married for ten years, though," I say, as we pass the closer cabins. They all have outdoor showers, and I'm hoping against hope that there are also indoor ones. "Which made you around thirty when they met. You weren't exactly a boy."

"I guess maybe it makes her feel more comfortable putting some distance between us," Myles says smoothly. "My dad's much older than her. It can't always be easy."

I change tack. "Does Liam know about our agreement?"

Myles swallows. "Yes. But he's promised not to tell anybody else. I figured we may need a little help if the timing is awkward." He glances at me. "Are you upset I told him?"

"No." I told my friends after all. "I'm just surprised you did."

"Why?"

I've counted five cabins. Which makes the last one – standing in the distance at the edge of the lake – Myles'. "Because you're so closed up you don't tell anybody anything."

"Liam's my brother," he says quietly. "We talk a lot."

My heart clenches because I'm glad he's got somebody. And I realize something else. In that room, surrounded by his family, he looked almost lonely. Is that even possible?

We reach his cabin and he puts all the luggage down on the wooden deck. It's actually very pretty. It's built on stilts at the water's edge, with dark varnished wood and a high pitched roof. A jetty stretches out from the deck into the water.

He opens the cabin door and ushers me inside. I heave a sigh of relief when I see it doesn't look as basic as I feared. Light spills in from the windows, illuminating the wooden walls and floor. There are rugs scattered everywhere, and a cozy sofa and chairs around what looks like a handcrafted coffee table. One wall is taken up with a huge fireplace complete with stove and cast iron chimney, which spans the wall and escapes through the roof.

A floor-to-ceiling window looks out on the lake. On the far side of the room is a little kitchen, big enough for two people to cook together if they're feeling cozy.

"Where's the bathroom?" I ask, because I have to know if there's a shower in there.

Myles leads me to two doors, opening the second one. I peer in over his arm and let out a sigh. There's a toilet, a sink, *and* an enclosed shower.

"It's not as bad as you described," I tell him, relieved. "It's pretty."

"Good," he says simply, then opens the other door. "Your bedroom."

Like the rest of the cabin, it's basic but nice. A wooden four poster bed stands in the center of the room, covered in what looks like a home-made quilt. There's a dresser with a mirror on the wall, plus an easy chair next to the window that looks out over the lake.

"Where will you sleep?" I ask him.

"In the living room. It's a sofa bed." He catches my eye. "You'll have your privacy, I promise."

I'm not sure I want it, but I don't know how to tell him that. So I change the subject.

"You really built this?" I ask, even though I know the answer.

"With some help."

"It's beautiful," I tell him. "You did good."

He swallows. "Thank you." He inclines his head at the door. "I'll just go get your things. You can rest or freshen up."

"What time do we start tonight?"

"The cookout starts at seven."

"Okay." I smile at him. "By the way, I'm glad I'm here."

His eyes flicker over my face. "I'm glad you are, too."

After bringing in my luggage, he leaves me alone as I unpack, sliding my things into the drawers, freshly lined with scented paper, and hanging my dresses on the rail that's fixed into a recess in the corner of the room. I hear footsteps outside, and I see the shadow of him passing my window as he holds a phone to his ear, pacing along the deck.

Figuring I might as well test out his shower – because I'm still not sure I believe him about the warm water – I grab my toiletries and head into the bathroom.

Miracle of miracles, it's warm! I groan as I step under it, letting the spray clean the dirt from my face and body. I don't even care that my hair's getting wet, I'll blow dry it and tie it in a knot at the back of my head. If we're having a cookout it'll get smoky anyway, and I'll have to wash it again in the morning.

When I finally emerge from the shower, my skin is red and glowing. I take one of the towels that was stacked on the linen rack and twist it into my hair, using another to wrap around my body.

Myles is back in the cabin when I walk out of the bathroom, fiddling with a coffee machine on the kitchen countertop. He looks up and blinks as I walk toward him, wrapped in only a towel. And again I marvel at the strangeness of the fact that I'm going to have a baby with a man who's never seen me naked.

"The water's warm," I tell him. "Thank God."

He smiles. "I told you."

"Yeah but you also told me it was unreliable." There's a buzz from the counter, and I see his phone there, the screen lit up.

"Work problems?" I ask. I need to call in myself. Make sure Ryan hasn't given everybody the week off.

"Some. But mostly my brothers. We have an annoying group chat going."

"Annoying?" I ask.

He switches on the coffee machine. "They're asking a lot of questions about you."

Maybe I should hate that, but I don't. "What kind of questions?"

"Beautiful, you don't want to know."

My body does something weird at his term of endearment. My nipples harden and my thighs clamp together. I have to look away, because I'm afraid he might see something in my eyes.

Something I don't want him to know.

My little crush on him.

I'm not sure when it began. For too long it's been clouded by my dislike for a man who is so closed up he'd give Fort Knox a run for its money. Recently, I've assumed it's gratitude, because he's selflessly giving me something I've dreamed about.

But now it feels like something else. Something deeper

and more personal. It's like he's opening his armor, chink by chink, and I'm slowly getting to see the real Myles inside.

And I like him. I really do.

Too much.

"Coffee?" he asks me. "I've brought decaf."

And that slays me a little more, because he knows I'm avoiding caffeine. Lauren and Sophie's warning bells start ringing in my head. *Bonding alert! Hormones are raging! Don't fall in love with the one man you shouldn't.*

"Coffee would be great." My voice is low and gritty. He pauses for a second, then reaches for one of the mugs hanging from a hook on the wall. There's a tic in his jaw and he won't look at me.

Does he know about my crush? Is he going to say something? That would be mortifying.

I take a deep breath and tug at the towel still wrapping my body. "So, if tonight is the cookout and tomorrow is the vow renewal, when do the Olympics begin?"

"The next day."

"And what events will you be doing?"

"Swimming. Rowing. Track and field. Shooting."

"Shooting?" I widen my eyes. "Not animals."

"Clay pigeons. It's my dad's favorite."

"Okay." I still won't tell my mom about that. Or any of this. Because Lauren is an amateur at sniffing the truth of my emotions out compared to Mom. I should probably just avoid her for the next five years.

"I didn't know you could shoot," I say, taking the coffee he offers me. His eyes glance down at my towel then back to my face again.

"Why would you? I don't go around waving a gun in the office like Bruce Willis in *Die Hard*."

"That would be kind of cool though. Shake the place up a bit."

He grins. Yes, actually grins. It takes all my self-control not to climb his fine body right there. "I'll bear that in mind. Why don't you take your coffee and get dressed? I have a couple more calls to make and then we can join the others."

"Okay." I nod. "I should take an ovulation test, too, before we go out." I'm logging them carefully.

He nods his head. "Do that, too."

And we're back to business. The reason why I'm here. Donor and recipient. I keep forgetting that, but I shouldn't because I wouldn't be here if it wasn't for our agreement.

"Are you sure jeans and a sweater are okay for tonight?" I ask him. "It feels a bit underdressed for a bachelorette party."

"It's fine. You want to be as covered as possible or you'll get eaten to death by the mosquitos."

I wrinkle my nose. "That sounds attractive."

"Don't worry, I'll cover you with bug spray as well."

"I knew there was a dark side to you."

"I just don't want you itchy all night. I've heard you complaining before." His voice is light and teasing. "And much like my family, the bugs here love fresh blood."

"You make them sound like vampires," I tell him.

"The bugs or my family?"

"Both."

He smiles and lifts up his coffee, taking a sip and closing his eyes. I take that as my cue to go to my room and get dressed. But as I open the door a weird thought washes over me and even though I try to push it away, it remains anyway.

He'd make a good dad.

And there it is.

I wish that thought hadn't come into my mind.

MYLES

. . .

I watch the door close behind her and breathe a sigh of relief because she must have noticed me looking at that tiny towel barely covering her body. She has the best damn legs I've seen, and yes I knew that from the red skirt that tormented me all those weeks ago, but now I've seen them bare and glistening and all I can think is that I want to touch her.

I swallow hard and pick up my phone, desperate for a distraction that doesn't involve knowing she's currently naked in my bedroom. It looks like my brothers' group chat is still going on without me. I roll my eyes because it's as predictable as ever.

So there's really nothing going on between him and Ava? – Eli

That's what he says. – Liam

I call bullshit. I saw the way he looked at her. And the way she looked at him, too. – Holden

I blink. She looked at me that way? I store that information away to think about later.

So, if he's not interested that means she's fair game, right? – Eli

What do you mean? – Holden

If I ask her to dance that's okay. Because she just works for Myles. – Eli

We don't shit where we eat. Remember? – Liam

I sigh and pull up the keyboard on my phone.

• • •

Nobody goes near Ava. Nobody touches her. Understand? –
Myles

Nobody replies for a moment. Then three dots appear next to Eli's name. I love my brother to death, but he doesn't know how to take no for an answer.

But you're not interested in her, so why not? – Eli
  Because I say so.– Myles
  Okay, okay. I get it. You want her for yourself. – Eli
  Eli… – Myles
  What? – Eli
  Just… Ah whatever. I have better things to do than listen
to you all gossip. – Myles

I put the phone down as Ava opens the door and walks out. She's wearing jeans and a t-shirt that skims her perfect curves. Her face is clean and her still-damp hair is knotted into a bun, escaping tendrils curling down her neck. I have to curl my hands into fists as to not touch her, because every cell in my body is urging me to do exactly that.

Feel her skin. Breathe her scent. Make her mine.

Fuck.

I stand, thanking God that my jeans hide any evidence of my attraction to her, and grab my phone. "I need to make some calls," I tell her. "Will you be okay here?"

She nods. "Of course." She bites her lip. "I'm not ovulating, in case you were wondering."

I clear my throat. "Okay."

"So you don't need to…" Her gaze drops. "Rush to, you know…"

"Touch myself."

Her eyes lift to mine. Two tiny circles of red appear on her cheeks. I want to touch them so badly, to feel the heat in them. I want to kiss her throat until she's gasping for more. I want everything about this woman, and I've no idea how to deal with that.

So I flash her a smile and run out of the cabin, heading for the tiny pier where I'll plunge my feet into the cold lake water and pretend to make calls until the urge disappears.

CHAPTER
NINETEEN

AVA

I groan and grab my stomach, wishing I hadn't eaten quite so much. When Myles said they were having a cookout, I'd imagined a little barbecue with sausages and burgers and a vat of chili on the fire. And there were those things, but there was also a hog roast and these amazing potatoes that were somewhere between steak fries and baked potatoes, and I ate way too many of them.

The cookout is taking place by the lake, a little further down from the brothers' cabins. From here you can see the house at the top of the hill, as well as the seats and wedding arch that have been set out for tomorrow. Down by the water there are trestle tables where we've been eating. In all there are about forty of us. I guess it's small for a ceremony, but a big crowd for this house. The air is filled with chatter and the twangs of the country band that's set up on a deck in the corner.

"Flag football time," Eli says, laying a pile of fabric squares on the table in front of Myles.

"Now?" Myles glances at his watch. "It's getting dark."

"Perfect time to play." Eli lowers his voice. "Deandra told me to keep Brooks and Linc occupied. I figure we can wear them out."

"Put them on the same team," Myles says. "That way they won't try to beat the shit out of each other."

"Already got it. They're on your team." Eli grins mischievously. "I get Liam and Holden."

"Can I play?" I ask, and they both turn to look at me with horror. "What?" I say, amused. "Can't stand competition from a girl?"

Myles shakes his head. "It gets… violent."

I eye him carefully. "I can take it." And I need to run off this food if I want to get into my dress tomorrow. "Anyway, I thought flag football was supposed to be no-contact."

"It is," Eli says, his lips twitching. "But by five minutes in, everybody forgets that."

Eli wanders off to find the other brothers, and Myles leans in to whisper in my ear. "I don't want you playing."

"Why not? Are you afraid I might beat you?"

"No, I'm afraid you'll end up with two black eyes. I'm trying to be chivalrous here."

"I know how to dodge somebody running for me," I tell him. "I did it enough times with the cops growing up."

He holds his hand up. "I'm going to park that thought for a minute. We'll come back to it later, because I want to know why you were running from the cops." He takes a deep breath. "If you play, you're on my team and you keep close at all times."

My lips curl. "You're a sexist."

"I'm not. I have every faith in your football prowess. I just don't have faith in my brothers. The rivalry gets fierce."

"I'll bear that in mind." The truth is, I've never played flag football. I've never had enough family around me to make one team, let alone two. But this is fun and I want to be part of it, if only for a few days. Myles shakes his head and smiles, exasperated.

We manage to recruit another three players, so there are five on each side. On ours there's Myles, Brooks, Linc, Julia's friend Sara, and me. Liam leads the other side, with Holden and Eli – who I really think are our biggest problem. They also have two of Julia's cousins to even things up.

I'm so excited for this game it isn't funny. I start warming myself up, shifting from side to side and Myles shoots me an amused stare.

"What are you doing?"

"Getting limber." I shift to my right leg.

He rolls his eyes and hands me a flag, and I tuck it into the back of my jeans. When Liam tosses a coin, Myles calls heads and we win, and I let out a whoop.

"Your team spirit is impressive," Eli tells me. "Have you played before?"

"Never."

Myles blinks. "But you know the rules, right?"

"Throw the ball, advance up the field, and if the other team is on offense, grab their flags." I shrug. "Simple."

"And stay behind me at all times," Myles says. *Spoilsport.*

Brooks takes the ball to start, with Myles behind him on the right and Linc on the left. Sara shoots me a smile. "Hi."

"Hi," I say. "I'm Ava."

"I know. Everybody's talking about you."

Oh that's weird. I open my mouth to ask what they're saying, but then the whistle blows and Myles is throwing the ball between his legs. The next minute is filled with running and shouting, the ball flying through the air at lightning speed. It goes from Myles to Linc to Brooks, who makes a run for it, but Eli is fast and grabs his flag.

"Gotcha, sucker!" Eli taunts.

"Fuck you," Brooks says, looking petulant.

"It's fine. We've advanced." Myles takes a deep breath. "Let's go for the second down."

The next ten minutes follow the same pattern. We throw and run and Eli's team runs us down. We're ten yards from the end zone when Myles calls for a huddle, and we gather around him.

"You're doing great," he tells us, and damn if Brooks and Linc don't light up like Christmas trees at his praise. I've noticed the same thing with all of his brothers this evening – they all stare at Myles like he's some kind of god. It's the same way they look at their dad. And maybe that explains it, because for a lot of their life it sounds like Myles has been their quasi-father.

They obviously adore him.

"Brooks and Linc, there's no way they're gonna let you score a touchdown. Eli and Holden are on you at all times," Myles tells them.

"Yeah, and they're on you, too," Brooks says. "It's like Liam's glued to your side."

"So we need to throw to Ava or Sara," Myles continues.

"Oh no, not me." Sara holds her hands up. "I'm only here to even up the numbers. And I've seen how fast Eli can run."

Four sets of eyes turn to me. "You want me to try to score?" I manage to squeak.

"Yes," Myles says. "That way we can take them by surprise. Stay on the left and Brooks and Linc, you stay on the right. I'll throw to Brooks and everybody will think he's either running or throwing to Linc. When they head to Brooks, be ready for his throw. And when you get the ball, run like hell, Ava."

I catch his eye and nod, my face serious. "I will," I agree. I'm trying not to laugh at how seriously they are taking this. God only knows how competitive they'll be when their Olympics start. What is it about grown men and sports?

My heart is pounding as we go back into our formation,

Myles at the front, Brooks and Linc behind him, Sara and me beside them. Liam's team is watching us carefully, their faces set as though this is the most important football game in the world.

There's a crowd watching us now. The music has stopped and everybody is silent. I can hear the blood rushing through my ears and feel the speed of my heart as it clatters in my chest.

Then the whistle blows and we're off. Myles snaps the ball back to Brooks and then we all run forward. Brooks calls Linc's name and Linc shouts something back, but I can't hear it because of the roar in my head. Instead, I watch as Brooks lifts the ball and it hurtles through the air toward me. My breath catches in my throat as I hold my hands up, and as if in slow motion, watch the ball land smack dab between my palms.

There are more shouts, but I start running like hell, my breath short as I see the end zone they've created out of sweaters. Somebody's chanting my name – is it Myles? – and other people are laughing and clapping, but my eyes are trained on the prize.

A stampede of feet is only a yard or two away, and I know this is my one chance to score. Somebody fumbles at my back and swears as though they've missed the flag, and I arch away and throw myself toward the end zone.

But instead of landing on grass, I feel a mass of muscle collide with my body, sending me up in the air until gravity does her thing and I fall back to the ground, the wind knocked out of me. I land on the grass with a dull thud, my head thwacking the earth, and for a moment I see stars dancing in front of my eyes.

"Ava!"

Tentatively, I wiggle my fingers and toes. They're still working. Does that mean I haven't broken anything?"

"Ava," Myles says again, his voice hoarse. He drops down and touches my face. "Christ, are you all right?"

"I'm so sorry," Eli says, and I assume he was the wall of muscle that caused the collision.

"You should be. You're twice her size, you asshole." Myles sounds furious. I try to sit up, but he pushes me back down. "Wait a minute," he murmurs. "I want to check that you're okay."

"Did I score?" I ask.

He gives the softest of chuckles. "You dropped the ball before the end zone."

"Damn." I frown. "I nearly had it."

"Forget about the ball, does anything hurt?" Myles asks.

"I don't think so," I manage. "Just my pride."

"It was a foul," I hear somebody – it might be Brooks – say. "She still has her flag. We should get a penalty."

"Nobody's getting anything. I'm taking Ava back to the cabin." Myles' voice offers no dissent.

"I can play on," I argue. "I think."

He touches my head. "Do you have any pain here?"

"No."

He runs his fingers down my face, then feels my neck. "I'd be happier if we got you seen by a doctor."

"I just fell over, it's no biggie," I tell him. He has this concerned expression on his face that makes my stomach do a little flip. "Let's not make a fuss, please?"

He presses his lips together and nods. Then he leans back and helps me up to sit, telling me to take a breath before pulling me to my feet. "If you get any twinges, you tell me, okay?"

Eli steps forward and swallows hard. "I'm really sorry, Ava."

"It's not your fault. I was so busy thinking about scoring a touchdown I didn't see you there."

Myles lets out a harrumph, but says nothing.

"Seriously," I tell Eli, who looks guilty as hell. "I'm fine." Or I will be once everybody stops looking at me. Myles is hovering around me as though he's afraid I might pick up the ball and make a run for it.

Eli gives me a tight smile. "I should have been more careful."

"Yes, you should," Myles says, then puts his arm around my shoulders. "Let's go, Tom Brady. Before you cause yourself any more damage."

"You really don't have to come back with me," I tell him after we say goodnight to his dad and his moms. "I'll be fine. You should spend time with your family."

"I'm not leaving you on your own. You might have a concussion." He's still got his arm around me. And it feels… nice. This enemy who's my friend. I slide my arm around his waist and for a moment he freezes, but then carries on walking. I can feel the heat of his skin through his long-sleeved Henley, and it makes my heart do a weird flip.

"I'm sorry we didn't win," I say, mostly because I want him to reply.

"I never realized you were so competitive."

"I'm not usually," I muse. "I guess you bring out the best in me."

"Or the worst?"

My lips twitch. "Maybe. Anyway, you'll just have to trounce them all at the Salinger Olympics."

"Well at least you won't be competing in that."

"Would that be such a bad thing?" I frown. "I'm as good as the rest of them."

"Of course you are. But every time you get the slightest scratch I'll have a fucking heart attack. And I don't know how many more of them I can take."

"I'm sorry," I say softly. "I just wanted to join in. I should know better at my age, but I didn't get to do stuff like that growing up."

"What?" His brow pinches. We turn a corner past the large oak trees and his cabin comes into view. There's a light on inside but apart from that everything is dark, illuminated only by the moon. It's reflected on the lake, a shimmer that moves every few moments as though insects are diving below the surface.

"I didn't have many friends." I shrug.

"I don't understand. Everybody loves you."

"No they don't."

He blinks. "Yes they do."

"You didn't. You hated me."

"What makes you think that?" His brows pull in tight as we reach the steps to his deck.

"Oh, the way you looked at me like you wanted to kill me every time we were on a conference call."

"How did I look exactly?" he asks slowly.

I try to form my expression into an approximation of his on all those meetings and video calls. My eyes are narrow, my lips pursed, and there are furrows in my brow about three feet deep.

He's studying my face like it's a map of somewhere he's never been before. Taking in every line.

"You mean like this?" he asks hoarsely, forming his expression into exactly the one I'm referring to. A little moody, a lot angry. It's like we're back in the conference room again.

"Yes!" I say triumphantly. "Exactly like that."

"That isn't a hating expression," he says, his face easing as the moodiness melts away.

"Then what is it?"

"You don't know?" he asks, his hand curling around the door handle. There's a depth to his eyes that I can't quite fathom.

"No," I say quietly. "I don't."

"It's a…" He exhales heavily. "It's a this woman is fucking

gorgeous, but she's out of my league and she wouldn't want me anyway because I made a really bad first impression and every time we see each other I just make it worse expression."

Absolute shock takes over me. "That's a very specific expression."

"It is," he agrees.

"Do you use it on all the women?"

He closes his eyes for a moment. "Let's go inside before all the bugs get in."

Myles flicks a light on as we step into the living area. I follow him, his words still echoing in my brain. He thinks I'm gorgeous. It's like a hundred-piece orchestra has taken up residence in my mind, playing the most beautiful piece of music I could have imagined.

"You liked me?" I ask, my voice tight. "Why didn't you say something?"

He closes the door behind me, his arm brushing my shoulder. He's close enough for me to smell his cologne, mixed with the sweet smell of fresh perspiration.

"Go to bed, Ava," he says.

I shake my head, my jaw set. "But I have questions."

"You think *you* have questions?" he asks. "I have a ton of them."

"Like what?"

"Like why didn't you have friends when you were younger?"

"I guess I had a few friends, I just didn't get to spend time with them out of school. A lot of the other moms didn't like mine."

He winces. "Why not?"

"Because she has very specific views and isn't afraid to demonstrate them." I'm leaning back against the door and he's so close our chests are almost touching. I have to look up to catch his eye. "What else?"

"Why were you chased by cops?"

"Same reason. My mom has very specific views and…"

"Isn't afraid to demonstrate them," he finishes. "But *you* don't seem to have specific views," he points out.

"I do," I say softly. "But maybe I'm afraid to demonstrate them."

"Why are you afraid?"

"Because I like to be liked." I'm feeling exposed. How come I'm the one answering the questions? All I want to know is if he was joking when he said I'm gorgeous.

"I noticed that," he says softly. "Why is that so important to you?"

"Who doesn't want to be liked?"

He shrugs. "Me."

I reach up to cup his face. His skin is warm and bristly against my palm. He closes his eyes as I trace the line of his jaw with my thumb, his breath exhaling in a pant. And it makes me feel like he wasn't joking.

He was deadly serious. And so am I.

"*I* like you."

He squeezes his eyes shut even tighter. "You should go to bed."

I ignore him, so sick of this push and pull between us. I need to know what he's thinking. I need answers, dammit. "Do you like me?" I ask softly.

He swallows hard, his throat bobbing. Up close it's like watching a miracle. A testosterone filled one.

"You said something to me a minute ago," I whisper. "That me getting hurt gives you a heart attack. What does that mean?"

"That I'm almost certainly going to be in the hospital before the end of the weekend." He's still not giving anything away and it's killing me. There's this frisson between us that's making my skin feel electric. He's big and he's masculine and he makes me feel so achy inside. I've never been into power plays between men and women, but right now if he flung me over his shoulder and carried me into the bedroom I'd be putty in his hands.

I roll onto the balls of my feet, my face inches from his. Myles' lips part enough for him to exhale softly. His gaze is wary, as though I'm a wild animal and he has no idea what I'm going to do next.

To be honest, I have no idea either.

"Myles, do you like me?" I ask him again.

"Yes." His voice is strangled, like he's admitting it against his will. "But I'm not going to do anything about it."

I frown. "Why not?"

"Because we work together. And I'm the asshole you love to hate."

"You're the asshole who's going to be my baby's father. And I don't hate you. Quite the opposite, in fact." I want him. My body wants him. Damn, my mind wants him, too.

He's silent, but his eyes tell me everything his lips won't. They're hot and they're piercing and I feel like he can see into my soul. I want to dive into them.

"Ava…"

"Kiss me."

I know this is stupid. If Lauren was here she'd be screaming at me to stop. It will complicate an already messy situation. But I can't help it, I burn for him.

I want him like I've never wanted anyone else.

He closes those beautiful eyes, squeezing them tightly as though in pain. His jaw is so tight I could cut cheese on it. He opens them again, inhaling sharply. "It's been a long—"

My lips tremble because I already feel the rejection. Then he shakes his head and says, "Fuck it."

The first thing I feel when his body presses against mine is the thick ridge of him digging into my stomach. If I wasn't winded earlier, I am now, because it's more than in proportion to this big, strong man. He brushes my hair over my shoulder, his fingers trailing over my neck, sending a pulse of electricity directly to my nipples. They harden against his chest.

Even on my tiptoes, he has to stoop to align his face with mine. His eyes blaze into mine, and I can feel every emotion that's running through him. I open my mouth to tell him to hurry up, but before I can say anything his lips crash into mine.

I think I let out a little moan. My arms curl around his neck and his slide down my back, cupping my behind before he lifts me up against the door. I'm the filling in a Myles and door sandwich, my back jammed against the wood, my front pressed into his beautiful, muscled body as he rocks his hips against me.

His lips part, his tongue sliding into my mouth, and this time my moan is loud. Whatever this man is doing to me, my body likes it. No, it *loves* it. My skin is tingling and sensitive, and the blunt force of his erection against my stomach makes me want to sing with joyful abandon.

The rough growth of a day's beard scrapes my chin as I kiss him back, my fingers playing with the short hair at the nape of his neck. Then I pull my mouth from his, dipping to kiss the hard lines of his throat, and for the first time he lets out a groan that rumbles through my body.

He tastes so good I think he might be my new favorite meal. With one hand still under my ass, he pushes the other between us and under my hoodie, sliding the base of his thumb over my breast, letting out a throaty noise when he feels the peak of my nipple.

But then he pulls back, leaving me breathless and aching. I look up at him, confused, and see the fire in his eyes.

"I kissed you," he says, as he struggles to catch his breath. "So now you should go to bed."

"But…"

He brushes his fingers against my jaw, his touch so light I barely feel it. "Ava, please, go to bed."

My heart is beating so fast I'm scared it might fly out of my chest. My skin is tingling and desperate for more of this man. I'm so confused and turned on and desperate to feel the weight of him on me.

I think I might die without it.

"Myles…" I whisper.

"Don't say anything," he urges. "Just go."

"But you… we…" I take a deep breath, trying to calm my speeding pulse. "Why did you stop?"

"Because if I don't stop now, I'm not sure I'll be able to later."

My breath is still unsteady. "Then don't. Don't stop. I won't stop you."

His eyes flash. "Don't say that."

"Why not?"

"Because I'm trying to be a gentleman," he rasps. "And I haven't forgotten why you're here."

"Why I'm…" It dawns on me. "To get pregnant?"

He swallows. "Yes. And you're not ovulating yet."

"So if I was, you'd still be kissing me. Touching me. Would you take me to bed?"

He squeezes his eyes shut. "Please stop. I'm on the fucking edge right now. Do you know how impossible you are to resist?"

"Then don't resist me." It seems simple. I want him. He wants me. Why can't we do this? "I want to feel you inside of me." There it is, the truth. I want this man like I've never wanted anything before.

"If I slide inside you, I'll come. And I don't want to come."

My mouth opens but no sound comes out.

"If I'm going to impregnate you this weekend, I'd like the odds to be good," he continues. "And I'm not lessening our chances now. Not when I've been abstaining for a week."

"A week?" I repeat. "But you…" I stop because I have no

idea how to say this. "You must have, you know, relieved yourself?"

He lifts his head from my shoulder, his smile crooked. "How come you can beg me to take you to bed but you can't say masturbate?"

My cheeks redden and his grin widens. "Why haven't you…" I take a deep breath. "Masturbated?"

"Because I read that it can reduce sperm count."

My brows lift. "You've been reading up about it?" I don't know why it surprises me. This is Myles we're talking about.

He shrugs. "I like to know what I'm getting into."

"What else have you been reading?"

He runs his palms up my back. It feels warm and good. "I like to research a subject before I go all in."

I'm intrigued now. And more than a little bit touched by him being all in. "Tell me the weirdest thing you've read."

He dips his head to press his lips softly against mine. My whole body sighs. "There's a study in *Evolutionary Psychological Science* which concluded that the duration of cunnilingus predicts the amount of a man's ejaculate."

"There's what?" I whisper. I'm floored. Not just because Myles said cunnilingus and now I'm picturing him doing exactly that. And yes, he'd be good at it, because Myles Salinger is good at everything he does.

But also because people study this. There're actually people who volunteer to be… um… orally pleasured in the name of science. I'd take my hat off to them if I was wearing one.

"You heard me," he says, his voice thick. Yes, I did. Now all I can think about is that Myles has been reading up on men giving women oral sex for scientific purposes.

"How many people did they study?" I'm literally fascinated. And more than a little turned on. He's still holding me loosely. I shift against him and he steadies me again. Yeah, he's turned on, too.

"If you'll stand still I'll tell you." He slides his hands down my thighs. Why didn't I wear shorts tonight? Oh yeah, because of the bugs.

"I'm still," I point out.

"They reached the conclusion by watching porn. Measured the length of time the man gave head to the woman, then compared it to the ejaculate volume."

"They must have had their eyes glued to the screen."

He grins. "It's a hard job…"

"Literally."

He laughs and it sends a shot of warmth through me. When he kisses me this time it's so soft it makes my chest ache. "You really should go to bed," he murmurs.

"Yeah." I nod. "But I don't want to."

His gaze is like a warm blanket being wrapped around my body. I feel so needy yet so safe with him. It's disconcerting.

"When I'm ovulating…"

He exhales heavily, his eyes never leaving mine. "Then we'll talk."

"About…"

"I wish you'd use complete sentences," he says. "It would make it so much easier for me if I didn't have to guess what you're thinking."

"I'm sorry. I just find talking about this stuff difficult." I press my lips together and give myself a silent pep talk. "Okay, when I'm ovulating will you kiss me again?"

The corner of his lip twitches. "Yes."

"And will you… touch me?"

He blinks. "Yes."

"And if you wanted… and I do want… would you do more?"

"Define *more*."

Oh, he's going to make me work for this. I keep my gaze on his even though I want to look away. I'm not going to let him beat me. "Would you slide your hard cock inside of me until my eyes roll back and I'm gasping your name?"

His eyes widen with shock and I feel a thrill of victory. "Fuck, Ava."

"Exactly. Will you fuck Ava?"

He swallows, his eyes dark and narrow. "Yes," he rasps, pinching the bridge of his nose with his fingers. "Now will you go to bed before I lose my goddamned mind?"

CHAPTER
TWENTY

MYLES

I barely slept last night. Some of it was due to having to contort my body to fit the way-too-small sofa bed, but most of it was because of her.

The woman who's currently laying in my bed, her warm limbs tangled in my sheets.

The woman I've been lying to myself about.

The one I want more than I want air to breathe.

It's early and as I swim away from the cabin, the only sound I hear are the echoing coos of the mourning doves as they call to each other from across the lake.

My brothers' cabins are all dark, and even the main house looks quiet. In an hour there will be mayhem as everybody wakes up to get ready for the ceremony, but for now I appreciate the peace.

Not that my mind is peaceful. It's too full of *her*. I feel like I've been walking around with a constant hard-on. It was bad enough when she was walking around the cabin half-naked.

Now she's not only half-naked but has told me exactly what she wants.

Me. Inside of her.

And now I can't think of anything else. I want to kiss her. I want to consume her. I want her to forget everything except my name. And I want to hear her scream it out loud as I fuck her to oblivion.

Jesus, this cold swim isn't doing me any good. Nor is the contrived distance between us. I tread water and reach down to adjust myself, wincing because it's almost painful. If I were anywhere else, with anybody else I'd just fuck myself stupid and be done with it.

In the distance, I see my father walking down to the water's edge. He spots me and lifts his hand up.

I wave back and thankfully the excitement abates. Nothing like seeing your seventy-three year-old father looking more calm than you are, even though he's about to renew his vows to his thirty-something wife.

"Myles!" he calls out. There's a fluttering of wings where he's scared the doves.

I swim over to him and climb out of the lake, water pouring off my body. "What's up?" I ask.

"Actually, I need your help," he tells me, and I try not to sigh.

Because somebody *always* needs my help.

"What is it?"

"Can you come talk to the celebrant with me?" he says. "We need to sort out who's doing the readings."

And now I know exactly who'll be doing the readings. And making sure the ceremony goes smoothly. And it won't be my dad.

AVA

· · ·

The string quartet begins to play, their achingly sweet music filling the air, and the woman sitting next to me pops a mint into her mouth and starts sucking it noisily. I'm in the back row of the seats that have been laid out for the vow renewal ceremony. Myles is at the front, sitting between his mom and Liam. His family tried to get me to sit with them, but I refused.

I need a little space away from Myles. Last night was... intense. But this morning when I got up he was working and then had to come up to the house to help his dad get things ready. I offered to come with but he insisted I stayed and got ready at my leisure. We haven't talked about our conversation but the promise of more is still there.

I can't sit still because just thinking about it makes me squirm.

I also had to do a pee test. I'm still not ovulating. That's probably a good thing because I don't want all these witnesses around for when I'm dragging Myles back to his cabin to keep his promise.

There are about eighty people here in all. Some of them I recognize from last night, and they gave me a nod as I walked up to the house and sat down on the chairs laid out on the lawn. Others have driven in just for today, like the mint monster next to me. She's already on her third. She bites down on it and it makes a cracking sound in my ear. Isn't she worried she might break a tooth?

Somebody sighs and then everybody turns around to look at the entrance of the aisle. I do the same, and I can see why they're sighing because Julia Salinger is beautiful. Her platinum blonde hair is swept up into a low chignon that makes her look timeless. Her dress is an ivory lace, high at the neck, tight at the bodice and hips, then out like a fishtail to a trailing train.

She could be getting married at any time in the last century, and she'd still look chic. And when Myles' dad catches her eye she blushes like a schoolgirl instead of the thirty-something she is.

"Beautiful," he mouths to her as she makes her way down the aisle alone, naturally catching the rhythm of the string quartet. There are no groomsmen or bridesmaids. Apparently, Julia just wants everybody to have a good time and not fuss over her.

She's so nice and I can see exactly why Myles' dad loves her.

Thinking of Myles, I glance over to see if he's watching her, too. But he isn't. He's sitting ramrod straight, looking dead ahead of him. He's wearing a tux like all the other brothers, and it makes his shoulders look wider than ever. There's a gap between the top of his shirt collar and the sharp line of his hair and my fingers tingle when I remember how I played with that gap last night.

"Mint?" the woman next to me asks, holding out the now half-empty bag.

"No thank you," I reply.

She shrugs and puts another one in her mouth.

Julia arrives at the front and her husband takes her hand, looking lovingly into her eyes. He strokes her cheek and she tips her head to stare up at him, as though they're in a world of their own.

The celebrant clears his throat noisily. "Friends and family of Julia and Rupert, we're here today to bless their decade long marriage, and to renew the words of love and commitment they first said to each other all those years ago."

"She must have been a child bride," Mint monster mutters. I bite down a smile.

"Marriage isn't just the commitment of one person to another," the celebrant continues. "It's a message to the world that love still exists, even during times of strife and pain. And though it's old fashioned to say, it's the bedrock of society. Of family. Even of humankind. If we can't commit to the ones we love, how can we commit to our fellow humans?"

"Yeah, well he's got a vested interest," the woman next to me mutters. "If people don't get married he's out of a job."

She has a point. I smile at her and whisper. "I'm Ava."

"Marie." She holds out her bag of mints again. "Sure you don't want one?"

"I'd love one," I whisper, and put one in my mouth. They're surprisingly good.

The celebrant is still talking. I must have missed a bit because he seems to be segueing into the next section.

"But before we hear their vows, Rupert has asked his son, Myles to read a poem to us all."

Myles is doing a reading? He never mentioned it.

He stands with a smooth, easy movement, and strides to the podium, placing a piece of paper down on top, and nodding at the celebrant. The expression on his face is unreadable, but I'm pretty used to that. His eyes scan the guests until they find mine. They stay for a moment, and I stare back at him, not breathing. Then he looks down at his piece of paper and blinks.

"Sonnet One Hundred and Sixteen by William Shakespeare," he says, in that full, deep voice. The guests are all silent, there's not even the crunch of a mint.

Then Marie pipes up, "Who invited Henry Cavill?"

I squirm in my seat again, but thankfully Myles starts to read.

Let me not to the marriage of true minds
Admit impediments. Love is not love
Which alters when it alteration finds,

• • •

My heart does a little leap at the sound of his voice, true and clear. His face is impassive, but the way he says the words tells me he understands them. That love once found is unmoving. Never changing.

He carries on speaking and I'm captivated. I can't stop looking at him, and when his gaze falls on mine I feel it to the tip of my toes.

I think he feels it, too, because the very corner of his lip quirks as he comes to the end of the sonnet.

He glances down at the words and then back at me again. My heart starts to batter against my ribcage. His lashes sweep down, and for a moment I feel frozen in time. I ache for him.

I can imagine laying in his arms in a meadow, the sun shining through dappled leaves, as he holds up a book and reads poetry to me, his other hand stroking my hair.

Love is an ever-fixed mark. Isn't that what he just read? Does he believe that? My heart starts to beat faster, because I think even I believe it. I think I could easily fall in love with Myles Salinger.

The problem would be falling out of love with him. I'm not sure that would be possible.

Once Myles is seated again, I somehow regain my composure. Julia and Rupert read their vows, and Julia starts to cry as Rupert promises to be by her side forever.

"Bet he said that to the other two as well," Marie says.

Luckily, the string quartet starts up right then, playing a version of *When a Man Loves a Woman* by Percy Sledge. Julia and Rupert sit to the side and talk softly to each other, while the guests start to murmur about how lovely everything is. I look at Myles again. He's in exactly the same position as he was before. Ramrod straight. Unmoving.

And now I'm fantasizing about how I make him lose control. I saw a glimpse of it last night and it was intoxicating.

"He's handsome, isn't he?" Marie says, elbowing me in

the side. "Troubled, though. Apparently they weren't sure he'd even come."

"Oh," I say politely. "I'm glad he did."

The string quartet fades away and the celebrant walks back to the podium and reads out his final remarks. Then he asks us all to stand up, as Julia and Rupert walk hand in hand down the aisle, stopping every few seconds to kiss and hug their guests.

It feels like forever before they reach the back where we're sitting. Julia gives me a big smile and grasps my hand. "Thank you for coming," she says softly. "And for making Myles come."

Marie snorts behind me, and I realize the double meaning. My cheeks blush, but luckily Julia doesn't notice as they've already moved on to more guests. Everybody's gathering their things now, ready to walk down to the lake for champagne, and Marie stuffs her mints back in her purse and zips it up.

"Are you a friend of the bride or the groom?" I ask her.

"Neither. I'm married to him." She points at the celebrant who's walking behind Julia and Rupert. "I have to sit through these things forty-eight weeks out of the year." She leans forward and whispers, "I can always tell which ones will make it and which ones won't."

I remember her saying it keeps her husband in a job. Ah well, I guess seeing that many marriages probably makes her cynical.

"Do you think these ones will make it?" I ask, intrigued by this professional wedding guest.

"Hmm," she says. "If they're renewing their vows after ten years together, I think they will."

———

"Here you go, I thought you'd like another one." Eli hands me a mimosa, and I take it even though I'm not drinking alcohol. My last glass was just juice, but he doesn't need to know that. I'm pretty sure Myles doesn't want his whole family knowing that we're actively trying to get me pregnant.

"Thank you." I smile at him, intending to pour it away when he's not looking.

"It's the least I can do after yesterday." Eli grimaces. "I'm sorry about body slamming you. I really thought you were going to run around me."

"I would have if I was looking," I smile to let him know all is good. "I was so focused on making a touchdown that I forgot there might be people in the way."

He laughs. "I'm the same on the rink. But it's kind of expected that we body slam people there."

I keep forgetting that Eli is a major sports star. He's shorter than Myles by an inch or two, but just as broad. His hair is slightly lighter, but he has the same defined jaw and piercing eyes. I imagine he's popular with female supporters.

"How long have you played for the Razors?" I ask him.

"Ten years. Before that I was with the Caps."

"The Caps?" I really need to brush up on my hockey knowledge.

"The Washington Capitals." He looks amused. "I signed with them in the draft straight from college. I was lucky." He shrugs. "Anyway, Myles asked me to look after you for a bit while he does his thing." He inclines his head to where Myles is surrounded by family.

"You don't have to do that. I'm fine people watching."

He frowns. "You are?"

"Yeah." I shrug. "I'm an only kid, I've learned to entertain myself."

"I used to dream of being an only kid." He grins and it really lights up his face. They sure know how to make handsome men in this family. "I'm glad I'm not, though. I wouldn't be playing pro if it wasn't for Myles."

I blink. "Myles helped you with hockey?"

"He drove me everywhere. Took me to college tryouts. Made me get up at the ass crack of dawn when all I wanted to do was sleep." Eli smiles softly, as though remembering those days.

"What about your parents? They must have taken you to practice, too?"

"Yeah, sometimes. But my dad's..." he wrinkles his brow, "unreliable. And Mom went through a really rough time when he left. Myles pretty much dragged us all up, even if we didn't want it."

I look over at the man who seems to be the center of his family, whether he likes it or not. He's inclining his head to listen to the words of an older lady, who's touching his arm and smiling up at him.

"Anyway, I know you say you're fine, but if I don't introduce you to some people Myles is gonna kick my ass," Eli says, offering his hand to me. "Just humor me and we'll both get out of this alive, okay?"

"Sure."

I'm introduced to friends and cousins, uncles and business colleagues. When I tell them I'm a co-worker of Myles' they look almost disappointed.

"When I heard he was bringing a plus one, I thought this might be it," his Aunt Lucy says. "Our Myles might finally be settling down."

"Sorry to disappoint." I give them a light smile. "We just work together."

"And what is it you do?" Lucy asks me, blinking as the dazzling sunlight catches her eyes.

"She's an editor, like Myles," Eli tells them. "She publishes the Dandy Lion series."

"Oh. You're *that* editor," Lucy says, and I immediately wonder what Myles has said to his family about me.

I glance at Eli, who is grinning. "Myles is a huge Dandy fan," he says.

I know this because Myles has told me. But it only feels polite to pretend I don't. "But he has Endo," I point out. "Isn't that much more his thing?"

Eli shrugs. "Endo is the kind of character Myles always wished he could be. Dandy is the kind of person he is."

Why did he want to be like Endo?" I ask.

Eli looks at me carefully. "Because he had all the responsibility and none of the fun. Endo's the opposite of that. Always doing things and regretting them later. Traveling into space when he's supposed to be at school or doing chores."

He's right, Endo does all those things. It's why I've always thought he was a bad role model for kids. But what about the kids who don't get to have fun? Kids like Myles, who are too busy shouldering responsibilities to have adventures or let their imaginations run wild.

Sure, Dandy is a great character. But he's good and kind and doesn't break the rules. He doesn't provide the kind of escape that Endo does.

I look over at Myles and he's now talking to Brooks and Lincoln, his two youngest brothers. They're listening intently. And I realize that everybody listens when Myles speaks.

He's the fulcrum of his family. Everything revolves around him.

Even me.

Or especially me. I don't know any more. All I know is that I want this man more than I've wanted anybody in my life.

And I can't think of anything except that.

CHAPTER
TWENTY-ONE

AVA

It's almost evening by the time I actually get to spend any time with Myles. We've started talking a couple of times, but he's been dragged away to solve a dispute between two uncles, or to speak to the caterers about timings for the day. Now that Eli has opened my eyes to it, I can see that everybody leans on Myles. And I start to wonder who he has to lean on.

"Okay?" he asks me, his eyes dipping to my face. I've just come back from the cabin where I had to pee on another stick.

"Yep. Still not there. You can keep your pants on for a few more hours."

He rolls his eyes but still manages to look amused. "Have I told you how beautiful you look today?"

No he hasn't, and now that he has I feel myself warm up. "I almost didn't look this amazing. Can you believe my date forgot to tell me there was a vow renewal ceremony?"

His eyes widen in mock horror. "What kind of man would do that? You should ditch him."

"I've thought about that, but he owes me."

"He owes you?" Myles repeats. "What does he owe you?"

I catch his eye. "Pleasure."

Myles blinks and I try to not smile. I've actually taken him by surprise and I like it.

"That sounds intriguing," he says, his voice mild. "Why would he owe you that?"

I roll onto my tiptoes and steady myself with my hand on his shoulder. He still has to dip his head for me to whisper in his ear.

"Because he promised me last night," I tell him. "But we have to wait for the right moment."

He opens his mouth to reply, but then his father calls out for everybody's attention. The crowd of people around the lake hushes and turns toward him, where he's standing next to Julia. She's still wearing her dress – I don't blame her, if I looked that good I would, too – but the train has been pinned to her waist so it doesn't drag in the grass.

"Hello everybody," Rupert says, curling his arm around Julia's waist. "I promise to not take up too much of your drinking time, but I just wanted to say a few thank yous before we get into celebrating tonight." He inclines his head at the wait staff, who are holding trays full of champagne. They start to weave through the crowd and hand out glasses. "And of course I'd like to toast my new-old-wife."

Everybody laughs.

"But seriously, a day like today couldn't happen without the help of so many people. The lovely Linda and Deandra," he says, nodding at his ex-wives, "have worked so hard with Julia to make this the perfect day. And I feel very lucky to be surrounded by my loves of the past along with my love of the present and future." He leans down to kiss Julia's cheek. "So thank you, angels."

Linda and Deandra beam back at him.

"And my boys." He looks around because the six of them

are scattered among the crowd. "Thank you for all being here. And for making me the proudest father I could be." His eyes crinkle.

"And finally, but not last. Never last. I'd like to thank Julia for being everything a man could want in his partner for life. She's kind, gorgeous, funny." He lifts a brow. "And most importantly, she knows how to keep me in my place."

Julia shakes her head, smiling.

"And on top of that, she's given me one more thing. The thing that we've been wishing for over the past ten years. She's going to make me a father again."

A collective gasp comes from the guests. Myles' face doesn't alter one bit. The only sign he's even heard his dad is when he tightens his grip on his champagne glass. Linda and Deandra let out a squeal and run up to hug Julia, who looks like she's about to cry with happiness.

From the corner of my eye I see Liam, Myles' closest brother, glance at him. Myles shrugs. I guess none of them knew.

"And with that bombshell, I'd like to raise a toast to my wife and our future child." Rupert lifts his glass. "To Julia and our baby. Thank you for making me the happiest man in the world."

"To Julia and the baby," everyone choruses, before lifting their champagne glasses up. Myles drains his own glass, then holds his hand out for mine. I pass it to him – I'm not drinking it after all – and he drains that one, too.

MYLES

I drain my glass of whiskey and gesture at the barman to refill it. The bar was built at the side of the wooden dancefloor the construction company erected by the lake, and for one night only it's full of people.

But I only have eyes for one.

She's laughing with Liam right now, as he leans down to say something in her ear. Her face lights up, her pretty lips curl, and all I can think is that I want her like I've never wanted anything in my life.

So why are you getting drunk at the bar and not dancing with her?

Mostly because I'm a fucking idiot. But also because my dad and Julia blindsided me. I thought my days of having new siblings were over. I thought I'd done my duty, but now it feels like it's starting all over again.

I'm about to be a brother again. And yes, so are Liam, Eli, and the rest. But their experience of brotherhood is different to mine. Mine is more like being a father.

I love them all, but I've spent most of my life taking care of them in one way or another.

Eli holds his hand out to Ava and she takes it, glancing over at me before letting my brother lead her to the dance floor. A pulse of irritation washes over me but I push it away. I asked Eli to take care of her earlier, after all. Despite our group messages the other day, I know he has no intention of trying anything with Ava. He was just trying to goad me, and right now he's just trying to entertain her.

I should be happy that she's having fun. And I am... but...

It should be me dancing with her. It should be me making her smile. But the truth is, I have no idea how to do that. She's so full of sunshine, and she deserves somebody who always brings that out in her. Not my grumpy, black soul that only brings things down.

"Another?" the bartender asks, noticing my empty glass.

"Yeah." My word slurs. That's a new one. I don't drink often, and never to excess. But there's a softness to my thoughts and I kind of like it. I like watching her, too, especially when she doesn't know I'm watching. And yes, I'm aware that's potentially icky, but damn, I like this woman.

I just don't know how to handle it. How to make her happy. And there's nothing I want more than that. To make her smile, to make her glow, to make her pregnant.

I'll do anything for her. Even sacrifice myself.

————

AVA

As the sun slides down behind the mountains and we finish dinner, the music strikes up and just like last night, people start to fill the dance floor. I dance with Eli, who apologizes again, even though I've told him it's fine, and then with Liam who turns out to be the best dancer ever. When the song finishes, I look around to find Myles, but he's not at his table or with his family.

Eventually, I realize he's still at the bar, a whiskey in his hand.

"Hi," I say, offering a smile. "I've been looking for you."

"What can I do for you?" His voice is low and throaty.

"Are you okay?" I shake my head at the bartender when he offers me a drink. Myles, on the other hand, holds out his glass to be filled up, and I wonder how many times he's done that.

"I'm just great. I'm going to be a brother again, did you hear that?"

"I was with you," I remind him. "And yes, congratulations."

He lifts the glass to his lips and swallows a mouthful of his fiery drink. "It was supposed to be you."

"What was?"

"Being pregnant. With my baby."

"My baby," I correct, because I can't think of it as his. As ours. I'm already messed up about him, I don't need to mess this baby up, too.

"Potato potahto," he says, taking another mouthful of whiskey. He looks at me over the rim of his glass. His eyes are wide and a little hazy. They're the only giveaway that he's drunk.

"We should go back to the cabin," I say, because I don't like this.

I feel like he's on the edge of something, about to topple over. I want to save him and that's stupid because he's not mine to save.

"Why?" he asks, running his finger around the rim of his glass. "Do you need me to impregnate you?"

"You make it sound so romantic," I joke, wanting to see his beautiful smile again.

But he's all serious. "I want you to get pregnant. I want to see your stomach swell. I want to see you bloom."

I exhale heavily. "You won't see any of that. You'll be back in New York and I'll be in Charleston."

He runs the tip of his tongue along his bottom lip, capturing a bead of whiskey. "You could come with me. You know Jean-Baptiste wants you there. You could stay at my place. I'd take care of you. You know I would."

"You've drunk too much," I tell him, because I can't let him put ideas like that in my head. I don't need him to take care of me. I don't need him to care.

But I want him to, and that's just stupid.

"Do you know I got drunk once when I was eighteen?" There's the slightest slur to his words now.

"I didn't realize alcohol made you so chatty," I say. "I'd have gotten you drunk months ago."

He smiles again and leans forward until I can feel his warm breath against my cheek. "It was the only time. And I had to go to the hospital because Brooks had broken his arm at a friend's house and his mom and Dad were away with my mom on a cruise. I've never sobered up so quickly in my life. I realized then that I can't ever lose control."

"Everybody gets drunk when they first try alcohol," I tell him. "It's a normal growing up experience."

"I didn't. Not after that."

"You're drunk now," I point out.

"I'm…" His brows knit as he thinks it through. "Mildly intoxicated."

"Potato potahto."

"Are you using my words back at me, Miss Quinn?" He reaches out to trace my jaw, sending a shiver down my spine.

"I'm pointing out that you may not be in complete control right now. And anything you say you might regret in the morning."

"Like I think you're the most beautiful woman I've ever seen?" he asks, cupping my jaw. "Or that I haven't stopped thinking about being inside of you since last night?"

I open my mouth to reply, but no words come. Just a heat that rises up from my belly and suffuses my skin.

"Do you know how out of control you make me feel?" he asks, though it doesn't appear he expects an answer. "How much I want to make you pregnant?" he whispers. "How much I want to make you happy?"

My heart beats wildly in my chest. He drops his brow until it's touching mine, his gaze full of emotions I can't quite name. "Ava Quinn," he murmurs. "So nice. So fucking nice."

I swallow.

"You know what I want to do to you? I want to corrupt you. I want to make you feel so good you can't walk for three weeks."

"You're going to regret this in the morning," I whisper.

"I'm not. I'm really not. Sometimes the truth just gets so big it has to get out there. Sometimes it hurts too much to keep it in."

"Myles," I whisper. "We're at your father's vow renewal. We're surrounded by your family. You need to keep quiet."

"I don't want to keep quiet. I want them to know. I want them all to know. You're mine, Ava. You're fucking mine."

I slide my hand into his and tug. "Come back to the cabin. *Now*." I'm using my best school teacher voice, cultivated by years of visits to elementaries.

He blinks. "Will you stay with me if I do?"

"Yes." I nod. "I'm not going anywhere."

There's a look of trust in his eyes, and it kills me more than anything else. "Who looks after you?" I ask him.

He gives me a strange look. "What do you mean?"

"Who looks after you when you're so busy looking after everybody else?" There has to be somebody. I have Lauren and Sophie. We take turns being each others' rocks. And even my mom. I know I keep a lot from her, but if I needed her she'd be there.

But who does Myles have?

He shakes his head as though my words don't compute. "I look after myself."

"Tonight, let me look after you," I say, sliding my fingers between his. He looks down at our intertwined hand and his brow scrunches. "Let me take you back to the cabin and make you happy."

"How will you do that?" He lifts a brow.

"Not like that." I smile. "Let me make you a drink. Make a fire. Give you a shoulder massage. Let me take care of you the way you take care of everybody else."

His eyes scan my face like he's looking for answers. My chest contracts because he's just so beautiful, even when he's drunk. "Okay…" he says slowly. "But you need to promise me one thing."

"Name it and it's yours."

"Don't make me fall in love with you. Liam said I shouldn't."

My eyes widen. "I won't," I say solemnly. His hand tightens around mine and we start to walk away from the bar, past the dance floor where the music is louder. He says something but it's swallowed by the beat.

It sounds like, "It's too late. I already have."

But it can't be that, can it?

CHAPTER
TWENTY-TWO

AVA

I send Myles to take a shower while I make the fire and brew some coffee. It's not actually cold enough for a fire, but somehow it feels comforting watching the orange flames lick at the grate.

The machine has just finished sputtering when I hear the click of the bathroom door. A rush of steam escapes first, and as it disperses I can see Myles standing there, wearing only a pair of dark blue sweatpants. He's rubbing his damp hair with a towel, and there are beads of water running down his ridged chest.

"It's hot as hell in here," he says, looking at the fireplace. "Do you feel cold or something?" He sounds almost normal. The shower must have sobered him a little. Hopefully caffeine will do the rest.

"I knew you'd be walking around the place half naked." I shrug and pour out a coffee for him. "Here you go. No creamer. You need the hit."

He lifts the mug to his lips then winces. "Christ, that's hot too. Do I have some kind of fever?"

"You need to sweat it out," I tell him. "It's all that alcohol running through your veins. Go sit down."

He lifts a brow but does as he's told, and I really try to not look at the defined muscles on his back as he leans over to put his coffee on the table, then collapses into the sofa.

"You sure I can't get you a t-shirt?" I ask him.

"No. I'll soak it in ten minutes."

"Okay. I'm just going to put on something more comfortable," I tell him, because I feel completely overdressed now. And as much as I love this gown, if I'm going to be taking care of Myles Salinger, I need something more flexible on.

It only takes a minute for me to change into a pair of pajama pants and a tank top. When I walk back into the room he's leaning forward on the sofa, his hands clasped, his elbows resting on his thighs. He seems to be staring at something in the fireplace. Or maybe just lost in his thoughts.

"Right then," I say, hoping to pull him from wherever his mind has him. "Let's start with a massage."

"You're really going to massage me?" he asks.

"Yep. You need to loosen up. Seriously."

"You want me to lie down?" He quirks a brow.

"It's okay. I'll just do your shoulders." I open the lotion I grabbed from my toiletry bag and spread some on my hands. "This works better with oil, but I don't have any."

"Next time."

His words send a shiver down my spine. Ignoring it, I place my hands on his shoulders, my fingers spread out at the base of his neck. I dig them in, squeezing gently as I lift the muscles, frowning when I feel how stiff they are.

"That feels good." He gives a low moan that shoots straight to my thighs.

"You're so tight," I whisper. "Try to relax."

"This *is* me relaxed."

I chuckle and start the massage properly, leaning forward as I dig into his muscles, using my fingers and thumbs to ease the knots in them.

"There. Right there." He groans. "Jesus, where did you learn to do this?"

"My mom took me on a retreat once. There was a masseuse who took pity on me."

"You should do this for a living," he says. "Actually, no. You should do this just for me. Every day. Whenever I click my fingers."

It takes ten minutes for me to get him to relax. Eventually I feel his muscles soften, and his shoulders spread his breath more even as I finish the final muscle. But when I go to pull away, he grabs my hand, pulls it around him, until my palm is against his chest.

I can feel his heart beating. It's slow and steady. Unlike mine.

"I'll make a bargain with you," he says, his voice gritty. "You want my pleasure? I want yours first."

He remembers that conversation? I blush. "You've drunk too much. You should go to sleep." I kiss his shoulder, his neck, but when I go to pull away, his hold is too tight, and I don't try very hard.

He threads his fingers through mine, moving them until my thumb brushes his nipple. He lets out a soft sigh, and it hits me right in the groin. "We're not supposed to do this tonight, remember?"

"We're not supposed to have sex. There are other ways to give pleasure," he tells me. There's no slur to his words at all. Even his gaze is steady. He's all control again and it's tantalizing.

"But if you…"

"Full sentences please, Ava." Oh yes, he's back. And bossy as hell.

"If you come then you'll be annoyed."

"I wasn't talking about *my* pleasure, I was talking about yours. About making you come."

My face flames. "Oh." I pull my lip between my teeth. "But you want to have sex with me soon?"

"Yes," he says, his voice gritty. "I want to fuck you seven ways 'til Sunday. I want to keep you in my bed and do it so many times that I'm certain you're knocked up."

"Wouldn't you rather use a cup and syringe?" I tease.

"I'd rather chop my right hand off than jerk off into another cup."

My breath catches. "That's good. Because I want to have sex with you, too."

His hand tightens over mine. "Jesus," he breathes. "I'm hard as a fucking rock." He tugs until I'm leaning over him and the sofa, then turns his head to brush his lips against mine.

I let out a soft moan and the next minute he's standing and lifting me over the back of the sofa, laying me down on the cushions. I start to laugh. "I could have walked around."

"Would have taken too long," he mutters, as he climbs back onto the sofa, brushing the hair away from my face before he kisses me long and hard.

I kiss him back, my fingers threading into his hair, my legs wrapping around his hips. He wasn't lying, he's hard as steel, and my body pulses and buzzes in reaction to the feel of him.

"Definitely… not… having … sex… tonight…" I gasp as he slides his hands down my side and buries them beneath my tank.

"Definitely not," he agrees, his voice tight. He scoots back to push my top up, revealing my naked breasts and aching nipples. He dips his head and captures a nipple, sucking it until my back is arching from the cushions. He pushes me back down with a firm hand, then slides his palm over my stomach, his fingers reaching for my waistband. "Can I touch you though?"

"Please," I breathe, and the next moment he's dipping his hand inside, groaning when he feels how wet I am for him. He touches me lightly – too lightly – and I buck again.

"Be still," he tells me. "Stop squirming."

"I can't help it. You make me squirm."

His thumb circles me and a strangled sigh escapes my lips. He kisses me again, and I can feel his smile. "No sex," he reminds me. "But you're definitely going to be coming on my fingers."

"That's not fair," I say as he tugs at my top and throws it on the floor, then follows with my pants. I'm naked in front of him again. I'd be embarrassed but the way he's looking at me makes me feel so safe. So warm. "I'm supposed to be taking care of you."

"You are." He kisses my breast. "This is what I need, beautiful. You beneath me, warm and full of need. Letting me make you come."

"But I'll be one up on you."

He kisses his way down my stomach then looks up at me, his eyes dark. "I told you, it's an exchange rate. One for one."

"So I get yours tomorrow?"

"If you're ovulating."

"And I won't come?"

He laughs. "Oh, baby, you'll come again. That'll be a down payment for the next round."

"I feel like we're negotiating a business deal," I say, my words turning to a gasp as he kisses my inner thigh. I'm aching for him. My whole body feels like it's on pause, just waiting for his touch.

"This isn't business. It's strictly pleasure." He reaches the apex of my thighs and blows softly on me, making my muscles contract. "Do you know how good you smell?"

"I need to shower…"

"Oh no you fucking don't." His face is right there. He slowly parts me with his fingers, and a low sound rumbles from his throat. "So damn pretty," he says. "Everything about you. But especially this."

I open my mouth to respond, but then he's kissing me there. Not just kissing. Worshipping. Devouring. Adoring. He takes a long lick, then swirls his tongue, his fingers digging into my thighs to keep them apart.

"So good. So good." He sucks at me and a whole new pleasurable sensation melts at my nerve endings. Then he slides a finger inside me, circling at my core, his tongue licking and loving, making me cry out his name.

"More," I beg, and he adds another finger but it's still not enough. I'm not sure anything could be – anything but the part of him I can't have. He curls his fingers and they hit a spot I didn't even know was there, making me scream out and buck until he's pushing me down again.

"I'm so close," I tell him hoarsely.

"I know, beautiful. Give it to me." He licks me again, but his eyes are still capturing mine. It's all kinds of dirty and I love it.

"I want you to kiss me when I come," I tell him. "I want you naked on top of me."

"Your wish is my desire, princess." He doesn't pull his fingers out of me, just shucks off his pants with his free hand and slides over me, his thumb taking the place of his lips as he circles and teases and takes me higher than I ever thought I could go. He kisses me and I taste myself on him, his tongue licking and sliding until my whole body is a mess of need.

"I need to feel you." I reach for him, circling my hands around his cock. He mutters a low oath.

He moves over me as I circle my legs around his hips once more, his body aligning with mine. His hard length is sliding against me, and he has to pull his fingers out before he strains his arm. I cup his face, kissing him hard, then whisper, "Let me feel you inside of me."

"I can't," he whispers desperately. "I can't come. I need to wait."

"I know. Just for a minute. Just the tip." I'm almost begging now. But I've never wanted anything as much as I want Myles Salinger.

He winces. "Do you know how much I want you? How long I've thought about this?" I feel him move against me, thick and hard.

"I'm getting the idea."

"Okay," he manages. "Just the tip." Then I feel him push against me, parting me, and I'm so close to orgasming it isn't funny. I clutch his biceps because if I don't I think I might fall. They flex as he slowly pushes into me, and my eyes roll into the back of my head.

I'm on fire. Exploding. Cries escape my lips as I spasm around him, pulling him deeper, calling out his name, my body bucking beneath his weight. My legs clamp tight and he kisses me, swallowing my cries, then his eyes go wide and he practically leaps off me, his erection bobbing as he jumps back.

"Fuck fuck fuck." He looks around wildly. "George Washington, John Adams, Thomas Jefferson..."

Pulses of pleasure are still wracking through me. I stare dizzily at him. "What are you doing?"

"James Madison, James Monroe, John Quincy Adams," he chants.

"Are you trying to conjure the former presidents?" I ask sitting up, my skin flushed. I feel like I'm floating on a cloud of pleasure. "Like Beetlejuice?"

He rakes a finger through his hair. His erection is still impressive, bobbing in front of him. "Andrew Jackson, Martin Van Buren, William Henry Harrison, John Tyler..." He lets out a mouthful of air as he slowly deflates. "I think it's okay. Damn, that was close."

"Your knowledge of our founding fathers and presidents

is impressive," I tell him, my body suffused in a warm, post-orgasmic glow.

"I was trying to take my mind off things." He frowns. "I nearly came inside you."

I widen my eyes and I slap my hands to my cheeks. "Oh no! I could have gotten pregnant."

"Smart ass." He shakes his head. "That's the last time I let you persuade me to break my rules."

I blow him a kiss. "I'm sorry."

"No you're not. And nor am I." He pulls his pants back on, and I already miss his beautiful body. "But I'm not coming inside of you until it's time."

"Well let's hope that's tomorrow then," I say, because I'm not exaggerating when I say I need this man. I want him, I desire him, I ache without him.

I want to have sex with him until he loses control.

"Let's hope so," he agrees, pressing his lips sweetly to mine. "Otherwise, I'm going to have to crack out the English Kings and Queens."

TWENTY-THREE

AVA

Watching the Salinger Olympics feels like sitting in the colosseum in Rome as gladiators face up to the lions.

Any sense of brotherly love is gone, replaced by pure competition. Right now, all six of them are lined up on the dock, waiting for Linda to blow the starting whistle for their swim to the other side of the lake and back again. The start was delayed because Lincoln pushed Brooks into the lake a second before the first whistle, causing a false start. And when Brooks climbed out, he and Linc had a fight that ended with Myles and Liam pulling the two of them off each other.

Is it wrong to say I'm enjoying every minute?

This is the third event of the day. The first was rowing, which was done in heats. Myles won that one easily, and I'm starting to suspect he spends a lot of time in the gym on the rowing machine. He has such a smooth movement that can only come from years of practice.

The second event was jousting on the floating platform out in the middle of the lake. I think that might have been my favorite, because watching Myles get pushed into the water by an oversized jousting stick is one that's going to stay in my memory.

Liam won that one by a single game. He's still grinning about his victory.

According to Deandra, who's sitting next to me, this morning's events are nothing compared to the ones this afternoon. There's boxing, running, shooting, and tree climbing.

"We tried to ban the boxing," Deandra tells me. "But the boys refused. They seem to enjoy beating the heck out of one another."

"Who wants some sweet lemonade?" Julia asks, carrying a tray down the lawn. Rupert immediately jumps up from his chair to take it from her. He hands a glass to each of us as Julia slumps in her chair.

"How are you feeling?" Deandra asks.

"I'm so tired. I thought you were meant to bloom in pregnancy," Julia says, shaking her head. She takes a sip of her lemonade and sighs.

"That's the second trimester. You're only a few weeks away," Deandra reassures her. "Just think, in about fifteen years your little one will be competing."

Julia's eyes widen. "Oh I hope not." She rubs her stomach. "Anyway, I'm thinking this is a girl. We need a little less testosterone around here."

"How long have the Olympics been going on for?" I ask them.

Deandra's brows pull together. "I'm not sure. I think my boys were young teenagers. They were running wild, so Myles decided the best way to keep them under control was to wear them out. He'd run drills every day and told them they had to train for the Olympics. They did it for years, but then it stopped."

"He got busy," Julia murmured. "At work."

"But they're back now," Rupert says, smiling warmly. "It's good to have all my boys here."

They're such a complicated family. I used to think my mom and I had a difficult relationship, but at least there was only two of us. We both knew where we stood. But the dynamics between all the branches of the Salinger family are almost incomprehensible. No wonder Myles gets exhausted by it all.

Not that he looks exhausted now, as he stands on the dock laughing at something Eli just said. He looks virile and masculine and everything that takes my breath away. He's wearing a pair of navy swim shorts, his chest bare and tan beneath the warm summer sun. The muscles on his back ripple as he slides his goggles over his eyes and Linda calls for them all to line up again, ready to dive into the cold lake.

When she blows the whistle they all dive in together, their bodies slicing into the surface like a knife through warm butter. I hold my breath as I wait for them to surface, and when they do, they're all five yards across the lake. I spot Myles immediately, his dark hair wet and glistening, his stroke easy and fast as he pulls and kicks himself through the water.

There's hardly an inch between all six of them. What Brooks and Linc lack for in skill they make up for in energy, their feet crashing against the surface as they try to keep up with each other, almost ramming into the other as they try to get in front. Brooks reaches for Linc's head and tries to push him under and Linda blows her whistle wildly to get their attention.

"No dunking," she shouts, but I don't think they can hear.

They reach the other side in a single wave, then turn to launch themselves back into the water, swimming toward us this time, and they're still so close it's impossible to call. Deandra and Julia are shouting out their names, trying not to show favoritism by cheering on each of them. My heart is racing as they get closer, and all I want is for Myles to win.

"Come on Myles!" I scream out, giving in to the excitement. "You can do this!"

Rupert chuckles. "He's saving his energy for the sprint."

Everybody's standing now, breathless as we wait for them to reach the dock, and Linda is watching with hawk-like eyes, ready to call a winner.

Two hands slap the wooden planks almost simultaneously, followed in quick succession by the other four. Linda frowns and looks from Myles to Holden, the quietest of the brothers who appears to be an A1 athlete, too.

"It's Myles," she says. "By about two milliseconds."

"It was Holden," Myles says. "I saw him hit first."

"No way, man." Holden shakes his head. "I saw you in front of me. It was you."

"Hey, I'll take it if you two don't want to." Linc pulls himself out of the water. Even though he's a fair bit younger than Myles, he has the same body shape and smile. He just gives it more easily than Myles does.

Linda looks over her shoulder at us. "Did anybody else see?"

"Maybe you should call it a draw," Julia suggests.

"Hell no," Liam says. "We don't do draws."

"Then it's Myles," Holden and Linda say in unison.

Myles' eyes alight on mine. If I thought he looked good in his trunks from behind, it has nothing compared to the full frontal view. His hair is dripping wet, his chest gleaming, his swim shorts plastered to his thick, muscled thighs. He looks like James Bond walking out of the ocean, and I have to mentally pinch myself not to let out a sigh.

"You okay?" he asks, wandering away from his brothers.

"Just watching the spectacle." I hold out my glass of lemonade. He takes it and swallows it in one gulp. From the corner of my eye, I see Julia looking at us.

Damn, I should have gotten him a fresh one. Sharing drinks isn't something that colleagues are supposed to do.

"Who do you think won?" Linda asks me.

"Myles," I say immediately.

The corner of his lip lifts. He's still staring at me. And I'm really trying not to think about that body of his and what he can do with it. We're in polite company here.

"You're biased," he murmurs, but he looks pleased about it.

"Always," I whisper.

Linda walks over to the huge chalkboard with the Salinger brothers' names written on it, and a table of scores. She allocates them each some points, giving Myles the most, then tallies up the totals so far and adjusts them at the end.

"Myles is winning going into lunch," she says.

"Of course he is." Deandra laughs. "He's always winning."

"I won't be this afternoon. Not with the running and the rifles."

"Who usually wins the running?" I ask him.

"Eli. The guy's a speed demon."

"And the shooting?"

"It's a close call between Linc and Brooks, when we let them hold a gun."

"When you let them?" I question.

"We have to ban them from the event when they're really pissed with each other." Myles picks up a towel and rubs his hair with it. "Those two riled up with guns is asking for trouble."

"Eek." I grimace.

"Right?" he murmurs, looping the towel around his neck. "I'm heading back to the cabin to shower before lunch. You coming?"

"Sure." We start walking in tandem toward his cabin. "What time do the Olympics restart?"

"At three. We'll go 'til six then we add up the scores. If there's a tie we go to a tie breaker."

"What's the tie breaker?" I ask him.

"Table tennis."

I start to laugh.

"You can laugh all you like, but it's table tennis to the death. One year Linc threw the paddle against Liam's head and left a scar."

"Ouch." I smile at him. "You're winning right now. Do you think you'll win it outright?"

"No idea. Probably not. The water's my specialty."

"Why's that?"

He shrugs. "I grew up in that lake. It's the only place I liked to be during the summers when I was a kid."

I picture him all young and gangly, floating around the lake as the sun turned his skin a deep bronze. And then I realize that one day our child might be just like that. A preteen, all emo and beautiful and ready for life.

Myles will never get to see that. It somehow makes me sad.

And then I think about his family again, and the question that's been playing on my mind.

"Can I ask you a question?"

"Tell me what it is, and I'll decide if I want to answer or not."

That's fair enough. I'd be the same. "You were upset last night when your dad made his announcement about the baby," I say, my words as careful as his expression. "Was that because you're jealous?"

He blinks. "Of my dad? Or of the baby?"

"I don't know."

He swallows. "I'm not jealous," he says slowly, measuring out his words. "I'm slightly annoyed that I'll have another sibling to step in and look after. I'll get over it, I'm sure."

"Why would you have to step in?" I ask, frowning.

"My father's seventy-three. By the time this kid is a preteen he'll be almost ninety. You think he's gonna play football with him? Steer him away from gangs and fights at school and channel his energy into something good? You think he'll be there the first time the kid gets drunk at some stupid teenage party and spends the night throwing up? Even if he wasn't an octogenarian he wouldn't be there. He never was for us." He takes a deep breath. "That's why I never wanted kids. Why my relationships never worked."

"Because you already brought up five kids of your own," I say softly. I'm not going to lie, when he says he doesn't want children it physically hurts. "But why would you agree to be the father to mine?"

He looks at me and reaches out to tuck a stray lock of hair behind my ear. I feel the burn of his fingers as they trail against my skin. "Because I know our child…" He shakes his head as though he's made a mistake. "*Your* child will never need what my brothers needed. Because he or she will have you."

"Don't you worry that he or she won't have a father?"

He shakes his head resolutely. "No. Because I know you, Ava, and I know you've thought this through. You wouldn't be doing this alone unless you thought you could be both mother and father to this kid. And you have friends and family and enough people who will be there to help you."

"But not you." I ignore the ache in my heart because he's not telling me anything I didn't already know. Hell, I was the one who told him I didn't need his help with anything. That this baby would be mine and mine alone. And I know I can do it. I've thought it through. I have guy friends who will be great role models, and enough support from everybody to have a babysitter every day of the week if I need one. And as I said to Myles all those weeks ago, even if I had a baby in wedlock, the chances were I'd end up being a single mom anyway. My eyes are wide open. I can do this.

"I told you," he says softly. "I'll be there if you need me. You just have to say the word."

But I won't. I won't be yet another person demanding his support and help. I won't be like his dad and mom and stepmoms.

He doesn't need any more people relying on him. His broad shoulders are carrying enough.

"Myles?"

"Yeah."

"What's it going to take for you to trounce your brothers at the Olympics?"

He smiles. "I don't know."

I lean forward to kiss his cheek. "How about the fact that I took a test earlier and I'm ovulating?"

His jaw twitches. He looks down at me, his eyes blazing. "Yeah," he says, his voice thick. "That'll do it."

I smile. "Good." I want him to win. I want him to get everything. Because I'm falling for this beautiful, complicated man.

And even though I can't have him, I can have a piece of him. And that's enough.

MYLES

"Christ," Linc says, rubbing his cheek. A shining bruise is beginning to spread across it, where Brooks managed to land his gloved fist directly on his brother's face. "What the hell does he have in there? Iron?"

It's the final event of the day. According to my mom's scoring system I'm leading Eli by one point, but I couldn't give a damn if I was coming last. Because I only have eyes for the woman leaning on a tree watching me.

Our eyes catch and damn if I don't get all heated for her again.

We spent most of lunch at the cabin making out. And then she begged me not to box because she hates violence. But it's tradition so I told her to disappear for that one. But now she's back and smiling at me because I'm not the one sporting any bruises.

"Okay then," my mom calls out. "It's tree climbing time."

I'm not gonna lie, I'm over this damn Olympics. I was

over it before it even started. I want to be in the cabin with Ava, doing everything I can to make a baby with her.

I want to be inside of her and never pull out.

Liam's drinking a beer. He's as laid back about this as I am. Eli is rolling his shoulders and looking up at the tree, as though working out the best way to get up there. Holden looks mildly bored, because let's face it, Holden isn't a natural climber. And Brooks and Linc are giving each other the evil eye.

Welcome to the Salinger family. No dysfunction to be seen here.

The tree climbing event is a time trial. Each of us has three tries to scale a huge oak tree in the quickest time possible. The fastest time stands. And since the winner scores six points, it's all open right now. Any of us except Liam and Holden could win the Salinger Olympics.

Mom tells us we'll attempt in reverse age order, starting with Linc and ending with me. Linc clicks his neck and ignores whatever Brooks is whispering at him. Then Mom blows the whistle, and my youngest brother hurls himself at the tree, using his hands and feet to shimmy up the trunk before grabbing a low branch. He swings onto it and there's a sickening crunch as it shears away from the tree, dropping him three feet before it pulls away altogether and he tumbles to the ground.

"Shit. I need a do-over," he says, kicking the trunk.

"That's your first try," Mom says mildly. "You still have two more."

"Let the professionals show you how to do it," Brooks says, flexing his arms. Linc grits his teeth but says nothing. I wonder if I'll have to break up another fight.

After the second round Eli is ahead, with me two seconds behind. He looks all kinds of pleased with himself and I'm good with that.

Let's face it, we're grown men. All way too old to be climbing trees.

Ava is watching me with a smile playing at her lips. I beckon her over.

"You okay?"

She nods. "Glad to see you survived the boxing."

"I went against Liam. We landed a couple of punches then pretty much sat the rest out."

She glances over at Linc. "Looks like he didn't sit it out."

"That's Linc. He likes a fight." I don't even want to tell her the number of times I've had to save his scrawny ass.

"I got that impression."

"So, are you going to win the tree climbing?" Ava asks me. "If you do then you win the Olympics, right?"

I shrug. "Ah, Eli's the climbing king. He'll probably win."

She rolls onto her tiptoes and whispers softly in my ear. "What if I told you that if you win, I'll not only let you come inside me tonight, but I'll wake you up in the morning with my lips around you?" Her voice is breathy. I'm immediately hard. Not that it takes much right now.

My jaw twitches. "That might do it."

She grins broadly at me. And for the first time in forever I feel like I'm not alone. That somebody is on my side.

It's a strange feeling.

This woman owns me even if she doesn't know it. She has since she walked into the New York office and gave it as good as she got. And yeah, she pissed me off, but she also turned me on.

And I'm not sure I can ever turn it off again.

A phone starts to ring and Liam grimaces, grabbing it from the ground where he left it. "I need to take this," he says. He lifts a brow at me, and I nod. We've been waiting for this call. The one where everything changes.

Mom checks her watch. "Will you be back soon? Dinner is at seven and I want everything cleared up before then."

"Go ahead without me," Liam says. "I can't win anyway."

"Are you sure?" I ask quietly. It doesn't seem fair that he loses because of a phone call. Especially one that involves me.

"Yep." Liam winks at me. "Seriously, I need to answer. I'll catch you guys later."

He accepts the call and wanders off – I assume to his cabin. It's about sixty yards around the lake from mine. Linc and Brooks start to trash talk each other so Mom blows her whistle sharply and calls for their attention.

"Last round," she calls out. "Climber with the slowest time goes first. That's you, Holden."

He smiles goodhumoredly and rolls his shoulders. "Okay, I'm ready," he calls out, looking up at the tree with his eyes narrow.

Mom blows the whistle, and he launches himself at the trunk. He takes a different route than last time, grabbing a notch to his left and pulling himself up. He's methodical as he pushes himself higher, and when he reaches the top he shaves a second off his last time.

But he's still last.

Linc and Brooks follow. Brooks has this determined look on his face and when he beats Eli's fastest time he lets out a whoop and swings from a high branch like Tarzan.

Now it's my turn. I look up at the green canopy to plan out my route. I'm as methodical as Holden in some ways, but I know when to take risks, too. When I know where I'm going, I walk up to the tree and nod at Mom. "I'm ready."

The sharp trill of the whistle cuts through the silent air, and I take a running jump at the tree, then pull myself onto a craggy knot, my other hand grasping for the branch. My muscles ache, my hands feel raw, and I'm fucking over this.

Then Ava starts calling my name. Actually, she's screaming it. And I don't know whether to laugh or jump down and take her back to the cabin.

I'm still laughing when I reach the top, and Mom calls out

that I've taken the lead. Ava's jumping up and down now, clapping her hands. I wink at her and she blushes.

And damn if I don't climb down as quick as I went up, because I want to see her. My skin is covered with a sheen of sweat and I'm still trying to catch my breath, but dammit this woman.

She drives me crazy in all the best ways.

I walk over to her and she looks as breathless as I feel.

"You okay?" I ask, pulling my soaked t-shirt over my head.

"I'm great," she says, her eyes scanning my chest. And yeah, that's what I wanted.

"It's just that I heard you squealing," I tease. "Wondered if you'd hurt yourself."

She makes the cutest frown. "I wasn't squealing."

"Sounded like squealing to me." I grin and she rolls her eyes.

"I'm just trying to show a colleague some support," she says archly. "You looked like you needed it. Plus, aren't you getting too old to climb trees?"

I ignore her question because I'll show her exactly how fucking young I feel later. "Do you support all your colleagues by grunting like a pig?" I ask instead.

"You said I was squealing," she points out. "Not grunting."

I lean in closer, my lips brushing the shell of her ear. "I'm going to make you scream later," I whisper.

"That's not very colleague-like," she says softly. A blush steals its way over her face. Christ, I want her.

"No. That's because you're not my colleague right now," I remind her.

Mom blasts her whistle again, interrupting our conversation, and Eli begins his final climb. He's taking the same route as I did, notch for notch, branch for branch. But his arms are stronger and he reaches the top a second before I did.

Brooks and Linc let out a roar, and I grin.

"Way to go, Eli!"

He pumps his fist in the air like he's just won the Stanley Cup.

Ava gives me the strangest look, and I smile at her. "What is it?" I ask.

She slowly shakes her head. "I just had you all wrong, that's all."

She sounds serious. I blink. "In what way?"

"I used to think you were a taker. I was wrong. I've never seen anybody give so much as you do."

The way she says it, so softly, sends a shiver right through my heated body. My heart canters in my chest and it has nothing to do with the tree I just climbed.

It's her. It's always been her. I have a feeling it always will be.

And I don't think this is about donating sperm anymore. Or even being friendlier work colleagues. This thing between us has taken on a life of its own. Grown like crazy into something that could consume us both.

I want her and she wants me. And I can't think of anything beyond that.

———

AVA

It's almost nine by the time we walk back to Myles' cabin. He holds my hand all the way, and it feels so nice. Cicadas buzz and fireflies flicker in the trees and I realize I'm going to miss this place when we go home tomorrow.

After the medal ceremony – and yes, they really did have medals – we had dinner by the lake. Liam came back halfway through, and pulled Myles aside for them to have a whispered conversation. Then they joined us at the table and nothing more was said about his disappearance.

"Is Liam okay?" I ask as we walk along the edge of the lake. The moon is reflected off the surface. It's almost full now.

"He's fine. Why?"

"I was just wondering." I shrug. "He disappeared for a long time."

"It's just a work thing," he says casually. "He has his fingers in a lot of pies and if his investors want to talk to him he has to be available. It's not a nine-to-five job."

"Do you miss working in finance?"

He shakes his head. "I prefer what I'm doing now. I let Liam take care of the money. He's good at it."

"Well I'm glad about that." I squeeze his hand.

"Why?"

"Because if you hadn't gone to work for Mediatech we wouldn't have met," I say.

His jaw twitches. Have I stepped over the mark? I shouldn't be gushy, should I? He's still just doing me a favor, even if that favor is going to be mutually enjoyable for both of us.

"And I wouldn't be able to have a baby," I add, even though that's not what I meant at all.

He nods but says nothing, and I feel the weight of the silence pushing between us. "Were you sad you didn't win the gold medal?" I ask, because I need to change the subject and fast.

"Sad that I didn't win a child's plastic necklace? No, Ava, I'm not sad." He sounds amused at the idea of it.

"That's good. Second place is always sexier anyway."

He tips his head to the side. "Is it?"

"Yes." I nod. "Think of all those guys who won the silver medal. They're much more appealing than the gold winners."

"Name one."

"Okay." I tap my chin with my finger, desperately trying to find a good example to back up my hypothesis. "Um… give me a minute."

Myles starts to laugh. "I can give you an hour and you probably won't come up with one."

"Give me an hour and I'll Google it. There has to be someone. Anyway, it doesn't actually matter. All I have to do is close my eyes and see you climb that tree and I get shivery all over."

"You liked that?" He looks genuinely bemused.

"I like you," I whisper.

We reach the cabin and he opens the door, standing back like a gentleman to let me in first. As I walk, inside he flicks on the lights and follows me, pulling the door closed behind him. I pull off my sneakers and let out a soft sigh because now I can wiggle my toes.

"Sit down," he says, inclining his head at the sofa. "I'll take a shower and then I'll fix you a drink."

"I can make the drinks," I reply, but he shakes his head.

"Sit, Ava."

I do as I'm told as he disappears into the bathroom, pulling the door closed behind him. I shift on my bottom then tap the cushions with my fingers, trying to ignore the fact that Myles is most certainly getting naked in there.

And after he showers, he'll come out and we'll make love.

Or a baby. Make a baby. Because he's not in love with me. But I think I'm in love with him, so I'll be making love.

This is confusing. And excruciating. I blink and shake my head.

Taking a deep breath, I stand up and walk over to the bathroom. Then, like a creeper, I put my head against the door. I hear him turn the shower on, the stream of water hammering against the basin, then there's a pause in the sound as he must be stepping underneath the spray.

Naked. Wet. I swallow hard.

Then I push the door open and steam drifts around me.

"Ava?" He turns in the shower. The glass is misted and I can't see much. Just the outline of his magnificent body. It's enough to make me shiver.

"Yeah, it's me. Can I come in?"

"You're already in."

"In the shower. With you." I don't want to be away from him for a moment longer. I need to be close to him.

"Of course."

The words are barely out of his lips before I'm pulling off my sweatshirt, then unfastening my bra and throwing it on top of the pile of clothes he's already made. My jeans quickly follow, along with my socks and panties, until I'm as naked as him.

Just on the wrong side of the shower glass.

I open the door and realize that this isn't going to be the romantic shower I'd envisaged. For a start, the cubicle is small. Really small. And Myles Salinger is big, too big for the shower on his own. With me in there too, there'll be barely be room to move.

He holds his hand out and I take it. His eyes are dark as he drinks me in, his gaze sliding from my face to my chest and then down. Water escapes the door, making a puddle on the tiles, so I hurry inside and pull it firmly closed behind me.

I was right about the squeeze. My body is pushed against his, our wet skin sliding against each other as he pulls me into his embrace. He looks down at me, brows slightly pulled together. "Are you okay?" he asks.

"You ask me that a lot," I murmur. "And yes, I'm okay."

"I ask you that because I need to know the truth. And if you're not okay I want to make things better."

The thing is, he does make things better. Just by being here. By holding me. "You don't need to make things better," I whisper. "I'm not a member of your family."

"I know that." His reply is terse, and I immediately regret the form of my words.

"I didn't mean it like that," I tell him. "I just want you to know that I'm not another person you need to care for." I manage to reach up and cup his jaw. He still looks confused. "I don't want to be your burden," I whisper. "I just want to be your lover. At least for tonight."

He takes my hand and presses his lips to my palm, then slowly slides his hands down me, like he's trying to imprint every curve into his brain. He thickens against me, the hard ridge pressing into my stomach. If this cubicle was bigger I'd drop to my knees right now and show him exactly how much I want him.

Instead I reach up for his hair, sliding my fingers into his wet locks. "Can I wash your hair?"

He blinks, surprised. "If you want to."

I really do. I reach behind him and somehow manage to get some shampoo into my hands. I have to roll onto my tiptoes to be able to place my palms flat against his head, and it's awkward as hell. My breasts squish against his chest and my chin grazes his shoulder. I rub and scrape my fingers against his scalp and the shampoo foams up. He lets out a soft groan as I reach the nape of his neck.

This man likes to be touched. And I'm totally here for that.

When I'm done, he lifts his head up and the foam washes out of his thick, dark hair, sliding down his broad shoulders and over his chest – and me. I'm still on my tiptoes, my body smashed against his chest, and it only takes a lift of my chin until my lips are a breath from his.

"Kiss me," I whisper.

The corner of his mouth lifts. He slides his hand down to the small of my back, making my spine tingle with delight. Dropping his head until his brow touches mine, he stares deep into my eyes.

It's like time stops. I could get lost in him. There are

depths in there that I want to plunder. His lips part and two tiny lines appear between his brow.

"Ava…"

"Yes?"

"What is this?"

"It's…" I try to find the words, but I'm not sure they exist. It's him. It's me. It's everything in between. It's the oceans and the land and the sky and the clouds. It's Myles Salinger holding me so close in the tiny shower he once built with his bare hands. It's a man who spends so much time taking care of everybody else that he forgets to take care of himself.

"I don't know," I whisper, because if I say any of that he'll think I'm crazy. Hell, *I* think I *am* crazy.

He laughs just for a moment, then presses his lips to the corner of my mouth. It's soft and barely there. He moves them until his mouth covers mine, and it's still so soft and achingly sweet. He cups my behind with his hands, leaving me in no doubt of how much he wants me. And that's good because I want him, too. I want to take him and give to him and spend the rest of the night making him feel good.

I want to feel him move inside of me until we both reach new heights.

"You're beautiful," he murmurs as I arch myself against him. Our kiss deepens, gets harder and needier, our tongues crashing together as I moan softly against his lips. He lifts me up, pushes me back against the shower wall, and I feel his hardness slip and slide against me. My breath catches as I realize that with one thrust he'd be there.

"No, not here," he mutters, as though he can read my mind. His face is as flushed as mine, our bodies soaked with soapy water, as he turns off the spray. Cold air immediately suffuses me, and he doesn't waste any time, pushing the door open and grabbing a towel to wrap around my shivering body.

He takes another and gently blots the water from my hair,

then wipes my face, my shoulders, and my chest. There's a silence between us as he drops to his knees, drying my feet, calves, and thighs.

"You need to get dry, too," I whisper.

He takes the towel he's used on me and rubs it over himself. It feels strangely erotic. Like we're sharing everything now. Showers and towels and, I don't know, *emotions*.

When we're dry, he doesn't say another word. Just peels the towel from my body and throws it on the floor. Then he lifts me up again, his muscles contracting as he pulls my chest to his, and I wrap my arms and legs around him like an over-eager monkey, loving being picked up by this strong, gorgeous man.

CHAPTER
TWENTY-FIVE

AVA

It's a few strides from the bathroom to the bedroom, and I cling to him like a limpet for every step. The bed is only partly made from this morning, but he doesn't blink an eyelid. Just drops me onto the mattress and stares down at me, his throat undulating as he swallows.

"Listen to me," he says, his voice soft as cotton. "You need to do what I say."

I lift a brow. "Is this some kind of fetish? Do you like control?"

He shakes his head. "No. It's life preservation. I haven't come in nine days. If you touch me the wrong way I'll explode. I need to be inside of you. I need to feel you come around me. I've fantasized about this for a very long fucking time."

"How long?" I whisper.

"Too long."

"Since you came to Charleston?"

He shakes his head.

"Since you offered to donate to me?" I ask, desperate to know.

"Before that," he admits. "A very long time before that. In New York. When we first met."

My heart does a little stutter. "But you hated me."

"No I didn't, Ava. I didn't hate you. I didn't understand you. But I wanted you."

My brows knit. "Why didn't you say something?"

"Because you hated me," he says. "And understandably so. We were making fun of your biggest source of pride. And I regretted it as soon as I saw your face. But I didn't know how to make it right, and maybe I liked having a reason not to act on my attraction to you."

"Because you don't like commitment," I whisper.

"Because I'm not good at it," he corrects me. "Because I didn't want to let you of all people down."

His admission touches something deep inside of me. "Come here," I say, holding my hand out to him. He joins me on the bed, laying on his side. I turn to him, reaching out to cup his beautiful, rugged jaw.

"Myles?" I say, and his jaw twitches beneath my palm.

"Yes?"

"You've never let me down. And I can't say that about a lot of people."

He presses his lips to the tip of my nose. "Let's keep it that way, by you doing what I ask of you."

"Of course." I nod.

"Good," he breathes, moving his lips to mine. His kiss is slow but deliberate, sending shots of pleasure to my thighs. I wrap my arms around his neck, delighting in the freedom of movement here compared to the shower. Then I kiss his jaw, his throat, his shoulder, down to his chest, pressing my lips to his tight nipple.

"Is this okay?" I ask him.

"Yes…" His breath catches as I softly suck at it. "No!" he

says quickly. "Fuck no." I pull away and he closes his eyes. "Jesus, this is goddamned torture."

"Maybe we should do this one quickly," I suggest. "Then take our time with round two."

"It's our first time, Ava. I'm not whamming and bamming you." He tucks his finger beneath my chin and lifts my face until our eyes catch. "I'm going to worship you. And you're going to scream. Then every time you touch yourself you're going to remember how it feels when I'm inside you."

My body clenches at the thought. I know what Myles is like when he's intent on something. He doesn't stop until he gets it. And now he wants me.

Who am I kidding? He *has* me. I'm completely his.

But from a purely intellectual standpoint I'm interested to see what he does with me.

"Tell me what to do," I whisper.

"Just lay there. Let me take care of you." He pulls me up until our faces are aligned, then rolls over so that I'm on top of him. There's not an ounce of fat on this man. How is that fair? I frown and run my hands over his arms just to make sure.

"You're grimacing," he says. "Why?"

"Because you're too perfect."

"You want me to be more…" he pauses. "Imperfect?"

I shake my head. "No. Don't change a thing." I brush the hair from his brow, trying to imprint his face into my mind. "I like you exactly like this."

A soft rumble comes from his throat, like a contented animal. An almost-purr. His eyes narrow and he pushes himself up to sitting, and my body follows his until I'm straddling his lap.

"Ava…" He kisses me sweetly. Softly. Even though he's not inside of me every part of me feels full. My throat is constricted, my chest is tight. I yearn for him.

I don't know if he can see it in my eyes. I don't know if he knows that this isn't just about getting pregnant for me anymore. It's about him. Myles Salinger. A man I've fallen head over heels for. But whatever he reads in my gaze, it makes him nod.

And before I can take a breath, he lifts me off him and lays me on the bed. My back is against the comforter, my front exposed to the air, making my nipples tighten and peak as he stares down at me.

He starts at my neck, kissing and licking my throat, sending bolts of pleasure through my veins. His fingers stroke my sides, soothing the need, as he moves his lips down to my breasts, kissing the swell of them.

His hands stroke them, his thumbs brushing my nipples and I let out a gasp. He replaces one thumb with his mouth and sucks the same way I sucked at him, and now I know why he had to make me stop.

This is too good. I'm too sensitive. It won't take much to send me over the edge. As though he can read my mind, he kisses lower, his mouth warm and soft against my skin, his fingers gently parting my thighs until I'm exposed to him.

"You're so beautiful it hurts," he murmurs, staring down at the most sensitive part of me. I'm glistening. I'm aching. I'm needy.

"Show me."

His lip twitches and he leans in. As soon as his mouth covers me I close my eyes, crying out because he's everything. He knows exactly how to play me. How to use his fingers and mouth until I'm crying out his name. He kisses and licks until my body is a mess of desire and heat, my thighs trembling as he brings me to the edge.

When I tumble he lets out a deep groan, holding me close as I convulse beneath him. I'm still gasping as I reach for him, pulling him up until he's braced over me, and my fingers close around his hard length, and slide the tip of his cock against me until he knows exactly what I need.

"Is now the right time to have the birth control talk?" I whisper.

He laughs. "Shut up and let me make love to you."

So I do. I release him because this man knows exactly what he's doing. I stroke his face, his hair, his neck, trying to show him that I care.

He presses against me and my body opens up to him. I feel myself stretch around his thickness, swallowing hard as he slowly pushes inside.

My hips lift to welcome him, and he lets out a groan, his hands moving down my side to still me as his body presses hard into mine.

"I knew it," he whispers. "I knew it would be like this. So good. So warm. So tight." There's a note to his voice that touches me. It's like he's fighting something that I can't see. I kiss him softly, because I need him to know we're on the same side.

I can't tell him I love him, but I can show him.

I slide my hands down his back, feeling the jutting muscles of his behind. I dig my fingers into them and he groans. "Myles?" I whisper.

"Yes?" There are a million emotions in his answer. "What do you need?"

"You. It's always you."

He smiles and it's like a little miracle. His eyes soften as he kisses me again. "Always?"

"Always," I breathe. "But if you don't move soon, I think I'm going to die."

"I wouldn't want that," he murmurs. "I have plans for you, Miss Quinn."

He rests his elbows on either side of me, lifting his body so he can get a better look at my face. His eyes don't leave mine as he slowly pulls out and I feel like I'm on a roller coaster, going up, up, up. Then there's the pause, the moment before oblivion, and I teeter on the edge, waiting for him to move once more.

When he does it's glorious. A hard, satisfying thrust that makes me babble something incoherent and wrap my legs around his hips. I tangle my fingers in his hair, pulling him down so we can kiss again, our tongues and lips worshipping, his hard thickness grinding inside of me, his soft groans swallowed by my mouth as I refuse to break our connection.

He cups my face tenderly, still resting on his elbows, his movements on the edge of control as he slides against me.

Every thrust of his body makes my own contract with pleasure. Every kiss makes me feel tender, exposed. He pulls out, almost to the edge, then moves forward again, dragging himself against me, making my toes curl and my breath shorten as we chase each other to oblivion.

"Are you close?" he whispers against my lips.

"So close." I'm surprised, and the shock must come through my voice because he smiles as he kisses me. He shifts, resting on his left elbow, moving his right hand between us until his fingers find me.

Right. *There.* Oh God.

He circles them, matching the rhythm of his hips, and my eyes roll back with pleasure. I sink my fingers deeper into his ass, my nails scratching him until he grunts, his muscles flexing at my touch, his body going into overdrive. My insides tighten around him, and he groans again as he breaks our kiss. He looks down, his eyes darkening as he watches himself move in and out of me, his fingers maddeningly teasing as he brings me to the edge.

"Myles?"

"Yes," he rasps, and I realize he's also on the edge.

"Am I annoying you by talking?" I manage to gasp.

His chest lifts as he laughs. "No. I like your voice." He's still moving. Still making me see heaven.

"Can we do this again? Don't let this be a one-time thing?"

"Whenever you want, sweetheart. You just have to say the word." He twists his hips and it does something to me, creating a delicious friction that boils deep in my belly. Then I feel it. The pause before the rush. The glorious moment when I reach the edge.

And it's bigger than before, because he's inside of me. He's making everything feel like it's the first time.

When I come, I scream his name. He grits his jaw and lets out a strangled sound, then follows me into oblivion, spilling inside of me until I'm full of him, so hot, so full, so completely sated.

It takes a minute for me to catch my breath. I look up at him and there's the tenderest expression on his face. It makes me think that maybe, just maybe, he feels this too.

Maybe he'll fall the same way I have.

"I hope we made a baby," he whispers, and it makes my chest ache. Because I'd forgotten all about that.

But yes, I hope we did, too. I want him to be my baby's father. I want to be connected to him forever. And I don't want tonight to end.

CHAPTER
TWENTY-SIX

MYLES

I wake up to an empty bed. Then I hear the flush of the toilet and the pad of her feet as she tiptoes back into the bedroom. She's wearing my t-shirt and nothing else. It falls to her thighs and reveals her smooth, tan legs.

The ones that were wrapped around my hips an hour ago. I harden at the memory of it.

She notices I'm awake and climbs back in, snuggling against me. I put my arm around her as her cheek presses against my chest and something weird happens inside of me.

"I never thought you'd be a cuddler," she whispers, tracing her finger in a circle on my skin.

"I've no idea what gave you that impression," I tease, because I know exactly what did.

"Me either. You're such a teddy bear at work."

I lift a brow. "It's hard to be cuddly when everybody hates your guts."

She looks up, the smile melting from her lips. "Everybody doesn't hate you."

"Yeah, they do. And it's okay, I understand. If somebody came from Charleston to the New York office and started changing everything I'd probably feel the same way."

"They just don't know you," she whispers, and it makes my stomach clench. Does she know me?

Maybe she does. But not everything. And I know that I'll have to tell her soon.

"You hated me, too," I remind her.

"No. I just didn't understand you." Her gaze lifts to mine. "But I do now. And there's nothing about you that I hate."

It's not exactly a declaration of love. But I'll take it.

She kisses my chest. "I wish I'd not hated you sooner."

"We didn't exactly get off to the best start," I point out. "You screaming at me before we'd even been introduced."

"Only because you were disrespecting Dandy. You know as well as I do that protecting a character's integrity is everything."

"Yeah, I do. Which was why I was telling the interns to erase the cartoon and never draw something like it again when you walked in."

She lifts her head up. Her brows drawn together. "You were?"

"Yes."

She blinks. "So why didn't you say something? You just looked at me like I was some kind of banshee."

"What would you have done if I'd walked into the office on my first day and started screaming at your intern because her filing system sucks?" I ask.

Ava blinks. "Um..." She lets out a mouthful of air. "I'd have stood up for her and told you that if you have a problem come and talk to me about it."

"Exactly."

She looks mortified. "Oh God..."

"Stop it," I tell her. "It's water under the bridge. I just want you to understand that I've never hated you. Or even disliked you. Yeah, I was annoyed but then you kept ignoring me and I realized that we were never going to see eye to eye."

"I should have talked to you," she says, crestfallen. "I shouldn't have assumed…"

"It didn't stop me from wanting you." I don't think anything could have. She's a force of nature. She's springtime warming up the cold earth. She's everything.

I want her to be mine.

"I'm sorry," she says softly. "I just wish I'd taken the time to get to know you."

I dip my head to kiss her brow. "We should go back to sleep." Not that I'm desperate for our night to end. In a few hours we'll be attending the big family brunch before everybody goes their separate ways. I just want to stay here, but I'm pretty sure they'll come searching for us if we don't show up.

But she doesn't look sleepy. Just contemplative. "When we're back in the office I'm going to tell everybody how wrong they are about you."

I shake my head. "Don't ruin my reputation. Maybe I like instilling fear in them."

"But why?" she asks. "Why don't you want them to like you?"

I blink. "It's not that I don't want them to like me. I just don't care. The only person whose good regard I'm concerned about is yours."

"You don't have to worry about me," she whispers. "You've already charmed me. You make me weak at the knees."

"Do you think anybody would notice if we stay here for the next few weeks?" I ask, reaching for her leg and curling it around my hip.

She frowns. "I wish we could."

I lower my head to kiss her, and I'm as hard as a rock. "We might not be able to stay forever, but we have seven hours until we need to be packed and at brunch," I tell her. "So do we go to sleep or…"

"Or," she says with certainty. "Definitely or."

"Good choice, Miss Quinn." I flash her a dirty smile. "Now roll over onto your front. I'm going to *OR* you until your eyes roll into the back of your head."

———

AVA

"It's been so lovely to meet you," Linda says, grasping my hand in hers. "You should come again, next time we all get together."

I look to my left, but Myles is out of earshot. He's talking to Liam again. Liam looks worried but Myles lays a reassuring hand on his shoulder.

"Thank you for being so hospitable," I say, giving her a genuine smile. The Salinger family is huge and complicated but somehow they make it all work. More than that, there's so much love here I can feel it seeping through my pores. Linda, Deandra, and Julia have such affection for each other and for Rupert. I know he hurt Myles, but I don't think he's a bad man.

Just a careless one. He assumes everybody is as laid back as he is and when they're not he has no idea what to do.

He's the next to hug me. "Thank you for being here," Rupert says, patting my arm. "You make Myles very happy, I can see that."

"Oh," I say because that's not what I expected at all. "We're not together."

"Of course you aren't." He winks. "But if you were I'd say you're good for him. And he'll be good to you, he always is."

Deandra and Julia say their goodbyes to me next, and then

I'm encompassed in a series of bear hugs from the Salinger brothers. Eli hugs the hardest, and Holden is gentle, but Brooks and Linc are definitely the most enthusiastic. I'm going to miss them all. Their dynamic and their affection for each other.

I might even miss the fights.

I turn to Liam and he's looking at me with a curious expression on his face. I smile and he winks back, then we hug tightly. He looks so much like Myles, but he doesn't have his intensity. He's more laid back like their father.

"I hope you got what you came for," he says softly, and I'm reminded that he knows our secret.

"Thank you." I nod. "I appreciate that."

Two tiny lines appear along his brow. "Can I ask something of you?"

"Okay…"

"Don't hurt him. He's a good man. The best. But he's not indestructible."

I blink because that's such a strange thing to say. How would I hurt him? If anybody's going to get hurt it's me.

"Are you ready?" Myles asks.

"Yes." I nod, and he carries our luggage down to the car, sliding his foot beneath the fender to open the trunk. I climb into the passenger seat and tie my hair back, because he's taken the roof down and I know it's going to get messy.

And as he pulls away, I feel a little lost. I also wonder if I'm taking more back with me than just some memories of good fun.

Maybe there's a baby inside me. Maybe there isn't.

But what I do know is that I'm different than when I arrived.

TWENTY-SEVEN

AVA

"So, do you want to come to my place, or should I come to yours?" Myles asks as we cross the Turnpike Bridge over the Allegheny River. "I have a few phone calls to make, but I could pick you up after."

Charleston is spread out ahead of us, shielded by the mountains. It's such a tiny city with its sparse high rises. It's more of a town, really. I think that's why I love it so much.

"We're spending the night together?" I ask.

"You're still ovulating, aren't you?" he asks mildly.

I lift a brow. "And if I wasn't?"

I can't see his eyes because he's wearing sunglasses, but I swear the skin around them has crinkled. "Then I'd come over anyway and we could watch something together."

My heart does a little leap. I can picture him on my couch, his long legs spread out, his feet on my coffee table. I'd be snuggled next to him while we binge watch the latest detective show on Netflix.

The image shifts. Changes. *There's a baby monitor on the*

table next to Myles' feet. It crackles and a baby's cry echoes from the speaker. He jumps up and winks at me.

"I'll take this one."

"So what do you say?" he asks, interrupting my extremely weird and embarrassing daydream.

"Come to mine. I need to do some laundry. And we both need to go to work tomorrow."

"Yours it is." He nods. "I'll bring dinner."

"Myles," I begin, because this needs to be said. "You don't have to come over if you don't want to. You don't owe me anything just because we did… what we did."

He shakes his head. "Shut up."

I try not to laugh. He's so rude and yet so sweet. Such a lethal combination.

He drives through the historic district, weaving through cars parked on the road and the occasional kid throwing a football. The parks are full of children, running around in shorts and t-shirts, enjoying the late afternoon sun. It's one of those perfect summer days that makes you nostalgic and happy at the same time.

He finds a space a few yards down from my house and pulls in, cutting the engine and climbing out. By the time I'm out of the car and joining him, he's got my suitcases out of the trunk.

"Thank you," I say, rolling onto my tiptoes to kiss his lips. "For everything."

"I'm coming in," he says, grabbing the cases. "If you try to carry these you'll give yourself a hernia."

"If you insist." They really are heavy. Heavy as hell. And even though I feel it tarnishes my feminist card, I let him carry them up the stoop and into the house.

And then he carries them up the stairs and I follow behind, marveling at just how good he looks in jeans. Don't get me wrong, the man is lethal in a suit, but in jeans he's just…

The sound of my phone shrills through the hallway. I run down to where I've left my purse and dig it out. I don't recognize the number but I answer anyway, mostly because I like to occupy scam callers so they don't swindle somebody else. My record for keeping them on the line is ten minutes. I'm hoping to beat that one day.

"Hello?"

"Is this Ava?" a woman's voice asks.

"Yes, that's right. Who am I talking to?"

"I'm Lisa, Raeanne Jackson's daughter."

The name rings a bell. I let it play around my head for a moment. "Raeanne as in my mom's friend?" I ask.

She sighs. "Yes, I'm afraid so. I have some bad news."

My mouth turns dry. "What kind of news?" I immediately want to hit myself for not calling my mom while I was away. Is she sick? Is she hurt? Worst cast scenarios rush through my head.

"I'm afraid she and my mom have been arrested for indecent exposure. They were protesting naked outside of the governor's mansion."

"Indecent exposure?" I say faintly. Dear God, not again. What is it with my mom and streaking?

"I'm sorry." Lisa sounds as resigned as I feel. There's a certain camaraderie in being the daughters of protestors. "They're at the South Central Jail. We need to go pick them up and bring them back for court tomorrow. From what I can tell it'll just be a fine, but seriously…" She sighs. "Aren't they too old for this kind of thing?"

I run my hand over my face. I don't know about my mom, but I'm definitely too old to be getting her out of jail. "South Central you say?"

"Yes. We'll need to post bail so they can come home tonight."

Of course we will. I think of my credit card and the bashing it took when I went on my extended vacation. I have enough money – *I think* – but it's going to make things tight.

"I'll see you there," I mutter. "And thank you for calling me."

"No problem." Lisa sighs again. "Why can't we just have normal moms?"

I think it's a rhetorical question because she disconnects, and I'm left holding my phone and frowning.

Myles walks down the stairs and I blink because I'd forgotten he was still here.

"You okay?" he asks. "You look a million miles away."

I take a deep breath. "I'm fine. But I'm going to have to take a raincheck on tonight."

"Is there a problem?"

"Nothing I can't handle." There's no way I'm telling him about this. He'll want to help and I don't want him to. He has enough problems with his own family. He doesn't need to add mine to the mix.

"Are you sure…"

"I'm sure, Myles." I give him a soft smile. "I'll see you at work tomorrow, okay?"

His jaw tics. "Okay. But if you need anything you know where I am."

"I appreciate it," I whisper, because I do. I appreciate everything about this man. I lift my head to kiss him because I need him to know it. "Thank you for everything. It's been amazing."

"Thanks to you." He pulls me closer, kissing the corner of my mouth, my jaw, my cheek. "You made everything bearable."

"Are we talking about the sex now?"

He grins. "No. That was unbearable."

My mouth drops open and I push him. He doesn't budge an inch. "Stop that."

"I'm not going to stop anything," he murmurs. "Especially not touching you."

"You'll have to stop it at work tomorrow," I remind him. "That's how rumors start."

"We'll worry about that in the morning." He shrugs. "I guess I should go home and do my own laundry."

"You don't know how sexy that is. Will you strip down when you do it?" I ask, teasing.

"Why would I strip?"

"Like that guy in that jeans ad from years ago," I tell him. "And also because it fuels my fantasies about you."

"In that case, I'll definitely strip." He kisses the tip of my nose. "Call me later when you've done what you need to?"

I grimace, because I know I have a long night ahead of me. "I'll definitely try. And send me a selfie of you doing the laundry. I need to know that you're keeping to the plan."

"Only if you can tell me why you're being so secretive."

"I'm not being secretive, I'm being discrete. It's different." I pull away from him, wishing more than anything that my mom knew how to dress appropriately. "I'm sorry to ruin our plans."

"I'll survive." He checks his watch. "Talk later, okay?"

"Okay."

———

"I don't understand it," my mom says. "How can a human body be indecent? It's perfectly decent. It's natural, there shouldn't be a law against showing it off."

"It's not natural to dance naked around the Governor's Mansion and chant that he's a…" I try to remember the exact phase. "Mother forker."

"We didn't call him that." Mom's nose wrinkles as though I'm the one who's been arrested. "We said he was assaulting Mother Nature."

"Same thing."

"No it isn't. We didn't use vulgar language."

This is the thing about my mom. She'll do something crazy like run naked around a mock-colonial mansion, then bristle when you use a cuss word in front of her. It's just one of the many ways I'll never understand her. She's a law unto herself and gets furious when the real actual law stops her from doing what she wants.

"You can't go around taking your clothes off every time you want to make a point," I tell her.

"Why not?" She frowns. "I think we made our point perfectly. Did you see the photographers outside the jail? We'll be in all the papers tomorrow. If it gets more attention to our cause then I'll strip off every day."

"Please don't do that." I rub my palms against my eyes. "I need to work. I can't spend all of my time and money bailing you out."

"I told you I'd pay you back," she says testily.

"You don't need to. They'll return it if you turn up to court tomorrow." I frown. "You *are* going to court tomorrow, right?"

She glares at me as though I'm being stupid. "Of course. There'll be journalists there. Raeanne thinks we should strip in court but I'm worried that they might sentence us to six months in jail. I think we're better off protesting outside of the penal system."

Thank God for small mercies. I shiver at the thought of my mom serving time in prison. Not so much for her but for the other inmates. They'd all be begging for an early release to escape her.

"But you're going to keep your clothes on in the future, right?" I ask. "Because if they catch you again they won't go so lightly on you."

"Of course," she huffs. "I'm not silly. And anyway, Washington DC doesn't count, does it?"

"What do you mean it doesn't count?"

"It's a different jurisdiction. So we'd start again with a warning, wouldn't we? Raeanne and I always strip naked when we're protesting in DC."

"You did it once, Mom. And you got away with it. You won't next time. And there's no way I'm driving all the way to DC to bail you out."

She waves her hand. "What else did you have to do tonight?"

"Laundry."

She smiles. "Then I saved you from yourself. You're so serious, Ava. You need to lighten up a bit. You know what you need?" she asks, looking at me critically.

I sigh. "What?"

"Some good sex."

"Mom!" My jaw drops to my ankles. "You can't say that."

"Of course I can. I'm old not decrepit. I know the power of an orgasm."

My stomach turns. These are words I never want to hear my mom say. I consider putting my hands over my ears and singing loudly. "Please stop now."

"But somebody needs to tell you, sweetheart. You need to relax. Have fun. Meet a guy. Let him ruin your insides."

"I thought you hated guys." I ignore the part about ruining my insides. That's not a direction I need this conversation to go in.

"I love men. I just don't need to plight my troth to one."

"Plight your what?" I shake my head. "Never mind. Can we change the subject?" I glance at my watch. "Actually, it's getting late. I should go home. I need to let the office know I'll be late tomorrow."

"You don't have to take me to court," she says.

"I'm taking you." Because I still don't trust her not to strip naked. I should probably call Lisa and suggest we keep Mom and Raeanne separated. Together they're a lethal combination.

"Whatever," she says, but secretly she looks pleased. And I feel guilty because she doesn't ask for a lot. Just a little of my attention. Apparently getting naked and arrested is the only way she can do it.

My phone buzzes and a text message appears from Myles. A smile immediately pulls at my lips as I open it.

And then it freezes when I see the image attached to the message. Myles, naked from the chest up, scowling at me through the camera.

Just doing laundry.

My body doesn't know what to do first. Blush because dammit, Myles Salinger naked from the chest up is something to behold. His skin is golden, his muscles taut and firm. But it's his face that draws me in. The way he's grimacing at the camera, as though the last thing he wants to do is take a selfie.

And yet he's doing it. For me. And it warms everything inside of me. Not just the buzzing desire that always takes over me when he's around, but the other, emotional side.

The one that appreciates Myles for who he is, not what he can do.

"Oh my." Mom lets out a low whistle. "He's even sexier when he's naked."

"Mom! Stop staring."

"If he wanted me to stop staring he wouldn't have sent that photo."

"He sent it to me, not you," I point out.

"Yes, and why is that?" she asks, her voice worryingly sweet. "I thought you two were just friends."

"I never said that." I never said anything. I always find with my mom that the less I lie the better. She always catches me.

"So you're not *just* friends?"

I let out a long breath, really wishing she hadn't seen that. "It's complicated."

"That's what we used to say when the guy wouldn't

commit," she says lightly. "Is that what he's doing? Using you for your body?"

"Maybe I'm using him for his." It's not a lie because I have been. Until we went away I was using him for the one thing I wanted most.

"I'd use him every day of the week and twice on Sundays," she says. "Does he go to the gym or is he naturally buff?"

"Mom!"

"What? I'm just taking an interest in your friends." She frowns. "Isn't that what you want me to do? You complain that I know nothing about you and then you hide things like this from me."

"When do I complain that you don't know me?"

"When you graduated college."

"That was fifteen years ago," I point out. "I'm okay with you not knowing about me now."

"But I want to know about you," she says softly. "I'm your mom, I care about you."

Guilt washes over me. "I know. And there's nothing to know about Myles and me. As I said it's complicated."

"Do you love him?"

My heart hammers wildly against my chest. "Yes."

"What's so complicated about that?" she asks, confused. "As much as I hate the patriarchy, love is a biological thing. We can't help it. It's mother nature's way of making us bond with our mate. It's humans that have subverted it and made it into subjugation. But love, Ava, that's a wonderful emotion."

It is. But there's an ache in my throat that won't disappear. "We work together," I tell her.

"So what? You're at the same level, aren't you? There's nothing wrong with that."

"He lives in New York," I add.

She shrugs. "He can move or you can move or you can have a long distance relationship. There's a lot to be said for that. You get to live your own life, build your own dreams, and get regular orgasms."

I'm never going to get used to hearing my mom say that word.

I open my mouth to tell her all the reasons why it couldn't work. But it actually boils down to one. "I want a baby," I whisper.

A smile pulls at her lips. "You do?"

I nod.

"That's wonderful. Oh Ava, I thought I'd put you off motherhood for life. I was such a bad role model."

"No you weren't." My eyes prick with tears. "You were a great mom."

"I was embarrassing. I know that. Your friends never came around when I was there. I wanted to be different. I tried a few times. I never wanted you to feel like you had to hide me away."

I guess that's what I did do. I hate the thought of it. She's a good person, she just approaches life different than I do. But I love her so much.

I grab her hand and squeeze it. "You were the best mom," I tell her. "And my friends love you. Sophie and Lauren are always asking about your latest escapades."

She smiles. "They're good friends to you."

"Yes they are."

"But sometimes we need more than friends," she says. "Sometimes we need lovers or partners or fathers to our babies." She lowers her voice. "Do you think Myles wants a baby?"

I don't know whether to laugh or cry. I feel closer to her than ever but I can't tell her what we've been doing. It's too personal. Too painful.

Too confusing.

"You're right," she says, taking my silence for a negative. "It's too soon for you to think about that with him. You two need to spend time together, maybe move in together first." She nods her head. "But don't take too long. I know we're all superwomen nowadays but Mother Nature can be a bitch as well as a goddess. And your biological clock isn't getting any slower."

And there we go. Another reminder that time is running out. If I told her what we were really doing she'd want to know every little detail. I'm just not ready for that.

"I should go," I tell her. "I need to unpack and get some sleep if I'm going to be back here in the morning."

She pats my hand. "Of course. Thank you for taking care of me."

"You're welcome."

CHAPTER
TWENTY-EIGHT

AVA

There are thirty messages flashing on my phone when I walk out of the court room. Most of them look like they're from work, so I ignore them and hug my mom, who's going off for a victory brunch with Raeanne and their gang.

Being fined five hundred dollars and getting a stern talking to from the judge doesn't seem like a victory to me, but hey, I'm not my mom.

And that's okay.

It's a short drive from the courthouse to work. There's an empty space just outside the building and I grin as I steer into it. Some days are just good ones, and that's how today feels. The sun is shining, my mom isn't imprisoned, and in about three minutes I get to see Myles.

We spoke last night but we were both exhausted. He was one up on me, having done his laundry already. That's tonight's job, though I hope I'll be able to squeeze it in around Myles, because he already told me he's spending tonight at my place.

Matthew, the receptionist, grimaces at me as I walk in. "There's a big argument going on up there," he says. "That guy, the angry one. I think he's riled everybody up."

"That's how he rolls," I say lightly. Myles probably caught Ryan watching Netflix when he should have been working and laid into him. We've been away for almost a week, they've probably gotten into bad habits.

I pull the creaky elevator cage closed and hit the button for the third floor, and even though I spent the morning in court there's still a smile on my face. Maybe we can finish work on time today and head for the park for a dinner picnic. The sun is too delicious to sit inside all evening.

When I step out of the elevator and into the office the room hushes. Everybody turns to look at me. They're all gathered into a group by Ryan's desk.

"I've been calling you," Catherine says softly. "Have you heard?"

"Heard what?" I look around for Myles, but I can't see him. The door to his office is closed and the inside is dark.

"New York has taken Dandy."

I blink. "What?"

"I told you," she says to Ryan. "She didn't know."

"What was I supposed to think?" He shrugs. "She disappeared for days with the enemy and then this happens. And she didn't pick up your calls. Classic avoidance."

I wave my hands in the air. "Can somebody explain what's happening?"

"We got the email today," Catherine says. "Naomi has agreed that Dandy can be transferred to the New York office. We assumed you knew."

I shake my head. "I didn't know anything," I say. "Nobody told me." And there has to be some kind of mistake. Naomi promised she wouldn't take Dandy to New York. We have an excellent working relationship. If she was thinking about something like this she would have said something.

"Where's Myles?" I ask, realizing he must know what's going on.

"You tell us." Ryan shakes his head. "He disappeared about twenty minutes before the email arrived. Didn't say a damn thing, the sneaky asshole."

I sit down heavily at my desk. My head feels woolly, like I can't form a coherent thought. And I need to think right now.

Really think.

The first thing I do is boot up my laptop and read my emails. Sure enough, there's the announcement in the form of a press release. Naomi Acre has signed a new contract and Dandy will be edited and distributed from the New York office.

Then I grab my phone and read my messages. Two missed calls from Myles plus two messages. I pull them up.

Can you call me when you get this message? – Myles

It was sent an hour and a half ago, when I was in court with Mom. I swallow hard and read the second.

Ava, please call me. – Myles

I take a deep breath. There has to be some explanation for this. I press his name on my phone to return his call and huff when it goes straight to voicemail. I leave a message and then send him a text, too, for good measure.

What's going on? Did you know Dandy is going to New York? Why didn't anybody tell me? – Ava.

. . .

"We're going to lose our jobs, aren't we?" Ryan says. "Dandy was the only thing that kept us in profit. Without him, they'll close us for sure."

"Christ." Catherine drops her head into her hands. "I just bought a new house. I'm going to lose it."

"Wait," I say, because somebody has to. "Let me call Naomi. She'll know what's going on."

I pull up her private number. Naomi doesn't have a cellphone. She doesn't like computers, either. She writes longhand and has her words transposed by a secretary.

The phone rings eight times before it's picked up. "Hello, this is the Acre residence. Anna speaking."

"Hi, it's Ava Quinn," I say. I've met Anna before. She's Naomi's housekeeper and the person who reminds her to eat when she's caught up in writing. "Is Naomi there?"

"Oh, hello Ava. No she isn't. She's gone to New York for a meeting."

Damn. "Do you know how I can contact her?" I ask.

"I'm not sure. She's staying with some family friends. I can ask her to call you if she phones home? She'll want to know how Artie is doing."

Artie is her cat. And of course she'll want to know.

"Yes," I say. "Please ask her to call me." I tell her my number and ask her to write it down. Naomi probably hasn't taken her address book with her and I don't want her to have any reason not to call back.

"I will, dear," Anna agrees. Then she shouts. "No, Artie, not the cake." She takes a deep breath. "I have to go. Artie and coffee cake don't mix."

"Of course. Thank you."

"You're very welcome."

I hang up and stare at the phone for a moment. So Naomi is in New York. Which probably means she's meeting with

Mediatech. They're making plans and talking about Dandy's future and I'm not involved, even though I discovered him. It feels like a knife twisting in my ribcage.

"Ava?" Catherine says softly. "Are you okay?"

It's only then that I realize I'm hyperventilating. "No, I'm not." I feel betrayed and hurt and most of all I feel like I've let everybody down.

Ryan's right. Without Dandy, this office isn't going to survive. Dandy allows us to take risks on smaller authors. To work with schools and educators. That little friendly lion literally pays for the roof over all of our heads.

"Myles really didn't say anything?" I ask her.

She shifts and I know there's something she isn't telling me.

"Catherine?"

She takes a deep breath and leans forward. "I was next to his office when he was on a call."

"You heard what he said?"

She glances at Ryan's desk – where everybody is still gathered, then back at me. "I didn't want to make things worse by telling them."

"Telling them what?" I feel sick. My stomach is literally twisting.

"He said that they weren't supposed to be announcing it today. That they'd agreed to do it next week."

There's a ringing in my ears. The kind that you only get after a loud bang. For a moment I forget to breathe.

"Myles knew this was happening?" I whisper.

"I think so. I couldn't ask him because he stormed out without a word. I guess he was hoping to be in New York when they announced so he didn't have to deal with the fallout here." She bites her lip. "Did he say anything to you on your retreat?"

"Nothing," I whisper. He was too busy making me fall in love with him.

She gives me a tight smile, but there's no humor there. Just a dark camaraderie that ties us together. We're going to lose our jobs. And let's face it, there aren't a lot of openings in Charleston for children's publishers. We're the only one here, so either we retrain or we move.

Damn it, we were happy. I had plans. Myles knew that. He knew I'd need a job if I was going to be a single mom…

Christ. I could be pregnant now. Pregnant and out of a job and he didn't say a word.

I look around the office. Ryan still has his cabal of mourners, all talking and shaking their heads. In the corner, Ella the intern is crying on the phone – I imagine to her parents, poor kid. Since Myles has disappeared to God knows where, I'm the highest ranking employee and I feel the weight on me. The need to do something to help these people.

"Okay," I call out. "Everybody, gather around."

Ryan looks up, surprised. A few of them pause as though waiting for me to say something more.

"Don't panic, I'm not going to fire you. I just want to talk to you all."

Within a minute, they've formed a circle around me. I look at their faces. Some are tearful, some are angry, some – like me – just look confused. They're faces I've seen every day, some of them for decades. People who try to do their best, who try to make things that educate and entertain the children of America.

People who are scared because they don't know what the future holds.

I take a deep breath. "I'm so sorry that you had to hear about this by email," I tell them. "And I'll be letting New York know exactly how I feel about that. And for those of you who are wondering, I had no idea either. The first time I heard about this was when I walked through the door a little while ago."

That mollifies a couple of them. The others just grimace.

"But there's something you should all know. This decision doesn't reflect the excellent job every one of you has been doing. Dandy was ours. We found him, we developed him, we delivered him to the homes of children who fell in love with him. And you should be proud of that. Because you made a difference in the lives of children everywhere. You helped make this world a better place by promoting Dandy's values. Of kindness, of taking care of others, of treating people the way you'd like to be treated." I give them a soft smile. "And nobody can take that away."

"They can take our jobs, though," Ryan mutters. A few other people start talking.

I lift my hand. "I don't know what will happen to our jobs. But I'm going to find out and believe me when I say I'll push New York to make sure we're all taken care of. I'm sorry this happened. I'm sorry I wasn't aware of it and I'm sorry I didn't get the chance to fight it."

"You don't need to be sorry, "Ryan says. "It's Salinger who should apologize."

"Is that why he was here?" Ella asks. "To steal Dandy?"

My throat tightens. The fact is, I have no idea. He said he was here to review the branch and make suggestions for improvements.

Could one of his suggestions have been to steal Dandy while I was busy falling for him?

It doesn't feel like he'd do that. But then how well do I know him? I thought I did. I thought I knew everything about him, but if he can hide something like this from me then…

I don't know him at all.

"As I said, I'll be talking to New York. But in the meantime, I don't think there's a lot we can do. So I'd like you to do whatever is urgent in your inboxes, and at lunchtime you should all go down to The Hole in the Wall. I'll make sure you're paid for the day."

"You want us to leave?" Ryan asks, looking confused.

"I want you to be together. To take care of each other. Us sitting in here staring at our screens isn't going to help. Let's get this out of our system then tomorrow we can work out what happens next. Okay?"

He nods. "Okay."

"Good. So get your work done and get out of here. And tomorrow we'll find out what the hell is going on."

CHAPTER
TWENTY-NINE

AVA

The office is empty. I'm sitting at my desk staring blankly at my laptop and wondering what else I can do to make this better.

Myles still hasn't called back – there's not even a read receipt on my messages. And Jean-Baptiste has been conveniently in meetings all afternoon and unable to take my call. I've scheduled a half hour slot in the morning with him via his PA, but I wouldn't be surprised if it's canceled as soon as she talks to him.

It's like they just want us to disappear.

There's a tap on the door. I look over to see Catherine walk in. She's carrying a glass of wine.

"You should come down and join us," she says. "But just in case you won't, I brought the bar up to you."

I smile wanly. "How's it going down there?"

"Everybody's drinking like there's no tomorrow. Ryan's asked Derek to get the karaoke machine out." She winces. "There is going to be a lot of sore heads in the morning."

"Maybe starting early means they'll finish early," I say hopefully. "Get a good night's sleep."

"I wouldn't bank on it."

I glance at the wine she's holding out for me and think about accepting it and pouring it down the sink when she's gone. But there's been enough lies and subterfuge here today. Anything other than honesty seems wrong right now.

"Thank you," I tell her. "But I can't drink alcohol right now."

"Are you on antibiotics?" she asks. "Those things are a killer."

I shake my head. "I'm trying to get pregnant."

Her eyes widen. "You are?"

"Good timing, huh? I wasn't expecting to be jobless right now."

She pulls out a chair and takes a sip of the wine she brought up for me. "My mom always said there's no good time to have a baby."

"She's probably right about that."

"But I know you," Catherine says, leaning forward. "You wouldn't have made a decision like this without thinking it through. And I bet you've saved enough to keep a roof over your heads while you look for a new job."

"I have, but it'll run out within a year."

"You'll be snapped up. Hey, maybe New York will ask you to transfer there. That could be an option, right?"

"They asked me before. A year ago. But I don't want to move to New York," I admit to her. "I want to stay here. I love Charleston. I love being near my family and friends. I love that it feels like everybody knows everybody." And most of all I love working at Smith and Carson. Tears prick at my eyes.

"Oh sweetie." Catherine puts the wine glass down and reaches for my hand. "You'll be okay. You're a strong woman."

The thing is, I don't feel very strong right now. I feel vulnerable. Afraid. I made decisions thinking one thing, and now they're being tipped upside down.

My phone starts to ring. I look down to see Myles' name flashing across the screen. My chest tightens and I look over at Catherine. "I need to take this."

"Of course." She nods. "I'll head back to the bar. Come down and join us after, okay?"

"Yeah, I will." Because let's face it, sitting in this empty office thinking about the future isn't doing my anxiety any good. At least in the bar I'll be surrounded by my colleagues.

She carries the wine glass out of the office, no doubt heading back to the Hole, and I slide my finger across the screen to accept Myles' call. My heart is racing now. I have no idea what to say to him.

"Hello?"

"Ava. Thank God."

"Where are you?" I demand.

"I'm in New York. That's why I hadn't returned your call sooner. I've been on a plane. Listen, I need to explain what's happening."

"You don't need to explain," I say softly. "I know. New York has stolen Dandy."

He lets out a long breath. "I wanted you to hear it from me."

His words feel like a stab in the chest. "Maybe you should have told me last week. Or any time really."

"I wanted to, but Ava…"

"How long have you known?"

"A while." He sounds edgy.

"How long is a while? Did you know last week?"

"Yes, but the announcement coming today blindsided me. I didn't think they'd lock it down while we were away."

"So you knew last week and didn't tell me?" I can't keep the hurt from my voice. "You made love to me and you didn't tell me. You helped me try to get pregnant and didn't bother to let me know I might not have a goddamned job or a roof over my head."

"You'll always have a roof over your head. I'll make sure of that."

"I don't want your money, Myles. I don't want you to take care of me. I thought we established that already. I want a baby and I want to provide for it. You knew that yet you still did what you did."

"Ava, listen to me." He sounds panicky.

"You know when I would have happily listened to you?" I continue. "Last week. Or any time really. I'd have listened and we could have worked it out. Maybe I would've stopped trying for a baby. Maybe I wouldn't have come to your family reunion." God this hurts. My chest is so tight I can't breathe.

"I wouldn't have let you stop trying. This isn't the end Ava, it's just a different beginning."

Tears prick at my eyes. "Tell that to the thirty staff who you walked out on this morning. You know what they think? That you're a coward who can't even face them. You could have called them together, you could have reassured them, but instead you ran away."

"Is that what you think I did?" He sounds angry now. But I'm angrier and somehow that fuels me.

"It's what I know. You ran away to New York and you're probably drinking a latte with your friends, laughing that you managed to steal Dandy away." A tiny sob escapes my lips. I feel completely betrayed. "I trusted you," I tell him. "I thought you were a good guy after all."

I wait for him to protest, to ask me to listen again, to do anything to break the silence, but instead he says nothing. I shift in my seat, the anger slowly dissipating, replaced by a deep sadness that makes everything feel dark.

"I would never laugh at you," he finally says.

"You didn't tell me the truth either."

"Just try to keep the faith. Please Ava, believe in me a little longer. I'm not a bad guy, I'm just…" He exhales heavily. "I'm just trying to do my job."

"I can't…" My voice breaks. "I can't do this now. I can't talk to you." It hurts too much. My chest feels like it's about to explode, I can barely breathe. "I need to go."

"Wait…"

I hang up before I can hear anymore. His name flashes up again on my screen as he tries to call, but I ignore it. When it finally routes to voicemail, I turn the whole thing off because I can't be dealing with this now.

It's time to blow off some steam at The Hole in the Wall.

———

MYLES

I stare at my phone as Ava's recorded voice tells me to leave a message. I manage to mumble something – God knows what – and end the call with a frustrated sigh.

"You should have let her know what's going on," Liam says. "I told you that."

"Thanks for the advice," I say through gritted teeth. "Really helpful." I push my phone away on the table in Liam's boardroom and drop my head into my hands. "I never should have gone to the family reunion. I should have known Jean-Baptiste would pull something like this."

"Yeah, well we didn't exactly cover our tracks well. It's hard when you're schmoozing stockholders left, right, and center," Liam points out. That's what he's been doing for weeks. Gathering investors and creating a fund to buy Smith and Carson from Mediatech. We've been planning this for the longest time.

And now it's all shot to shit.

Without Naomi Acres and Dandy the Lion, Smith and Carson is worthless.

Even worse, we're still obligated to buy it. And all the investors' money – not to mention Liam and my personal funds – are tangled up in the purchase of a worthless publishing house.

In short, we're fucked.

A fact Jean-Baptiste giddily told me this morning when he called just before he sent the email out confirming that Naomi Acres would be publishing her next books directly through Mediatech. He somehow persuaded her that if she signed it would save Ava's job and she could come work in New York.

Which is bullshit, because Ava would never come here. But Jean-Baptiste is persuasive when he wants to be – especially when there's nobody around to contradict him.

If I'd been in the office I would have known this was going on.

But I wasn't. I was fucking distracted.

I try to call Ava again, but like last time it goes to voice-mail. Liam lifts a brow.

"She's not talking to you, bro."

"Don't you think I get that?" I ask him. If it wasn't for the fact that he's about to lose everything, I'd be on a plane back to Charleston right now.

Because I can't lose her, too. I can't.

"So how are you going to explain this to her?" he asks. "Because she sounded pretty pissed."

"I was just trying to protect her," I say, my voice thin. "If she knew about this she would have panicked. Let the cat out of the bag. Better to keep her in the dark until everything was done."

"Yeah," Liam says, nodding. "That worked out really well."

I look at him, annoyed. "What would you have done?"

"I would have told her that I was making decisions about

the company she's worked at for fifteen years. Heck, maybe I'd have even asked for her help. Had you even thought about that? If she'd known what we were doing she could have kept close tabs on Naomi. But no, you knew best. You always do."

"You didn't seem so annoyed when this was going to make a ton of money for you," I point out.

"It's lucrative, or it would have been," Liam says. "But it's not worth the pain. I did this for you, because you asked for my help, so don't turn all this around on me."

I squeeze my eyes shut because he's right. I have no right to lash out on my brother. When I was worried about Jean-Baptiste's plans to close down Smith and Carson he was the first person I went to. Asked if he could help fund a buyout.

And he agreed because we're family.

"I'm sorry," I say. "I'm just so fucking annoyed. I messed up. This is my fault."

Liam's silent for a moment, looking at me carefully. "It's not just your fault. It's mine, too. We're in this together." He runs his thumb along his jaw. "It's just you're so used to being the one solving all the problems, you don't know what to do when you can't."

"What would you have me do?" I ask, because I'm out of ideas. We're going to be broke. His investors are going to be broke. We'll both be out of jobs.

I mean, I am anyway. Jean-Baptiste made that clear. But Liam's business should be thriving.

"Talk to Ava," he suggests. "She knows Naomi better than anybody."

"She won't answer. So how am I supposed to talk to her?" I slump down, because losing money feels like nothing compared to losing her.

It's killing me to think of her so upset. Hating my guts and feeling like I deliberately misled her. And yeah, I know I'm an idiot. I shouldn't assume I know best.

Because right now I don't know anything at all.

"I'm not sure," Liam admits, shaking his head. "I was hoping you'd have some ideas about that."

Well in that case, we're all fucked.

———

AVA

"You couldn't have picked a worse time to stop drinking," Lauren says, shaking her head after I've filled her and Sophie in on everything that's happened. "I'm going to have to drink for the both of us."

"Me too," Sophie says, her face deadly serious. "I'll do it for you." She squeezes my hand.

They turned up at The Hole in the Wall just after four. I was shocked because I hadn't called either of them to let them know what was going on. It turns out that Ryan had sent Ella out to buy donuts from Lauren's bakery, and the poor kid had broken down and told her everything.

It had only taken one phone call to mobilize Sophie and they'd arrived here within the hour. And now they're as drunk as the rest of my colleagues. I'm literally the only sober one in the bar.

"I just can't believe it," Sophie murmurs when she finishes her glass. "This is your day from hell, honey. It can only get better from here."

"Well hopefully tomorrow she won't wake up and have to take her mom to court for indecency," Lauren says. "That'll be a bonus."

"And she won't lose her job tomorrow if she's already lost it today," Sophie agrees.

"Plus she can only get betrayed once, right?" Lauren sighs. "I can't believe you had sex with him and then he turned around and stabbed you in the back. What an asshole."

"Maybe we shouldn't call him an asshole," Sophie whispers. "What if Ava's pregnant? That's her baby's daddy."

"Eww." Lauren wrinkles her nose. "Good point though." Then she leans down and touches my stomach. "Ignore what I said, potential baby."

They've definitely had too much to drink.

"Did you just say Ava had sex with Myles?" Ryan asks.

My stomach drops. Apparently this day *can* get worse.

"Um…" Lauren looks at me.

I shrug. I literally don't care anymore. I don't care what people say and I don't care what people think. My world has crashed down and I'm too busy wading through the rubble.

"Yes, I did," I tell him. "But it was for a greater cause."

"Listen, buddy," Lauren says, poking her finger into his chest. "This stays between us, right?"

"Of course." Ryan nods, his eyes widening. He leans in closer, desperate to hear more.

"I'm trying to get pregnant and Myles was helping me," I say, my words jumbling together. "That's it. That's the news. I slept with him and now I'm not sleeping with him."

"Whoa." Ryan lets out a low whistle. "You could be pregnant with the spawn of Satan."

I frown. "Don't call him that."

"He walked out on us in our hour of need," Ryan says. "He's not exactly my favorite person."

"Ava's right," Sophie says. "Whatever happens we need to stop calling people names. Especially if he is the father of her baby."

"Can we stop talking about this baby?" I plead. "We don't even know if there is one."

"You're having a baby?" Ella asks. Somebody hears her question and leans in, and before too long everybody's gathering around our table, talking in heated voices about how I'm knocked up by the man they hate the most.

"I can't believe you're pregnant," Ella says. "You don't look pregnant."

"I'm not pregnant. Or not for sure." I sigh. "I could be or I couldn't be."

"It's like Schrodinger's baby," Lauren says helpfully. "Both there and not there."

Ryan shakes his head. "Can't you sue him? Didn't he take advantage of you?"

"No, I can't." I frown. "And I don't want to. He didn't take advantage." Despite my harsh words to him, I know this in my heart. "We're both at the same level, there's no power play here. We were equals."

"What was it like?" Catherine asked. "Is he as angry between the sheets as he is out of them?"

I widen my eyes at her. "Can we not do this? He deserves some respect." Yes, I'm angry with him, but less than two days ago I was in his arms. It's confusing and I don't need their opinions of him right now. I pull my lip between my teeth and try not to cry because all I can think about is how much I need him right now.

I wish he was here.

Sophie frowns at me. "Oh my God," she whispers softly. "You're in love with him."

Her whispering isn't very good, because everybody turns to look at her. Then they whisper to each other. About me and Myles and the baby we didn't want anybody to know about. If I could bring myself to care what people think I'd be embarrassed.

But I'm not. It's almost freeing. I've always cared what people think. I've always tried to be the good person doing the right thing. Taking the safe route through life. And look where it got me.

"Yes." I nod. "I am."

Sophie looks like she's about to cry. "I'm sorry."

"I know." I take a deep breath. "But it's literally the least of my problems now." I need to figure out if I still have a job and if I don't, find another. Then I need to find out if I'm pregnant. After that, I'll worry about Myles and my emotions and all the other things I have no control over.

"You need sugar," Lauren says. "And lots of it."

"We ate all the donuts." Ryan looks apologetic. "Sorry."

Lauren rolls her eyes. "It's okay, I own a donut shop." She looks at me and Sophie. "Want to get out of here?"

"Yes," the two of us say in unison.

Ryan frowns. "You're getting more donuts? Can I come along?"

CHAPTER
THIRTY

AVA

"*Ava, can you please call me back. I really need to talk to you.*"

"*It's me again. Call me. Whenever you get this just call me, dammit.*"

"*Ava, please. Just pick up my calls. I'm freaking out here.*"

The fourth message takes on a different tone. Calmer. More like the Myles I know and… *yeah.*

"*Okay, I get it. You don't want to talk to me. That's okay. Just send me a message to let me know you're all right. Before I pull my goddamned hair out.*"

Okay so the ending wasn't cool and controlled. But if I'm being completely honest I kind of like the fact that he's as riled up as I am.

I look up at Sophie and Lauren who are leaning in, listening avidly. Then I pull up my messenger and type out two simple words.

I'm okay. – Ava

Yes, it's a lie but I can't get rid of my nice girl tendencies all at once. These things take time and planning. When I see the message has sent, I turn the phone off again and lift up my second donut, smashing it into my mouth in a glorious haze of lemon and honey.

We got here half an hour ago – without Ryan who's probably still sulking – and I watched as Lauren chose all my favorites and laid them on a plate. It was only when I ate the first donut that I realized I hadn't eaten all day.

"Okay," Sophie says after I've demolished the second donut. "We need to make a plan."

Lauren rolls her eyes. "You and your plans."

Sophie holds her hands up. "I'm a weather forecaster. I like to know all worst case scenarios."

"Ava's lost Dandy," Lauren points out. "It's not like she's about to be hit by a tornado."

Sophie ignores her, rummaging in her bag. She pulls out a pad and pencil then looks at me. "Let's start with the worst things that could happen."

I blink. "You want me to say them out loud?"

She nods slowly. "Honestly, it helps. You take it out of your head and put it on the paper. And then if you want to go the final step you put the paper in a fire and burn away your worries."

"Ooookay…" I mean, it's better than eating a third donut, right? "Where should I start?"

"What's your biggest worry?"

It doesn't take a lot of thinking for this one. "That I'll lose my job. And my home. And I'll end up destitute and pregnant on the streets. Then the baby will be born and he or she will either be taken away from me or hate me because I chose to have them and couldn't provide for them."

"Oh oh…" Lauren leans forward. "Maybe the Salingers will steal the baby from you. Bring them up in complete luxury. And one day they'll seek you out and find you haggard and toothless on the streets."

"That's not really helping," Sophie says, shaking her head. "Let's circle back. Do you really think you'll be on the streets if you can't pay your mortgage?"

"Of course she won't," Lauren says. "She could move in with me. Or you, if she likes having her toiletries lined up like soldiers."

"Or your mom," Sophie says to me. I grimace at that.

"You could sue Myles," Lauren suggests. "He's independently rich, isn't he? You could sue him for child support."

"I'm not going to sue Myles," I tell her firmly. "And anyway, he keeps telling me he'll take care of me."

Lauren's lips form a perfect 'o'.

"Well, that's okay then. Your worst worry is never going to happen." Sophie strikes through the words 'be a homeless mom' with a flourish of her pen.

"I'll never take his money," I tell them.

Lauren frowns. "Why not?"

"Because I don't want it. I set out to do this alone. The only thing I wanted from him was, well, *you know*."

"His sperm," Lauren says. "You know the problem with you?"

"What?" I ask.

"You're too independent. You always have been. Remember our first day at college? There were all these gorgeous guys waiting to help carry our boxes up to our dorm room and you refused any help at all."

"I'm perfectly capable of carrying boxes," I point out.

But Lauren's on a roll now. "Have you ever not gone Dutch on a date?"

"I..."

"Or let a guy hold a door open for you?"

"Yes!" I say triumphantly. "I have."

Lauren looks me dead in the eye. "When?"

"I don't know." I frown. "But I definitely have. Anyway, I thought you were supposed to be making me feel better?"

"Would you let me if I tried?" she asks softly.

"What do you mean?" I ask her. I'm genuinely perplexed.

"You don't like people helping you. You like being the one to help others. And that's okay most of the time, until you hit rock bottom." She glances at Sophie. "We're your best friends. We love you. We just wish you'd let us help you."

I open my mouth to respond but nothing comes out. She's right. I hate being helped.

"You're a strong, independent woman," Lauren says. "But even you need support sometimes."

The thing is, I don't know how to accept it. I feel like a failure. All of this is my fault. If I hadn't been so busy wanting a baby and falling in love with Myles then I would have noticed something was going on. I would have talked with Naomi and she would have given me a hint.

Something to make me realize that Smith and Carson was at risk.

"We won't let anything happen to you," Sophie says, rubbing my arm gently. "We're here for you. We'll support you. You've taken care of us enough times."

"She's right," Lauren agrees. "Remember when I ended up stranded at that guy's place and you drove over to pick me up at three in the morning?"

"Or how you always stop and talk to those people raising money for charity when everybody else avoids them," Sophie adds.

"But I don't know how else to be," I protest. "I've always had to take care of myself."

"But you don't have to now," Lauren tells me.

My lip wobbles. My chest feels so tight I'm not sure I can keep breathing. I realize something.

I'm afraid of letting go. Of letting other people help me. I'm afraid that if I just relax something bad will happen.

Like Dandy being taken by New York.

And that's when I realize something else. That I'm the

same as Myles. We both substitute taking care of others for taking care of ourselves. It's our love language and when we can't do that anymore we don't know how to show love.

Lauren stands and walks over to the counter. "Okay, this calls for the big one," she says. "The chocolate popcorn caramel donut." She brings out what looks more like a cake than a donut. The top is iced in chocolate, sprinkled with caramel covered popcorn. Flakes of white chocolate are sprinkled all over, and to finish it off she sprayed it with gold flecks.

"If I eat that I'll die of a sugar overdose," I say, even though my mouth is watering.

"You'll still feel better in the morning than if you'd drunk a bottle of wine," Lauren points out. "Anyway, I'm cutting this one into three. We'll all have a piece."

Sophie and I watch in awed silence as she slices into the donut and chocolate sauce oozes out from the middle. Lauren puts each third onto a plate and hands them to us.

"Do people eat this and survive?" Sophie asks her.

"They not only survive, they come back for more." Lauren gives us a satisfied smile. "Go on, try it."

Sophie's the first to bite in. She lets out a low moan and closes her eyes. "Jesus, this is better than an orgasm," she says once she's swallowed it down.

"You're dating the wrong guys," Lauren points out. "But thank you."

I'm the next to try the donut, and Sophie wasn't lying. There's something so perfect about the mixture of soft sponge and oozy chocolate, along with the crunch of popcorn. "How do you keep the popcorn from going soft?" I ask Lauren.

"That's a trade secret." She winks, pleased. Then she eats her portion and a huge smile pulls at her lips. "Ooh, this could be my best yet. How can you think the world is a bad place when goodness like this exists?"

————

I toss and turn in bed for hours. I'd blame the sugar rush that came from Lauren's delicious donuts, but really it's all the worst case scenarios that are still rushing through my mind despite Sophie's attempts to coax them out.

When I was a child my mom told me that Mother Earth was once a person called Gaia. And that whatever happened to the world she would always try to bring things back to an equilibrium. That for every bad thing that happened, Gaia would make sure that at least two good things would cancel it out.

It was reassuring then, to know that good people always succeeded in the end. That Cinderella always became the princess, that Sleeping Beauty always woke up, that Belle's love made the beast become the prince again, and she got to live in a palace full of beautiful books.

Belle was always my favorite. Maybe because, like me, she was an only child. But I also loved her because she got to do things. She didn't have to sit around waiting for a pageboy to bring her a shoe, or for a prince to kiss her. When she heard the beast was in trouble she ran as fast as she could over there and fought for him. And when he was about to die, she saved him with her kiss.

I might be in my thirties, but there's a part of me that still believes good people get good things. Or at least there was until today. Now I don't know. I feel a bit adrift. Maybe this is what it's like to finally grow up.

Just before four in the morning I hear the rumble of an engine outside. Then the car door bangs and I wonder if my neighbors have been out partying again. But instead of the usual thunder of feet up their stairs – which adjoin to mine – someone thumps on the door.

My door.

I hesitate, wondering if I really heard that. But then it

comes again, and I hear shouting as well. And I know that voice. My insides twist up and I swallow hard.

My body feels heavy as I swing my feet to the floor and head down the stairs, not bothering to cover myself with a robe because this is Myles and let's face it, he's seen it all before. But I regret it when I pull the door open and I see he's not alone, though.

Next to him is Liam, who lifts a brow at my skimpy camisole and shorts.

"Um…" I look from him to Myles. "What's happening here?"

"Can we come in?" he asks gently. My heart clenches at the softness in his voice.

"I was asleep," I say, trying to explain why I look so bad right now.

"I know you were. And I'm sorry." Myles runs his hands through his hair. "But I need to talk to you."

It's only when he steps inside that I get a good look at him. He looks like crap, too. His hair is disheveled, there are dark shadows under his eyes, and there's a day's beard growth on his jaw. His clothes are creased and they're never creased.

I get a grim sense of satisfaction from that.

"Ava." Liam nods at me.

"Liam." I nod back. "How are you?"

"Tired." He smiles and there are creases around his eyes. But he doesn't look anywhere near as bad as Myles.

"Can I get you a drink?" I ask. "Or some food?"

"No thank you," Liam says. "We ate on the way."

In the midst of all this early morning chaos I'd forgotten they were supposed to be in New York. "Have you just driven here from New York?"

"Yep. No flights into Charleston until tomorrow." Liam lets out a long sigh. "And this idiot was in too much of a fucking state to drive alone."

"Oh-kay, so you drove back. But what does this have to do with me?"

Liam looks at Myles. "You should explain." Then he turns to me. "Can I use your bathroom?"

"Sure." I direct him to the one nearest to us, then lean on the hallway wall and look at Myles.

Once Liam is out of earshot, Myles runs his fingers through his thick hair again. I have to slide my hands behind my back to stop myself from reaching out to touch him. He looks exhausted and vulnerable and everything that's not him.

But most of all he looks so damn gorgeous I could cry.

"I need your help," he says softly.

That's the last thing I expect to hear. "What?"

"I need you to come to New York with me," he says. "In the morning."

"But you've just come back from there," I point out.

"Because you won't answer my calls."

I blink. "You drove five hours because I didn't pick up the phone?"

He takes a deep breath. "Your friends wouldn't pick up their phones either. Nor would anybody at Smith and Carson. Except Ryan." He doesn't blink a lash. "Who tells me that our baby should be named Damian and that if he ever sees me again I'm, in his words, 'fucking toast'."

"He was in a protective mood," I say.

"So I gather," Myles says dryly.

"Are you mad that he knows?" I ask him, because I'd be mad in the same situation. "I didn't tell him. Not at first. He was just listening in when he shouldn't have been."

"I'm not mad, Ava. I'm exhausted and worried and so damn sorry you wouldn't believe it. And I'm running the risk of losing my brother a lot of money."

"Wait, what?" I put my hand up, slowing his words. "What do you mean losing Liam's money?"

"It's a long story." He glances at his watch. "Can I tell you in the morning? I think I'm going to fall over if I don't lay down soon. I just needed to see you for myself. I need to know you're all right."

My heart clenches. That good girl inside me whispers excitedly, telling me I could make everything better by telling him it's okay. That I'm okay.

That the whole world is fine.

But it isn't. Yes, he drove for five hours in the middle of the night, but it wasn't only to check if I was okay, it was to see if I could help him.

Which is crazy because I have no idea how to do that.

"Yeah," I say, too tired to question him further. "I'll be better once I've had some sleep."

He looks at me carefully, then opens his mouth as though he wants to say something. Then he frowns and shuts it again.

"Have you asked her about New York?" Liam sounds way too chipper as he walks back into the front hall. "Because we should go."

"Are you going back now?" I ask, alarmed.

Liam smiles. "Nope. I want to go to Myles' place and sleep on his nice comfortable guest bed for three hours before we have to come pick you up and do this all over again." He gives me a careful look. "You will come, won't you?"

I look at Myles. His gaze doesn't waver for a moment. It's set on me the way my heart is set on him. "Are we driving back to New York?" I ask softly.

Myles and Liam exchange a glance, and I realize I've pretty much confirmed I'm going with that sentence. Because I will go. I'm not completely sure why, but maybe it's the fact that Myles has thrown himself at my mercy. He's asking for help – something he never does.

"Yep, I'm not leaving my car here," Liam says. "Not with the cum trees on every corner."

I rub my eyes with my hands, wondering if this is all a donut-induced dream. "So, what time are you leaving?" I ask.

"We're leaving at eight," Liam says, putting emphasis on the 'we'. "I'll bring coffee."

"Better make it decaf," I mutter. "And whatever you do, don't bring donuts."

CHAPTER
THIRTY-ONE

AVA

"What do you mean you're going to New York?" Sophie asks, her voice echoing through my phone speaker as I pointlessly dab concealer on the dark shadows under my eyes. "How long are you going for?"

"I don't know," I tell her, putting the concealer stick back in my makeup bag. It's only making me look worse.

"Why are you going anyway?"

I shake my head at my reflection in the bathroom mirror. "I don't know that either."

"And Myles' brother is driving you?" she asks.

"Yes. His name's Liam."

"What if they're trying to kidnap you and sell you as a sex slave?"

I try not to laugh because Sophie always thinks of the worst case scenario. Now that she's revealed her anxiety-reducing methods to me it all makes sense.

"I don't think they're going to do that. Myles said something about saving Liam's money."

"By them selling you!" Sophie squeaks. "Oh God, I should come with. Just let me call work and tell them I'm sick."

"No." I shake my head. "Please don't do that. It's fine, I'll go see what's happening in New York and then I'll come home. We'll meet up this weekend, the weather's going to be beautiful. Maybe the three of us can go for a picnic on Sunday."

"If they set you free by then," Sophie says grimly. "Listen, are you sure this is a good idea? Yesterday proves that Myles can't be trusted. And you're hurt and vulnerable and almost certainly still high from all that sugar."

I've been asking myself the same thing. I'm not really sure why I'm going to New York, to be honest. Myles and Liam weren't exactly forthcoming about their reasons for needing me. But there's something in my head that's telling me I need to go.

That, and the fact I like to be needed.

By eight, I'm standing at my front door with my overnight bag at my feet. I've already called Catherine and asked her to hold down the fort for the day. I promise to call in later, and she let me know not to worry because half the staff will be out with hangovers anyway. To be honest, she doesn't sound too hot herself.

But then neither do I.

A car stops outside of my house and through the frosted window in my front door I see a blurry shadow walk up the steps. My heart starts beating wildly in my chest and I have to give it a stern talking to.

I wait for him to knock, because there's no way I want him to think I'm eager to see him. Then I slowly unlatch the top lock and press down on the handle, basking in the knowledge that last night he looked as shitty as I did. And hopefully today he's still the same.

But. He. Is. Not.

He looks breathtaking in a dark gray suit and crisp white

shirt, his pale blue tie perfectly knotted. I look down at my jeans and t-shirt and frown.

"Am I supposed to be wearing something professional?" I ask.

"No. It's fine."

Actually, it isn't. "But you look all charming businessman and I look a mess."

His eyes catch mine. "You look beautiful." The way he says it makes my thighs quiver.

"I have some business clothes in my bag if I need them," I say, reaching down to pick up my overnight case. Myles goes to take it at exactly the same time and our fingers brush, making me a hormonal mess.

Seriously, my body needs to get the memo. He's back to being Myles the enemy, or at least something close to it. Not a love interest.

"Thank you for doing this," he says as I lock up my front door.

"I don't know what I'm doing yet," I point out. "Or if I'm going to do it."

"But you're coming with us to New York. That's more than I thought you'd agree to." He gently untangles my fingers from the handle of my bag and hoists it over his shoulder. "And you packed light for a change."

"I've only packed for one night. If I stay longer Sophie's going to launch a rescue mission. She thinks you're going to traffic me."

His lips twitch. "Would you like me to call and reassure her?"

"No. She'll probably bite your head off. You're not her favorite person right now." I get a grim sense of satisfaction from that.

He says nothing, just walks down the step with my bag and opens Liam's trunk, sliding it inside. Then he opens the passenger side front and back doors.

"Front or back?" he asks.

The nice girl inside of me screams that I should take the back. I have little legs and he has long ones, and the backs of expensive cars like Liam's rarely have enough leg space.

"The front," I say.

He doesn't blink. "Okay." He steps aside to let me in.

"I'll move the seat forward." Ah there's the nice girl. "To give you some more room."

"It's fine, Ava."

When I climb inside, Liam's watching me with amusement. "Good morning," he says. "There's a coffee for you there."

"Morning." I smile at him because he isn't the one who lied to me. "Did you sleep well?"

"As well as I could, considering that asshole just paced the floor all night." He inclines his head at the backseat, where Myles has just about managed to wedge himself in.

"I was making a plan," Myles protests.

"You were muttering. Loudly."

"You'll thank me later." Myles shakes his head. "We also got you some fruit and water. And we can stop whenever you need us to."

"Okay." I pick up the coffee cup. "Um, is this decaf?"

"Naturally." Liam rolls his eyes. "Myles reminded me ten times."

I lift the cup to my lips and Liam pulls from the curb, weaving through the treelined street and taking a right so he can head toward the highway. The city is just waking up – we don't do early here – and it looks beautiful in the morning sunlight. My heart clenches as we leave the historic district and weave our way to the river's edge. When we cross the river, the sun sparkling like diamonds on the surface, I can't keep it in any longer.

"Is somebody going to tell me what's going on?" I ask.

Liam looks into the rear view mirror and raises a brow. I

can only assume he's caught Myles' gaze.

"We're trying to save Liam's ass," Myles says.

"No we're not. We're trying to save *yours*," Liam replies, shaking his head. "Because you persuaded me that this whole thing was a good idea."

"It is a good idea," Myles replies. It would be funny watching the two of them bicker if I actually had an idea what they were bickering about. "Or it would have been. If Jean-Baptiste hadn't found out."

"Um, hello?" I wave my hand. "You two are only making things more confusing."

"Myles is trying to buy Smith and Carson," Liam says. "And I've been raising the capital for it. Finding investors, hedge funds, that kind of thing."

I twist in my seat. "You're buying Smith and Carson?" I ask him. "Why didn't you say anything?"

"Because I didn't want you to have to lie to the rest of your team. Or your friends. Or New York. I know you're not very good at it. I was trying to protect you, or I thought I was."

"I can lie," I respond, feeling annoyed. How could he have been doing this without me noticing? But then I remember the way he was always disappearing for a day. The calls he took while we were away. His discussions with Liam. I assumed it was family business.

And it was. Just not the way I imagined.

"I know," Myles says. "And I should have told you. I'm just trying to explain my faulty reasoning."

"Why are you buying Smith and Carson?" I ask, feeling slightly mollified by his confession.

"I wanted to buy it because I knew Mediatech was going to close you down eventually. And when I heard rumors that they were in direct discussion with Naomi about moving Dandy over, I had to accelerate things."

"And then they jumped the gun and announced early so if

we buy Smith and Carson now we're pretty much buying a business with no tangible assets," Liam says, shaking his head. "Basically, we're fucked."

"How much money is invested in this?" I ask, my stomach twisting.

"A lot," Liam says grimly.

"A million?" I venture.

"More."

"Two?"

Liam shakes his head. "More. Myles had a lot of plans for expansion. We needed to fund those as well as buy the business from Mediatech. And when I say buy, I mean do a hostile bid because Jean-Baptiste wouldn't want the shareholders to sell with Dandy there."

"So you stand to lose millions?" I ask quietly.

"Me and my investors, yes." Liam nods.

"And me," Myles says quietly. "I'm about to lose it all, too."

"How long have you been planning this?" Because this isn't something you cook up overnight.

"For six months," he tells me.

I blink. "Six months? But Richard was still chief editor then."

"I know," Myles says. "But the writing has been on the wall for Smith and Carson for a long time."

"I don't understand. Why would you want to save it?"

"Because it's a good publisher. It has good staff." He exhales softly. "And it has you."

My heart clenches. I don't know how much more the poor organ can take. I feel like I'm on some kind of hallucinogenic trip where everything I thought I knew was wrong.

"I thought you hated us. Hated being here."

"It was never in my plan to move to Charleston," he tells me. "The idea was for Liam's investors to take over and I'd be the silent partner. But when Richard was shown the door, I needed to step in. Make sure Smith and Carson was still a going concern until we were ready to take over."

"But how can I help?" I ask. "I'm not good with numbers. And I certainly don't know any investors."

"We need you to talk to Naomi," Myles says. "We've asked for a meeting with her and she'll only do it if you come."

I swallow. "Naomi wants me there?" I thought she'd turned her back on me completely.

"She's your biggest fan. She's only just discovered that you knew nothing about the Dandy move. They'd told her you were on board with it. She's pissed."

"But she's already signed the contract, hasn't she?" I ask. "With New York?"

Myles nods. "We want you to persuade her to break it. That's the only way we can save this deal and save Smith and Carson. Otherwise…"

"It's goodnight, Vienna," Liam says.

"She'll never break a contract," I whisper. "She's too upright. Too straight down the line. She believes in keeping her word." She's like me. Believes that good things come to good people.

We've both been duped.

"Will you try anyway?" Myles asks. "Please?"

I look at him over my shoulder. Despite his perfect grooming he still looks tired. His eyes catch mine and for a moment the car is silent. Emotions course through me, making my fingers shake and my heart speed in my chest.

I was in love with this man only days ago. I would have done anything for him.

Will I still do that?

"I'll try," I tell him, even though I know it's futile. I'll try anyway because I wasn't just in love with him, I still am. And I don't want him or his brother to lose everything. "I just wish you'd told me about this before."

"I was trying to protect you," he says. "I know that sounds counterintuitive, especially after the past few days, but it's true."

"He tries to protect everybody," Liam says. "Ask him how that's going for him."

"Shut up," Myles says mildly. Then he looks back at me, his expression soft. "I'm sorry you had to find out the way you did. There's only one flight a day from Charleston to New York. I had to be on it to try to save things. I wanted to tell you face to face. I just couldn't."

"Everyone thought you'd run away to avoid the fall out."

"I know." He nods, his face grim. "I can see how it must have looked that way."

"I thought you did, too," I confess. "I'm sorry I said all those things to you."

"You don't need to be sorry." There's a yearning in his voice. "I'm the one who's sorry. For not telling you what was going on. For not realizing that New York had stopped trusting me. I should have known they were in negotiations with Naomi. Jean-Baptiste went behind my back when we were otherwise engaged." His eyes flash and I realize that he's annoyed as hell about that.

"Shoulda spoken to her earlier," Liam says. "I told you that."

"Yes, you did," Myles says tightly.

The drive to New York takes just over six hours. We only made one stop – the coffee had gone right through me, and Liam needed to check his phone and make some calls. I'm so aware of Myles' eyes on me constantly. It's like he wants to say something and has no idea what.

But I can't think about that now. I'm too busy thinking about Catherine and Ryan and everybody back at Smith and Carson. If I can't persuade Naomi to stay they'll be out of a job.

And so will I.

We arrive in the middle of the afternoon, and Liam drives into the center of Manhattan. The sound of car engines and horns and pneumatic drills fill the air as we slowly head bumper to bumper through the city. I've been to New York more than a few times, but it still feels like another planet. People rush here, and don't smile or spend the time of day with each other. And everything's so big. I crane my head to look at the top of the skyscrapers. Just like in Charleston, the sky is blue, but there's a haze to it, and I can spot three helicopters hovering like flies.

Eventually, Liam hits his indicator and pulls into a parking garage beneath a huge tower made of reflective glass. I wince as he turns into the smallest space I've ever seen, yet he manages to do it without scraping the sides of his beautiful car.

"Okay," he says, pulling at his door handle. "Let's do this."

Myles squeezes out of the backseat and helps me out of my own. The three of us walk toward the bank of elevators at the far end of the garage. Liam swipes a card and hits the call button, and within a few seconds the door opens.

"We're running a little late," Liam says, checking his watch. "Naomi and her agent will be here in twenty minutes. Do you want to freshen up?" he asks me.

"Yes please." I need a minute alone to center myself. Although, after everything that's happened in the last forty-eight hours, I'm pretty sure I'll need more than a minute.

The elevator shoots up smoothly to the forty-eighth floor, where Liam walks to the left and Myles puts his hand on my back to steer me to the right. A huge metal sign proclaims this floor belongs to Salinger Industries. Liam's done well for himself.

Or at least he has until he got involved with Smith and Carson.

"Are you okay?" Myles asks softly once we're alone in the corridor.

I swallow. "I don't know. I'm just... confused. And anxious." On the plus side, I'm pretty sure they're not going to sell me as a sex slave in this swanky office building.

"The bathroom is there," he tells me, pointing at a solid wood door to our left. "I'll get some food sent up. You need to eat."

"I'm not hungry."

"You've only eaten a banana today. And two cups of decaf. You need food."

I open my mouth to argue with him, but I know he's right.

"Okay. Thank you."

He reaches out to cradle my face and I feel the burn of his touch against my skin. "Thank *you*," he says. "For coming here. For trying to help."

My chest feels tight. I nod silently.

"The boardroom is the third door on the right when you come out. Liam and I will be in there."

"Are you sure I shouldn't be wearing business clothes?"

He shakes his head. "No, you look perfect."

He's still cupping my face. I feel a tight yearning inside me. "I should go..."

Myles nods and releases me. "Take your time. We can wait."

I take less than five minutes. Most of that is taken by me leaning against the wall and worrying that I'm going to fail. They all think Naomi and I have this close relationship, but really, how close can it be if she didn't tell me about this new contract?

When I walk into the boardroom the sandwiches are already there, along with those insulated casks of coffee you always see at office meetings, along with a jug of water and another with orange juice.

Myles jumps out of his seat. "Would you like coffee?" he asks. "We have decaf. Or orange juice if you prefer."

"Orange juice sounds great. Thank you."

"Take whatever sandwiches you want." He looks me dead in the eye. "There's no soft cheese, no cured meats. And the mayonnaise is safe."

It takes me a moment to work out what he's talking about. He's worried about me eating things that pregnant women can't.

I could be pregnant with his baby right now. The thought sends a shiver down my spine.

"Thank you," I murmur and load two little triangles onto my plate, along with an apple because I really need to counteract those donuts I ate last night. If I am pregnant, I need to start taking care of myself.

If I don't, I have a feeling that Myles will. Regardless of if we're together or apart, I know he wants the best for me.

Liam's phone shrills and he looks at the message. "They're here," he says. "You ready for this?"

"Do I have enough time to eat something?"

"Yes you do," Myles says firmly. Liam bites down a smile.

Lauren was right last night. I'm not used to being taken care of. I don't know what to do when it happens.

"Ava," Naomi calls out as soon as the boardroom door opens. I stand and she envelops me in a bear hug. I hug her back because despite everything, I truly like her.

Who couldn't like somebody who invented a kind lion?

"I'm so sorry," she continues. "They told me you knew. That you couldn't be at the meetings because you were working on something else." She frowns. "I would never have done this if I'd known you'd be out of a job."

"It's okay," I say, my throat tight. "You didn't know." Behind her is her agent. Elizabeth Horton is a bear when it comes to negotiating contracts. And protecting Naomi. As it should be. "Hi Elizabeth," I say.

"Ava. It's good to see you."

Myles and Liam come to shake their hands and Liam suggests we all sit down.

"Can I get you a drink?" he asks Naomi and Elizabeth. "Water? Coffee? Juice?"

"Just water for me," Naomi says, and Elizabeth asks for the same.

Once everybody is seated – Naomi and Elizabeth on one side of the shiny wooden table, Myles, Liam, and me on the other – Liam leans forward and rests his elbows on the surface. He looks at Myles who nods.

"As you know, my brother and I have agreed on an initial buy out of Smith and Carson, and we'd very much like you to be part of our publishing house."

Naomi winces.

"I understand that you've already agreed to a new contract with Mediatech, but we're asking you to reconsider."

"We've already signed," Elizabeth says. "It's too late."

"We're willing to work with you to break the contract," Myles says. "Ava has some exciting ideas to take Dandy into the future."

I do? Oh shit. I smile and nod. "Working with you has been the greatest privilege of my career." That's no word of a lie. "The thought of losing you from Smith and Carson breaks my heart."

Naomi sniffs. "I know. It breaks mine, too."

Elizabeth pats her hand. "But there are a lot of exciting things in Dandy's future. The team here in New York is talking about television rights, and possibly a movie. And all those merchandising rights." She smiles. "No need to be so despondent. And Ava, I'm sure if we talk to them they'll offer you a job here. That way you can still work with Naomi."

Myles shifts in his seat. I feel my pulse rise by about a thousand beats per minute. "I can't move to New York," I tell Naomi. "I love Charleston too much."

"I understand," Naomi says. "I couldn't spend longer than a few days here either. It's too scary."

Naomi doesn't like being anywhere but at her beautiful sprawling home in the mountains. I can't say I blame her.

"Is there any way we can change your mind?" I ask, looking first at Naomi and then at Elizabeth.

"I've never broken my word in my life," Naomi says. "And as angry as I am that they lied to me, I still can't do it."

My shoulders slump. So that's it. We're done for. And yes, I mean we. Because I'm in love with Myles, no matter how stubborn he is.

And I'm not letting him take the fall alone.

"Will you be all right?" Naomi asks. "You'll still have a job?"

I look at Myles. His expression is unreadable. "Ava will always be all right," he says. And I believe him. For the first time ever, I feel like I will be. My heart is breaking over Dandy and over the fact that Myles and Liam are about to lose big time on this deal, but the sun will still rise and life will still go on.

"Thank you anyway," I say. "For coming here and listening."

"I just wish there was something else I could do," Naomi says. "If only there was a way to divide Dandy into two."

And that's when an idea hits me like a bolt of pure lightening. I frown, because it can't be that easy, can it? I let the idea percolate in my mind for a minute as we all sit in silence ruminating.

Then I look at Elizabeth. "Is there a non-compete clause in Naomi's new contract?"

She shakes her head. "You know I'd never let them put one in. But if you're thinking what I think you're thinking, we've signed away the next five Dandy books. There's no way you could have him for at least five years."

"That's not what I'm thinking." My voice turns excited.

Myles looks at me curiously. Liam is just frowning. And Naomi is looking hopeful because I know she wants a happy ending as much as I do.

"How about we work together on a completely different project?" I ask, glancing over at Myles and Liam. Myles leans forward, looking interested. Liam looks at Myles.

"What kind of project?" Elizabeth asks warily.

"A brand new character," I tell them. "One with the goodness of Dandy but maybe with a little more edge." I don't look at Myles but I'm certain he's smiling. "Dandy's wonderful but he doesn't always take a risk. He doesn't always put himself first. And though it's great to be self-sacrificing, we want to teach kids that it's also okay to stand up for yourself. That there's a balance to be found. And I know you'd create the perfect character to do it."

"A brand new character," Naomi says, twisting her fingers together. "That sounds interesting."

"I'd work with you every step of the way," I tell her. "Remember when Julia Donaldson wrote *The Gruffalo*? And everybody thought she was a one-trick author? But then she came out with *No Room on the Broom* and showed them all how stupid they were."

"Maybe a girl character," Naomi says. "Or we could have two. A brother and sister."

"This already sounds wonderful." I grin as excitement shoots through me. "I love the idea of siblings." I look at Myles and Liam who are staring at me with wide eyes. "Do you think that would work for the business?"

Liam looks at Myles who nods. "Yeah," he says, his voice low. "I really think that could work."

For the first time there's hope in their eyes. And I can't keep the excitement down. Working with Naomi on Dandy has been amazing. But a chance to bring a whole new series and character to life? That's out of this world.

"It's a risk," I say, because I want to downplay expectations, especially my own. "But a calculated one. You're a name that sells books."

Naomi beams. "I'm excited." She looks at Elizabeth. "We can make this happen, right?"

"There's no legal reason why we can't," Elizabeth says. "We'd have to discuss terms, of course."

"Absolutely," Myles says. "We're more than happy to do that."

Naomi looks at me. "I'm so happy we can work together again. I hated knowing I was causing problems."

"I'm happy, too. This could turn out to be the best thing that's happened to all of us."

"And on that note, we should call your driver," Elizabeth says to Naomi. "I promised I'd get you home by tonight."

"That would be wonderful. It's always exhilarating to come to New York, but it takes me weeks to recover afterward." Naomi shakes her head. "And now I've got some new characters to think about."

We all stand and Myles, Liam, and I walk around the table. I hug Naomi while Myles talks quietly to Elizabeth. Then they leave and the door swings behind them and I collapse heavily into the nearest chair.

"I'm sorry," I tell them. "I know it's not what you wanted, but it was the best idea I had."

"You don't need to be sorry," Myles says. "You were amazing."

Liam nods. "Yep. I'm pretty sure I can keep our investors happy once we've signed on for the newest creation by Naomi Acres." He leans forward to kiss my cheek. "I can't thank you enough."

"You don't have to give me this job," I tell them. "I spoke out of turn saying I could work with her. I'm sure she'd understand if…"

I'm silenced by the press of warm lips against mine. Myles pulls me out of my chair and kisses me until I'm dizzy. I curl my arms around his neck to steady myself before I'm kissing him back, our lips moving, our hands stroking, as though we can't get enough of each other.

"I'm still here," Liam reminds us.

Myles pulls away, leaving me hot and breathless. I feel myself blushing while he doesn't look flustered at all.

"I'm sorry," he says. "I just needed to—"

"Shut me up," I finish for him.

His smile is disarming. "No, I meant I just needed you to know how fantastic you are. And of course we want you working for us. We want you to be the chief editor. I'll run the business side of things and Liam will be the silent partner."

"Is he ever silent?"

Myles shakes his head. "No."

Liam rolls his eyes. "I'm going to make some calls," he says. "And then I'm going to the nearest bar to drink so much whiskey my body won't know what to do with it." He winks at me. "Have a good evening, kids."

"Thank you," Myles says. The two of them share a look. "I'll call you later."

"Don't bother, I'll be busy," Liam says. "Just send greasy food over tomorrow. I'll need it." He lifts his hand in farewell and walks out, heading, I assume, to his office.

Leaving the two of us alone.

I look up at him, taking in his beautiful, beloved face. He's staring back at me with such passion that I can't believe he is capable of hurting me.

He's too lovely. Too caring. Too kind for that.

"Unless you want another five hour car ride, I suggest you stay here overnight and we'll get you back to Charleston tomorrow."

"That would be good." I nod. "Thank you."

"I can get you booked into a hotel. Or…" He takes a deep breath. "You can come to my place. There doesn't have to be any funny business. I have a spare room that you can have."

Tears prick my eyes because it's been a long day. I shake my head. "I don't think so."

He nods. "Fair enough. Let me get Liam's assistant to make you a hotel reservation. Anywhere in particular you'd like?"

"No, I mean I don't want to sleep in your spare room. I want to sleep in *your* room." He looks confused so I try to simplify it. "With you."

"I have no idea how big your apartment is," I continue. "But I want to use every inch. I want you to take me in the shower, in the kitchen, on your sofa. I want you to bury yourself inside of me until we're so breathless we can't form any words. I want to be in your arms because that's the only place I feel safe and tonight I really, really want to feel safe."

His jaw tics. "Fuck, Ava."

"Exactly," I tell him. "Exactly that."

He smiles and I remember just how glorious a happy Myles Salinger is. He reaches for my waist, pulling me into his arms and I immediately relax against him. When he kisses me this time, it's slow and deliberate and it sends electric tingles to the tips of my toes.

"I'm sorry I hurt you," he tells me when we break apart. He still has his arms wrapped around my waist. "I should have told you what was happening."

"You should have." I nodded. "I could have helped. But I should have trusted you, too. I thought the worst and that was wrong."

His gaze softens. "I'll never give you a reason not to trust me," he promises. "And I'll try to tone down the protective part."

I smile. "And sometimes I'll let you protect me for the hell of it."

"That sounds good."

I nod. "If we're agreed on that, can you take me home?"

"Yes. Let's go."

CHAPTER
THIRTY-TWO

AVA

We're like horny teenagers, barely able to keep our hands off each other as we kiss our way out of the cab and into his apartment building, then paw at each other in the *thankfully* empty elevator until we reach his floor.

It takes him twice the amount of time it should for him to open his door because I'm clinging to him like I'm never going to let go. From the way he pulls me inside and slams the door shut behind me, I don't think he wants me to either.

"Nice apartment," I murmur as he slides his palm up my neck, angling my head to kiss me again. My back is against the door, his solid body holding me in place as he kisses me so hard and deep I forget my own... what was I saying?

I slide my hands inside his jacket, feeling the warmth of his skin through his perfectly tailored white shirt. How the hell isn't it creased after those hours in the car? That's a question I decide to store away for another day, because I have more important things to think about now.

Like the way his muscles feel like steel beneath his hot

skin. Or the way he slides his hands down to my behind and lifts me up, sandwiching me against the door as I wrap my legs around his hips.

And oh, Lord, his muscles aren't the only thing made of steel. He's hard and thick and I find myself wishing I wasn't wearing jeans because they're so not easy access. He doesn't seem to mind, though, as he plunders my lips and strokes my sides until I'm a jelly-like mess in his arms. With my own still wrapped around his neck, he staggers back and mutters something about his bedroom and being too old for this.

"Did you just say you're too old for knee tremblers?" I ask him.

"Knee tremblers?" He laughs. "What the hell kind of thing is that?"

"When you stand up and have sex. A quickie. It's a knee trembler. My mom…" I trail off because this is another direction I don't want to go in. "Never mind," I say quickly. "Where's your bedroom?"

He puts me down and pulls me with obscene haste to the door on the far side of the hallway. His room isn't grand like I'd expected it to be. It's cozy and warm and has the most comfortable looking bed I've ever seen. I kick off my shoes and throw myself on the mattress.

Yep, definitely comfortable.

For a moment he stares at me. I return his gaze, waiting for him to pounce again, because my body has a thing for being attacked by this man. In the nicest possible way, of course.

But he takes too long and I start to squirm. "What are you doing?" I ask him.

"Just looking." His voice is thick. "And marveling."

"Marveling? What about?"

"That Ava Quinn is laying on my bed looking all flushed and beautiful like she wants me to touch her all over."

"I do," I tell him. "So hurry up please."

But he won't be hurried. He's a measured man. He clearly likes to drag things out. I remember the way he wouldn't come until I was ovulating. Which reminds me…

"You know I'm not ovulating anymore, right?"

"I can do the math."

"And you still want me?" I ask.

He looks incredulous. "More than ever, baby."

"Then what are you waiting for?"

He walks to the bed, his gaze never leaving mine. It's full of aching need and sends a shiver down my spine. He folds his fingers around my ankles and pulls me forward, his bedsheets ruffling around me, then he leans over me to unzip my jeans. I arch my back and do a weird shuffle to help him pull them down, then sit up and pull off my t-shirt.

His eyes darken more as he takes me in. "It's your turn," I tell him, because I will never, *ever* get bored of watching Myles Salinger undress.

I also won't get bored of his strong, muscled chest. Or those thick legs that can scale trees and run sprints before making me quiver like I've never quivered before.

When he's left only in his boxers, he climbs onto the bed, hovering over me. His knees nudge mine and I open for him, reaching my hands up as he lowers his lips to mine.

And if I thought kissing him fully dressed was hot, this is pretty much melting my world. My body heats as he slides his lips down my throat, my chest, then pulls at my nipple through the thin fabric of my bra. Desire flickers and licks at me as he unfastens it, exposing my chest to the air and making me shiver in the air conditioned room.

I push at his boxers and he lifts himself up to help me. Then he pulls down my panties, his fingers sliding down my calves as he pulls them from my ankles.

And I'm naked. In Myles Salinger's bedroom. He's kissing me again, and there's a funny feeling in my chest. It's like when you run too fast in the cold and your lungs get all heavy and you have to bend in half to recapture your breath.

"Myles," I say.

He kisses my jaw, my cheek, my eyelid. "Yes?"

"I need to tell you something."

He blinks, bemused. "What, beautiful?"

"I used to think I hated you." It hurts me to say it now, but I need it out there. I want complete honesty with this man. I want to open up and let him inside.

It's scary and it makes me feel vulnerable but it's oh-so-real.

"I used to think you hated me, too," he murmurs. He doesn't look hurt. Just interested in what I have to say.

And I realize this is how he always looks when we talk. The scowling wasn't anger. He was concentrating.

"But I love you," I tell him. "So much it hurts."

His expression softens. He swallows and stares but says nothing. It's only when he lets out a long breath that I realize he's been holding it.

"You have no idea how much I needed to hear that." His voice is soft. He tenderly brushes the hair from my face. "You're everything to me. *Everything*. You have been for so much longer than you know."

I put that thought aside to mull over later and reach for him, my hands sliding along his shoulders, my knees grazing his hips. He's there, just where I need him. I feel the pressure of his thickness, pushing against me, opening me up. My throat feels tight as he slides inside and all I can think is that I'll never get tired of this.

Never.

"I love you," he gasps as his hips find their rhythm. My fingers tangle in his hair and tears tickle at my eyes because I'm not sure how to deal with all this emotion. "So much, Ava. So much." His words are short and staccato, punctuated by his heavy breaths as we cling to each other. "You're mine," he says. It's half possessive, half in wonder.

"Yes, I am," I whisper, feeling the familiar burn deep inside of me. This man knows exactly how to touch me. How to coax every feeling out of me until I'm wrung dry. "Always," I whisper, because it's true. I've been his so much longer than I realized.

And I'm going to be his forever.

And when we tumble over the edge together, clinging to each other as we kiss hot and heavy, it's everything I've ever dreamed of.

He's mine and I'm his and tomorrow we'll tell the team at Smith and Carson that he's somehow managed to save everybody's jobs. That we all have a future thanks to him.

And if they cause him any problems, they'll have me to face. Because he's mine to protect. Mine to love.

"Is it too late to talk about birth control?" I ask him as he gently pulls out, making my body quiver all over again.

"Much too late," he tells me, pressing his lips to mine. "And I'm absolutely okay with that."

MYLES

"How are you feeling?" I ask her as she curls into my arms and smiles up at me.

"How do you think?" she asks. "You just rearranged my insides. Twice."

I laugh. "I hope not. I like your insides exactly the way they are." I kiss the tip of her nose, then her lips, savoring the taste of her. "Just like the outside."

"It might all change soon," she says. "If I'm pregnant."

I stare down at her. "I hope you are."

Her lip curls. "You do? I was wondering if you were regretting the whole thing."

"Why would I regret it?" My brows pinch together. "I'm in love with you."

"Yeah, but that wasn't part of the arrangement, was it? I was supposed to have the baby and take care of it myself. And now it's…" Her eyes cloud up. "Complicated."

"What's complicated about loving you and hoping you're pregnant?" I don't get it. It feels simple to me. She's my everything and she could be having my child. What man wouldn't want that?

Me a few months ago. But we won't go there, because right now it's all I want.

"So you'd be okay if I was pregnant?" she asks warily.

"I'd be ecstatic. I want this, Ava. I want you and I want our baby. I want it all." I shake my head, because she doesn't seem to understand how I feel about her. "I know it's not what you had planned. And if you still don't want me involved, I'll understand that. I'll hate it, but I'll understand. I already signed my rights away in a contract and if you want me to keep to that, I will."

Her expression softens. "Of course I want you involved," she tells me. "I want you to be the father of my children."

"Children?" I smile.

"If possible. I'm not getting any younger so we'd have to do it fast."

I grin. "Exactly what every man dreams of hearing."

She wrinkles her nose at me. "You're an ass."

"So I've been told."

"But you're my ass."

My grin widens. "There's no doubt about that. I've been yours since the day we met."

Her gaze softens. She reaches up to cup my jaw. "I love you so much."

"I love you too, beautiful."

Then she curls around me and falls asleep.

——————

AVA

I'm still cozy and warm the next morning when Myles wakes me up with an insistent kiss. It's like my body knows exactly how to react, so I reach for him, my hands sliding down his bare back, my chest arching to his.

"Not so fast," he murmurs. "You need to get up and shower. We have a video conference at ten."

Blinking, I look over his shoulder at the alarm clock nestled on his bedside table. It's almost nine. "Uh?" I say. "Who are we talking to?"

"Charleston. I called Catherine. She's making sure everybody comes in."

I swallow. "Shouldn't we do this face to face?" I ask.

"Ordinarily, yes. But the rumor mill is already circling at Mediatech, which means we have about two hours before the whispers reach Charleston. We'll announce the changes by video conference then drive back so we're there in time for the end of the day. It's Friday, I'll treat everybody to champagne. The real stuff."

"Um, they're not exactly your fans right now." I was hoping to have some time to talk to them all. To do some rehabilitation on his character. "They think you ran out on them. And on me." I grimace. "After trying to get me pregnant."

He doesn't look perturbed at all. I wonder what it's like to be so at ease with yourself that you don't care what other people think.

Maybe it'll rub off on me. Maybe he'll rub off on me. And then I'm all flushed again and he's lifting an eyebrow at me.

"Later," he tells me curtly. I pout.

"Before we leave for Charleston?" I ask hopeful.

"You're insatiable," he whispers, sliding his hand around my naked waist. "Don't ever change."

I honestly don't think I can. It's like some kind of dam has been breached inside of me. I love him and he loves me and now I can't stop thinking about how it feels to be under him.

Or over him.

Also laying spooned together – him the big spoon, of course, as he gently slides inside of me and we sleepily make love.

It was a busy night. No wonder I'm exhausted.

An hour later, I'm a little more awake. Myles has set up his home office so that we're both sitting in front of the video cam. On the screen we can see all the confused faces of the Smith and Carson employees as they take in what we've just told them.

"So, we're not working for Mediatech anymore?" Ryan says. "But we still have jobs?"

"That's right. Smith and Carson is being bought by Salinger Enterprises."

"And you're okay with that?" Ryan asks me. He's obviously their unofficial spokesman. I should have called him and Catherine earlier and told them exactly how much of a savior Myles is. But I was too busy watching him get dressed. If I thought watching him strip was enticing, watching him meticulously button his shirt and knot his tie is out of this world.

It took everything I had not to untie it so he'd have to do it all over again.

"Smith and Carson has a great future thanks to the investment from Myles and his brother," I say honestly. "And the fact we have Naomi on board is icing on the cake. We have a steady base to build from, and that's exactly what we're going to do. Look for brand new voices, work with those we already have, and continue to build our relationship with schools and educators. Honestly, I'm really excited about this."

Ryan nods, his lips pressed together. "But what about…" he nods. "You know."

"You're going to have to spell it out," Myles says. He doesn't look annoyed that they're questioning his integrity.

"You ran out on Ava after trying to get her pregnant," Ryan says, frowning. "I don't understand why she's forgiving you."

Out of view of the camera, Myles threads his fingers through mine and squeezes my hand. "Do you want to take this one or shall I?" he asks.

"I'll do it." I take a deep breath and look at the screen. Nobody moves an inch. "Myles didn't run out on us. Or on me. He came to New York to secure the funding to save Smith and Carson. He just didn't have the time, or go-ahead, to let us know what was happening."

"And you trust him now?" Ryan asks. He winces and I'm almost certain that Catherine has just elbowed him in the ribs.

I look at Myles. He's so beautiful it makes me ache. "Yes, I trust him," I say softly. The hint of a smile flickers at his lips. "I trust him completely and irrevocably. He only wants the best for us."

Ryan nods tightly, but says nothing. Catherine beams wildly. And the rest of the team looks too relieved about their jobs to care about what's happening in my personal life.

Thank God.

"So what happens next?" Catherine asks.

"You carry on working as normal," Myles tells her. "We have books to release and authors to work with. None of that will change. I'll be working on ways we can streamline things on the business end but none of you have to worry about your jobs. And if you can get through today, Ava and I will be there by early evening with champagne. And maybe some food, too."

Everybody starts talking at once. Some of them laugh about something, while others are leaning forward and whispering in each others' ears. But all of them look relieved.

"And how about you?" one of the accountants asks Myles. "You said that Ava will be the Chief Editor, so does that mean you'll be going back to New York?"

My breath catches in my throat. We haven't actually had this conversation. I have no idea what he wants.

I know that he loves me, but I don't know how that's going to work in practice. I feel my chest start to tighten.

As though he can sense my panic, Myles moves my hand down until both of our fingers are touching my thigh. He squeezes softly.

"I'll be mostly in Charleston," he says. "Because that's where the woman I love is. But I'll travel to New York for meetings when necessary."

A breath escapes my lips. It's my turn to smile, because I still can't quite believe this is true. I have the man of my dreams and the job of my dreams, and maybe, just maybe, the family of my dreams, too.

I didn't think that life would work out this way. That everything I ever wanted would finally be in my grasp.

But it's here. He's here. Sitting by my side, caressing my hand with his, making me feel safe and so in love.

Dreams do come true, and ever afters can be happy. I should have believed the books all along.

EPILOGUE

AVA

I stare at the stick as the first tiny line appears. Then hold my breath as I glance at the timer on my phone. The box promises a result in three minutes, but it's less than twenty seconds before the second line appears and my heart starts to clatter in my chest.

I'm pregnant. Don't get me wrong, it's early days. This test can detect the pregnancy hormone before I've even missed a period.

But the lines don't lie – and by the time I take a second test I'm convinced that it's true.

Myles and I are having a baby.

I wasn't upset when I got my period after the second month that we tried. I even wondered if it might be a good thing. We sat down and talked long and hard about it, but

Myles insisted that if I was ready to be a mom that we should keep trying.

And so we have. Not that it's been a hardship. We still can't keep our hands off each other. Every time he travels to New York I'm patiently waiting for him to come home, and then I pretty much launch myself at him as soon as he's through the door, unable to keep away from him.

Things at Smith and Carson are going well. I've been spending a lot of time with Naomi who's come up with a brilliant concept. Twin kittens – a boy and a girl – who are abandoned to the street before being adopted by a tiger. Yes, a tiger. It makes sense when you read it and it's so lovely, but also so modern.

We launch next year and I can't wait. Naomi is already the talk of the town.

I hear the front door open and I look at the tests again. He's back from New York and it's time to tell him. I run down the stairs to see him dropping his travel bag on the polished wooden floor. He looks tired but delicious, and I know that later I'm going to nag him about getting some sleep, but right now I need him awake.

"Guess what?" I say.

"Your mom's been arrested again?"

"Nope." I grin, because he actually loves my mom. I introduced the two of them properly the weekend after we got back and she told him that even though she hates the patriarchy she'll make an exception for him, as long as he keeps me happy.

Which he does. He's made it his personal mission. Damn, I love this man.

His mom and Deandra are equally as welcoming to me. We visited them in New York last month and they insisted on taking me out for lunch without Myles. It was fun – we had cocktails (well, mocktails for me) and tapas while Myles apparently paced up and down in Liam's office asking if it was too early to pick me up.

We've even been to visit his dad and Julia. She's really starting to show now. I don't think we'll ever be besties with them, but at least they're all trying to get along.

And this baby will have a huge family waiting to welcome him or her.

"What is it then?" Myles asks, pulling me in for a kiss. "Has Ryan beaten the world record for donut eating? Has Sophie discovered a cyclone that's going to level Charleston?"

That's another wonderful thing. He adores Sophie and Lauren and they love him. Some of that is due to the fact that he'll pick us up from anywhere at any time, no matter how drunk they are or how far away he is.

But mostly they see how happy he makes me. That's enough for them.

"No," I say, grinning. "I've just decided to set up a focus group. I thought it would be a good way to test out our future projects. Go straight to the source and ask the kids what they want from books."

He blinks. "Oh. Okay. When's that happening?"

"In about eight months." I tip my head to the side. "Or three years if we need them to be able to give proper feedback, I guess. Three more if they need to be able to read."

He stares at me, uncomprehending. "Why so long?"

"Because I have to grow it first," I whisper.

Understanding washes over his face. His eyes sparkle, as he reaches for me again, a huge smile on his face. "You're pregnant?" he asks.

"I just tested."

"Fuck, Ava…"

"That's how it happened." I love teasing him, and he makes it so easy. He smiles and strokes my hair and I feel warmth wash over me. "It's simple, really."

"No, baby," he says, his hands warm on my back. "It's not simple. It's a goddamn miracle."

"You're happy?" I ask him.

"I'm ecstatic." His grin widens. "You're having my baby. Why wouldn't I be happy?"

"Because it's somebody else to look after. You have enough people to worry about already."

"Yeah, well maybe I like worrying about you. And him or her. You're my people. It's my job."

"So you're ready to be a dad?" I ask him.

"I've been ready for a lot longer than you think," he admits, cupping my face and kissing me. "You've made me the happiest man alive."

Tears prick at my eyelids. "Thank you for being perfect," I whisper. "I can't believe you're here. And I have everything I've ever wanted."

"You're the perfect one," he growls, his eyes grazing my face like he can't bear to look away. "I love you, sweetheart."

And I love him, too. So much. I can't believe I ever felt differently about him. But that's the thing about life. Sometimes it likes to take you by surprise, jumping out and shouting 'boo' when you least expect it.

"When can we tell people?" he asks me.

"I don't know. Maybe wait until I'm three months along?"

He grimaces but nods. "You're right. But it's going to kill me."

"You could tell Liam," I suggest. "I'll probably tell Lauren and Sophie."

"Let's just not tell them together," he says, because Liam and Sophie have something against each other.

That's a whole other story, and Lauren and I think it's sexual tension, but still, they're going to have to get over it if they're going to be godparents to our baby.

"It's a deal," he says, pressing his lips to mine. "Oh, and one other thing."

"What?" I ask because what more could there be? I already have everything I ever wanted.

He lifts my palm to his lips and presses a soft kiss there, before folding my fingers over it. Then he gives me that sexy smile that nobody else ever sees. "We're definitely getting married before the baby comes."

Want more of Strictly Business?
If you're not quite ready to let Myles and Ava go, get a glimpse of their happily ever after in this exclusive bonus epilogue.
Just put the following code in your browser: https://dl.bookfunnel.com/hhkoceavx0

And if you enjoyed Myles and Ava's story, the next book in the Salinger Brother's series is STRICTLY PLEASURE - Liam and Sophie's story. Find out what happens when the two godparents clash!

DEAR READER

Thank you so much for reading Myles and Ava's story. If you enjoyed it and you get a chance, I'd be so grateful if you can leave a review.

WANT TO KEEP UP TO DATE ON ALL MY NEWS?

Join me on my exclusive mailing list, where you'll be the first to hear about new releases, sales, and other book-related news.

To sign up put this web address into your browser: https://www.subscribepage.com/carrieelksas

I can't wait to share more stories with you.

Yours,

Carrie xx

ABOUT THE AUTHOR

Carrie Elks writes contemporary romance with a sizzling edge. Her first book, *Fix You*, has been translated into eight languages and made a surprise appearance on *Big Brother* in Brazil. Luckily for her, it wasn't voted out.

Carrie lives with her husband, two lovely children and a larger-than-life black pug called Plato. When she isn't writing or reading, she can be found baking, drinking an occasional (!) glass of wine, or chatting on social media.

You can find Carrie in all these places
www.carrieelks.com
carrie.elks@mail.com

ALSO BY CARRIE ELKS

THE SALINGER BROTHERS SERIES

A swoony romantic comedy series featuring six brothers and the strong and smart women who tame them.

Strictly Business

Strictly Pleasure

Strictly For Now

THE WINTERVILLE SERIES

A gorgeously wintery small town romance series, featuring six cousins who fight to save the town their grandmother built.

Welcome to Winterville

Hearts In Winter

Leave Me Breathless

Memories Of Mistletoe

Every Shade of Winter

ANGEL SANDS SERIES

A heartwarming small town beach series, full of best friends, hot guys and happily-ever-afters.

Let Me Burn

She's Like the Wind

Sweet Little Lies

Just A Kiss

Baby I'm Yours

Pieces Of Us

Chasing The Sun

Heart And Soul

Lost In Him

THE HEARTBREAK BROTHERS SERIES

A gorgeous small town series about four brothers and the women who capture their hearts.

Take Me Home

Still The One

A Better Man

Somebody Like You

When We Touch

THE SHAKESPEARE SISTERS SERIES

An epic series about four strong yet vulnerable sisters, and the alpha men who steal their hearts.

Summer's Lease

A Winter's Tale

Absent in the Spring

By Virtue Fall

THE LOVE IN LONDON SERIES

Three books about strong and sassy women finding love in the big city.

Coming Down

Broken Chords

Canada Square

STANDALONE

Fix You

An epic romance that spans the decades. Breathtaking and angsty and all the things in between.